THE BODY IS WATER

"Satisfying . . . A lovely, loose, and liquid novel of a woman at a crossroads."

"Penetrating, drenched in memory, free of nostalgia, propelled by fierce urgency, and sometimes very funny."

"Witty, straightforward, and sound . . . Just as Elizabeth Evans and Mary Morris have done in their recent excellent novels, Julie Schumacher demonstrates that fiction about the routines and disasters of home life is really (when done well) not about those things at all, but about the search for lost mothers and fathers, the ones we lose at birth, the ones that are inside us and therefore invisible and inaccessible, the ones we lose through misunderstanding, intolerance, stubbornness, and the ones we want to become but never do."

"Vibrant and striking, resonant with the ideosyncrasies of life."

"Clever . . . telling . . . Julie Schumacher has a deft touch."

The Body Is Water

Julie Schumacher

AVON BOOKS NEW YORK

AVON BOOKS
A division of
The Hearst Corporation
1350 Avenue of the Americas
New York, New York 10019

Copyright © 1995 by Julie Schumacher
Inside cover author photo by Francisco Photography
Published by arrangement with Soho Press Inc.
Visit our website at **http://AvonBooks.com**
Library of Congress Catalog Card Number: 95-18208
ISBN: 0-380-72840-0

First Avon Books Printing: April 1997

AVON TRADEMARK REG. U.S. PAT. OFF. AND IN OTHER COUNTRIES, MARCA
REGISTRADA, HECHO EN U.S.A.

Printed in the U.S.A.

RA   10 9 8 7 6 5 4 3 2

For Lawrence,
who keeps the light burning;

And for Emma and Isabella,
who slept.

Acknowledgments

For their patience and interest and generosity in reading this book in various forms, I thank Melissa Bank, Lisa Bankoff, Paul Cody, Ed Hardy, Lamar Herrin, Liz Holmes, Paul Jacobs, Mary LaChapelle, Alison McGhee, Steve Polansky, and Stephanie Vaughn. To Gini Fleming, thanks for medical advice; to Dan Kelliher, thanks for assistance with the stars; to Larry Cantera, my thanks for the final title.

For her expertise in philosophy as well as in many other matters, I thank Barbara Schumacher; for their love of stories and their expertise in golf, I thank my parents.

For allowing me four years' worth of Tuesdays and Thursdays without real worry, I'm very grateful to the teachers at the University of Minnesota Child Care Center.

And for his undying and stubborn enthusiasm, I thank Lawrence Jacobs, my own Don King, who read this book and lived with it for half a dozen years.

Contents

1

June

Three months pregnant and unmarried, I was sitting at the kitchen table with my father, whom I hadn't gotten along with for fifteen years. Because I hadn't yet told him that I was pregnant, we were drinking tea in relative peace, looking out at the ocean, a mottled gray and unusually warm for that time of year.

He hadn't asked me why I'd come. At six-thirty in the morning he'd opened the porch door for his paper and found me sitting on the metal milkbox, sweat-stained and exhausted, the crumbs of a thousand saltines spread across my clothes. "It's me, Dad," I said, looking up.

I had just driven several hours through the dark, zigzagging my way southeast on minor roads around the Black Horse Pike as if drawn by a broken homing device to 5025 Amanda, Sea Haven, New Jersey. I clenched the wheel and drove, the towns got smaller, the pine trees spindlier and less hardy, until toward dawn I could smell the salt, the dead crustaceans, the vibrant, rolling, variegated sea.

I parked and climbed the outdoor stairs to the open porch, which noticeably listed to the right, and felt lethargy and indecision wrap themselves around me like a pair of creeping vines. With the house between me and the ocean sunrise, I sensed my father waking with a grunt in his gray-blue bedroom, rapping the thermometer on the wall with a callused knuckle, and beginning a new day by swearing at all the idiots, losers, and donkeys on the Sea Haven AM radio news. I sagged down onto the milkbox and wondered if I should have come.

"I can see it's you," he said. He picked up the paper, tightened the belt of his flannel bathrobe, and went back in. My father is an asymmetrical man. His right ear sticks out stiffly from his head as a result of some childhood trauma, and his left leg is shorter than his right. I followed him across the sand-colored carpet into the kitchen, where he put a badly oxidized kettle on the stove and pretended not to notice me at the table, rubbing my eyes. Scanning the one-page international section of the *Sea Haven Herald* for disaster, he mused aloud about a train wreck in Colombia, a riot in Pakistan, and a twelve-year-old British boy who had murdered his mother and then set fire to the house in which she had fed and clothed him for a dozen years.

"Do you have any tea?" I asked.

He shrugged, probably searching for an entry to his favorite topics: the corruption of elected officials; apocalypse; high and low tides; the disposal of garbage in towns built near water; the uselessness of all theory; death by hanging and electrocution; hurricanes; and the likelihood of a bomb causing a tidal wave in the immediate vicinity of his house in the narrow islands of southern Jersey.

"You're lucky you found this place still standing." My father dandled a tea bag in a cup, donning his doom-and-disaster voice like a smoking jacket. "In 1948, the first floor was underwater. The bay and the ocean met nearby. The only people outdoors who weren't bobbing facedown in the current had to paddle through the streets like gondoliers."

I waved his comments away. "I know; I've heard."

"In '69 we lost thirty yards of beach. All it takes is fifteen minutes; we could get swept out past the sandbar anytime."

I doubted my father knew where the sandbar was. He almost never went in the water but, living near the ocean, was a fatalist; he believed in the malevolence of nature, the endings of things.

I could hear Mr. Denzer, the man who rented the floor below us, vacuuming the rugs as he did almost every morning as close to dawn as protocol allowed. Mr. Denzer had been my high school gym teacher; behind his back we called him Mr. Clean.

My father took two paper plates from the freezer (the ants couldn't find them there) and two forks from the drawer; the table was set. He was drinking from a chipped white mug that said GREG H. across the front. Bee and I had given it to him when we were small—I don't know why we didn't buy one that said DAD.

"I guess you're surprised to see me here," I said,

watching him jiggle a mountain of undercooked eggs in a pan.

"I guess." He shook enough salt and pepper on the eggs to turn them gray.

"I probably won't stay very long. In case you're wondering."

"I don't wonder. You kids do whatever you want. I don't tell you when to come and go."

"It's your house, though, Dad."

"Of course it's mine. Who the hell else would it belong to? Genghis Khan?" He sat down at the table, dividing the eggs between us and hauling the plastic trash can up next to him on the kitchen chair. He liked to throw waste into the can as he made his way through a meal: napkins, paper plates, bread crusts. He almost always used paper plates. He would have used paper pots if there were such things.

"Dad," I said. "Don't put the garbage at the table. It isn't sanitary. And it makes me sick."

He leaned back, lifting the front legs of his chair high off the floor so that he could open the refrigerator without getting up. He grabbed the butter and the jam. "Who's visiting who? You were always squeamish." But he put the trash back on the floor. "So you're here to visit, just like that. Pick up and go. No worries, just flit from one spot to the—"

"I don't teach in the summer. I never have."

"No, you keep your own schedule. Anyway, you timed it right: Spunk here is planning a little voyage of his own." He nodded toward the black misshapen object at his feet. Our ancient dog, a Labrador/poodle mix, lay on the cool linoleum, legs splayed, genitals mashed against the floor.

"What's wrong with Spunk?"

My father made the motion of drawing a knife across his neck. "Heart conditions, arthritis, who knows what else. I have to give him three pills a day. This dog's on a lease, hour by hour. Hanging by the tip of his hairy tail." He buttered a piece of bread, wrapped an ominous blue pill in its center, and tossed the wad to Spunk, who painfully scuffled the three or four inches toward it without lifting his head or body from the floor. "I told your mother, that second time in the hospital, 'If you die on me in here, the very first thing I'm going to do is drive home at seventy miles an hour and kill that dog.'"

"I guess you lied," I said.

I tried to muster up some sympathy for the dog, but no one in the family had ever liked him. He was like a relative that way—we were stuck with him, through thick and thin. My mother had found him injured and abandoned on one of the dirt roads leading to the bay. In one of her moments of intense involvement—moments Bee and I always craved and wished were directed toward ourselves—she fed him hamburger and raw egg and bathed him in the sun with her own shampoo; even so, he was unfriendly, taciturn. "Look how much happier he seems," my mother had said, as the dog curled his upper lip. My father, who liked the dog least, ended up walking him by the marshes twice a day, jerking the leash when Spunk stopped to inspect dead rodents, cat turds, flies.

"I knew a fellow," my father said, nudging the dog

with a corduroy slipper, "who took vacations whenever he felt like it. Ran his life the way he wanted to—worked if he was in the mood that day and sat around the house if he wasn't." My father paused for dramatic effect. "He was one of the most miserable sons of bitches I ever knew."

"My job," I said, "is over for the summer. I can't eat this; it's impossible that a person your age can't cook an egg. I think I'm going to take a nap. We can talk later."

My father wiped the crumbs from the table with his forearm, clearly annoyed. He associated daytime sleep with foreigners, welfare, and disease. "Sleep all you want. If you wake up by tomorrow noon, we'll play some golf. I'll show you what they've done to the back nine."

"I don't play golf anymore. You know I don't."

"I know that you're willing to throw considerable talent, not to mention years of hard work and practice paid for with your father's money, down the drain. You'd rather sit in a dingy tenement listening to your neighbors beat each other up than go outdoors and have any fun. But that should just make our game more even." I watched him pop the plastic lid from the dog's medicine and put a pill on the tip of his own tongue. "I've gotten stiff."

From the first moment that I suspected I was pregnant, I suffered sudden bouts of nausea and despair. Now I fought back both at once. "You wouldn't be satisfied with me no matter what I did."

Spunk rotated his head toward me. His eyeholes seemed to have slipped so that they drooped beneath his eyes; his skin didn't fit his face anymore. His teeth were coated with thick saliva, and his gums were black.

"Satisfied?" My father downed the pill with his tea and scratched his head. "Where would you be if I was satisfied? That's not my job."

I pushed my chair away from the table and stepped out the back door, inhaling the smell of my former life. Four years earlier, when I got a master's in education, I took a job twelve hours away in Cincinnati. I had no particular reason to teach in Ohio—there were other positions open nearer-by—but it seemed like a good opportunity to try something new. I didn't like the principal, though, and left. The next year I taught in a district outside of Pittsburgh—a mild, suburban set of schools—but the Monongahela depressed me, so I left again for a job in White Plains, New York, where I was robbed by an angry student. Then through amazing luck and a recommendation I didn't deserve, I landed a truly good job in Philadelphia, in a school that was padded with money. The students were bright, the curriculum flexible, the pay scales high. Still, by the middle of the year I knew I would go. Each time I'd be offered a new contract, give all indications that I would sign, then wake up one morning in a generic apartment that didn't look like it belonged to anyone I knew and I'd throw all the paperwork into the trash. With every job, I was getting closer to my father's house, as if pulled back to Sea Haven by the tide.

Sea Haven was in some ways a beautiful island town. Two hundred yards from the back porch of my father's house was the Atlantic, or at least the five-

mile stretch of it I knew, still relatively free at this
time of year from lifeguards, rafts, folding lounges,
plastic buckets, and extended families from the suburbs of Philadelphia. It was the beginning of the season, when year-round families like ours had to brace
themselves for crowded grocery stores, parking problems in their own driveways, petty thievery, assault,
and occasional drownings by the pier. My father hated
the summer crowds. He'd taught my sister and me
when we were young to whistle whenever someone
took the shortcut through our yard. He would come
dashing around the corner of the house, usually wearing a pair of suit pants cut off with garden shears at
the knee, and direct the astonished criminals up the
block, where they would cross to the beach via a
scorching asphalt walkway marked PUBLIC. Summer
people used to have very little clout; now almost no
one lived in Sea Haven all year round.

The real mark of status in having a house right on
the beach was that we didn't generally use the beach
at all; we sat above it, on the deck built on top of the
bulkhead, surveying the day-trippers from a height of
six or eight feet. When their kites or beach balls landed
in our yard, we let them grovel up the steps from the
beach to retrieve their toys, but we never tossed them
back ourselves.

The beach was popular because it was smooth and
flat and wide; you could play tennis on the wet sand
when the tide was low. In the off-season the broad,
clean stretch of white looked like a huge, abandoned
stage. Other people remember houses or neighborhoods where they grew up; their formative events took

place in apartment hallways, refinished poolroom basements, leafy graveyards, barns, or square suburban malls—places defined by boundaries that enclose an hour or an afternoon. But my childhood unfolded in the open, a single line of houses on one side and everywhere else an endless, indefinable space. There were landmarks, of course—the fishing pier, the boardwalk, the periodic lifeguard stands—but these were markers instead of bounds. When we walked along the sand at night we knew our location by the lights of the houses, the glowing windows' shapes: the turret belonged to the Dohertys, the boxy squares to the Flynns on Daniel Street, the rectangular stained glass to Mrs. Borg. It seemed that our lives would go on and on in one direction. In some ways we were misled. Growing up by the ocean implied a boundlessness, a lack of finite events. We didn't believe in starts or finishes, or death.

Often visitors to Sea Haven, struck by the tiny size of our town, ask what it was like to live in a small homogeneous place where all the streets are flat and straight and the houses (thirty-four hundred of them) square. They fail to notice the different neighborhoods, as distinct to those who live here as Manhattan from Brooklyn. Sixty-eight blocks long and four and a half blocks wide, Sea Haven begins in the south at Sandy Point, widens to encompass the Fighting Cougars' playing fields and the volunteer fire department, then narrows again at the north end of the island, just past the boardwalk and the marina on the bay. We have one large hotel, the sixty-four-room Carlotta, named for a shipwreck, and one department store, Linders, which my father used to run. But as kids, when we

asked each other where we were from, we answered
not by street but neighborhood: "downtown" or "marina" or "bayside" or "Sandy Point" or "beachfront
south" or "marsh." I was one of the few kids who
lived right on the ocean, where most of the houses
were summer rentals. The year-round families tended
to live either near the marina, where they kept their
fishing boats, or in the middle of the island, two blocks
each from the ocean and the bay.

Sea Haven was divided in two between the vacationers and the residents, and more visibly between the
old houses and the new—that is, the expensive, modern, oddly shaped condos whose owners thought they
fit in because they flaunted "native" plants: tiger lil-
ies, dwarf pines, and cattails floated among the rock
gardens of their lawns. Their wood homes bristled with
balconies and porches, huge windows and decks cluttered with drink carts and umbrellas. The year-round
residents, on the other hand, preferred houses made of
brick, devoid of porches and decks; they sported dark
awnings to keep out visitors and the sun. American
flags and eagles graced their front doors, and folding
lawn chairs faced the street instead of the water, so
that their occupants could know who was traveling to
and from town. They had salty grass for yards or gave
up on lawn care altogether and decorated their property with plastic deer and wishing wells and stones.

"How about we survey the estate?" My father appeared behind me, dressed, albeit oddly, in a pair of
black tuxedo pants and a yellow sweatshirt. Once he
retired—not so willingly—as the manager of Linders,
he refused to patronize the shops by buying new

clothes. Almost everything he wore had been his father's; the suits and shirts were stored in the attic in
garment bags from decades long ago.

We walked down the rickety outdoor stairs, a flight
that my father and I had reconstructed after a hurricane
fifteen or sixteen years before. The morning after the
storm we'd driven back to Sea Haven from a motel in
Vineland and found some houses entirely gone: ours
was battered but in one piece except for the staircase,
which turned up in someone's living room a block
away—my father seemed pleased at how far it had
traveled on its own. Toward the bottom of the stairs
was a crooked, misaligned board, the only step I had
built myself. I'd gotten tired of holding the nail can
and the level, standing on the sidewalk and listening
to my father swear, so I measured and set a step while
he was gone. He caught me trying to take it out, having
seen that I'd done it wrong, and he took the hammer
and nailed it in furiously, leaving it as an example of
what I could do. "This one's Jane's work, this one
here," he used to say, putting all of his weight on the
board so it would creak. When people came to visit,
he put a CAUTION sign at the bottom of the stairs.

The backyard, as usual, was three or four inches
deep in sand. The deck, built on top of the bulkhead,
was designed to keep the sand from blowing over from
the beach but it never worked: the tiny lawn was a
smattering of thistles struggling to survive among the
dunes. Our neighbors on either side, who had perfect
lawns, paid every year to have the sand removed by
dump truck and to have carpets of grass unrolled from
north to south. Every year their plants were dead by

the middle of August, the grass white with salt, the evergreens gritty, the geraniums keeling over in the sun. The following May they began again. The Benedettis on the left, and the Cranes on the right, fortified their fences against us, weaving plastic sheeting between the pickets to keep our sand from blowing through. Periodically they offered to clear our yard, too, but my father refused. The sand was coming, he said, which meant that the ocean was coming with it, inch by inch, and did they think he would stand outside with a plastic bucket, hurling the water back out to sea?

We stood on the deck and studied the shoreline, packed with fat two-story condos so wide and close together that you could climb from one to the next through the bedroom windows.

"It looks fancier," I said, "more like a resort. I recognize fewer buildings every year."

"It looks like it was designed by blind epileptics," my father said. "If you came more often, you'd learn something about the way the world works."

"Tell me the current scandals."

He shrugged. "More of the same, only worse. People you thought would never sell are letting go. Mostly it happens like it did with Murphy. The kids come down and get rid of the parents—push them down a flight of stairs in their wheelchairs and call the realtor the next afternoon."

"Murphy sold his house?" I felt a wave of sympathy for my father as well as Murphy. "I can't believe it."

"Why not? After his heart attack his daughter sold

it for him, right out from under his nose. He signed the papers while he was still doped up in a hospital ward.''

"Karen Murphy? She's younger than I am.''

"Fat,'' my father said. "And a moron to boot. She undersold. They took it for less than 180,000 and tore it down the next afternoon. The thing that replaced it rents for 2500 a week. It looks like a giant doghouse.''

"How's Murphy doing?''

"He's got a scar like a railroad tie. He has a trailer in Marmora and doesn't come down.''

"That's probably good.'' Murphy was my father's oldest friend, a sweet, oversized man who used to stand on our deck, shaking his head at the new construction marring the view, and say, "Look at the bimbos, Greg. They don't know who's rich around here.'' A retired electrician, Murphy was richer, but probably didn't know how to spend his money. For a good time he used to drive to Sandy Point, bringing a cooking pot, matches, and a hammer; he killed blue crabs by tapping them gently between the eyes.

Almost all of my parents' friends had sold and moved inland. They'd bought their houses for fifteen or twenty thousand; it was too hard not to sell them twenty years later for ten times as much; they had children who wanted to go to college or they had empty retirement funds. At first they were happy to return on weekends in the brand-new cars bought with money from the houses' sale, but eventually they visited less and less, made awkward in their new Chevies next to the Jaguars and Mercedes and by the soaring redwood homes that replaced their own. Periodically a group of my parents' old friends came to spend the day, and they sat miserably on the deck in their ugly street clothes, drinking beer out of beaded cans and refusing to look either left or right. They stared at the ocean straight ahead, as if wishing it would rise up and carry the lot of them away. It was better to think of Murphy in his trailer home.

"I won't push you down the stairs in your wheelchair, Dad," I said.

"You may not have to. I can't insure this place if the rates go up much more." He studied the house. "That's why the goons from Jason Realty drop by once or twice a year. I even call them up sometimes. I say, 'Hey, why don't you send a couple goons to see me?' and they send them down. They sniff around with their little charts, then offer me five thousand more than they did last time. I think we're up to two-forty-five." He shook his head. His face, though thin, was now padded with jowls. "Look at this place. It warms my heart to see them sweating out here in their ties. I want them to offer me three hundred thousand the day it falls down."

"You'll never sell it," I said. The house was one of the few things that my father and I agreed on. While Bee and my mother used to complain about the sinking kitchen floor, and the constant gritty dampness in the rugs, my father and I loved the odd corners, the windows that began at your knee and went up nearly to the ceiling, and the red brick fireplace with my grandfather's initials in the hearth. My father and the house had become as one.

"No, the Indians were right." He climbed back

down off the deck into the yard. "The Lenni-Lenape. They left this place for hopeless swampland and moved on. Nothing but sassafras and clams. I have to sell it sooner or later. If I don't, how will you get your inheritance?"

"I guess I'll borrow from Karen Murphy."

"Ho," he said, cheerful, wheeling around. Bee said that the soaring property values made my father nervous, that living in a dump worth a quarter-million on a piece of land that might not exist in twenty years made him feel that he was the butt of someone's joke. Maybe to demonstrate a similar sense of humor, when he repaired things around the house he tended to make them look worse than before. He didn't bother to match the color of the exterior paint, and he used beams of all different types to hold up the porch, which always sagged. The house was light blue and gray and aquamarine, with peeling white paint on the windows and on the two sets of outer stairs that criss-crossed their way to the second floor. Porches—open in the front of the house, glassed-in at the rear—protruded from the second story. A gray deck jutted out from the third-floor attic on the ocean side. The house had a rusty outdoor shower for rinsing feet and three corroded copper seagulls nailed above the windows facing the beach. Next to the architect-designed homes on either side, our house looked like a squatter on private land.

My father picked up a broken piece of clapboard on his way to the sidewalk. "Do you want to have a look at the foundation?"

"Not now."

"Oh, come on. Try to learn something for a change." He got down on his hands and knees and rested his head against the sidewalk, peering into the dirt and pylons in the dark. "See the supports? One of them's rotted, right through. I wedged some cinder blocks in there but they may not hold."

The smell of the dirt and mildew made me sick. I wondered if, once I told him I was pregnant, he would throw me out of the house. Even if I would be miserable, I needed to be here, where my childhood and all my memories were preserved like fossils in ancient stone.

"Your grandfather remembered when this place was built. He stood on a stack of railroad ties and watched them drive the piles in."

I tried to picture my twelve-year-old grandfather in shorts and a matching jacket, gazing coolly at the Italian and Irish laborers who sweated within sight of the ocean in the midday sun. He had grown up in this house when it was new and died in it before Bee and I were born. Four generations of us had occupied this space, argued in it and inexplicably blighted each other's days in it, all while looking out at the ocean, crashing and advancing every year.

"I'm going to be sick," I said, and in fact I was, across the sidewalk and up the edge of the Benedettis' fence, all over the plastic weave between the pickets. I leaned forward, hands out, vomiting up saltines and eggs, grape juice and bread. As soon as I caught my breath I felt fine again. I wiped my eyes. "Sorry, Dad."

He was still on his hands and knees. "What the

hell.'' He slowly stood and surveyed the damage.

"Sorry," I repeated. We were standing by the first-floor windows, eye level with Mr. Denzer's kitchen.

"I'm going to have to hook up the goddamn hose." He shook his head. "Knock on the door and ask if Bill's got a scrub brush and some soap."

"Let me get them upstairs."

"No, Bill's got a bucket full of stuff." My father put his face against the screen. "Bill!" he yelled.

"Dad, please. I'm already going." I thought the heat and the smell of vomit would make me sick again, so I walked quickly around to the steps, checking my clothes. Bill Denzer was discreetly coming around from the front with a very clean brush, some soap, and a pail. They were probably sitting on a shelf labeled with a sticker that said PAIL.

"Welcome home," he said, smiling and ignoring my blanched complexion and trembling hands. "I saw your car. Does your dad need these?"

Even under the best conditions, I felt awkward around Mr. Denzer. He had been my teacher at Sea Haven High when I was fourteen; several years later, when my mother died and my father needed the money, he moved into the first floor of our house. We had it remodeled, closing off the stairs between the floors and restoring the old second kitchen down below. Except that his view of the ocean wasn't as good, Mr. Denzer's part of the house was nicer than ours.

"Thanks," I said, "I'll be back." I lurched away with the bucket, making sure that Mr. Denzer stayed behind, then dropped the cleaning supplies on the sidewalk behind my father, who was busy with the hose.

"I just bought these at the store," Mr. Denzer called from a little distance. He stood on the tips of his toes and held out a yellow Popsicle. He had always had a knack for kindness.

I thanked him, unwrapped it, and bit off the tip, letting the sweet ice dissolve slowly in my mouth. We sat together in the sun on the front stoop. Mr. Denzer wore gray jogging pants and a bleached white T-shirt. Without being overweight, he was stocky and round, like the trunk of a tree.

"I remember last time you visited—what was it, a year ago?—we talked a lot about teaching, here on the step. And here we are again, both of us still in the same profession. How is it going?"

"Fine," I lied. Mr. Denzer credited himself for inspiring me to become a teacher; in his eyes I was probably still seventeen years old and full of warped promise, a wild girl.

"I always knew you'd be good with kids. I knew it." He nodded to himself. "Some people have it and others don't."

"How's your coaching going?" I asked.

"Oh, you don't want to hear about that." He looked at me happily, open-faced; he smiled like a Unitarian. "You look better already," he said.

I ate my Popsicle and looked down the block. In another week the streets would be full of children on bicycles, their hair gradually whitening in the sun. "Sometimes," I said, "I think teachers are mainly intended to amuse their students. It's like a play. They sit in their seats and watch, judging: good or bad? Except at the end the actors get to punish certain members of the audience.''

"Oh, I don't think about it that way.'' He wiped up a drop of lemon juice from the concrete step; his hands were thick and immaculate, the nails filed evenly, cuticles groomed. "Just consider what you do. You open up the world of books. I had an English teacher I still remember perfectly. Her name was Mrs. Clauston. We read *Robinson Crusoe* in her class.''

Mr. Denzer was the type to love *Robinson Crusoe* for its practical applications. He probably studied it as a manual, trying to learn how to build a lean-to, hunt, and fish. His light brown hair had gotten thinner; the lines had deepened across his forehead and around his eyes. I had no idea why he continued living in my father's house. He must have been making enough money for a place of his own. "Everyone wants to believe they're doing something worthwhile,'' I said.

"Almost everyone *is*,'' Mr. Denzer said.

My father appeared beneath the outdoor stairs with the garden hose. "I think I got it all. Don't tell me you were eating again.''

"I'm fine now; I just needed to sit down.'' I turned to Mr. Denzer. "I always remember my mother here; we spread her ashes in the ocean. My father doesn't talk about her anymore.''

My father ignored this comment, walking away and shaking his head, coiling the hose, then reappeared with his sleeves rolled up. "Did you bring your suitcase out of the car?''

"No, it's in the trunk. Just leave it. I'll get it later.''

''When is 'later'?'' My father moved toward the trunk.

''Dad, don't open it,'' I called, but he had already popped the driver's side latch. Now he was staring down into the bowels of my rusty ten-year-old Dodge.

Strewn about the trunk were three plastic garbage bags and a suitcase full of clothes, fifty or sixty books, a spare tire, half a dozen pairs of shoes, a jewelry box, and a philodendron in a hand-made pot. I don't know why I'd brought the plant to a house that couldn't support greenery, but I'd tucked it into a corner of the trunk so that it wouldn't spill. ''Is the plant alive?'' I called.

My father looked up. ''You mean this?'' He held up some earth-colored roots without any leaves. ''I'm just curious—'' He brushed the dirt from his hands. ''—do you own more than one suitcase?''

''I was cleaning the apartment,'' I said. ''I wasn't sure what to bring. Leave everything there, Dad, please.'' Once my possessions entered the house, it might be difficult to get them out again.

My father hesitated briefly, then mumbled to himself and lifted the two smaller garbage bags from the car.

''I'll help,'' Mr. Denzer said.

I finished my Popsicle while they worked. My father set my stuff on the grass while Mr. Denzer swept up the dirt in the trunk with a broom. I felt disgraced, like a wayward child. I thought of the summer I'd come home early from sleep-away camp, abandoning half-finished projects, like my initials in hard spaghetti not yet glued to their posterboard. I had called, day after

day, to beg my parents to take me home. I hated the
ponies with their yellow teeth, I hated the woods that
were much too green and where there were too many
places to hide, and I lived in such terror of the out-
house, with its humid dark stench and hideous legion
of centipedes, that I relieved myself only in the lake
at swimming hour. Most of our recreation time I spent
on the steps of Bee's cabin on the other side of a dirt-
scuffed lot, crying and eating oatmeal cookies sent in
the mail by other children's parents.

Bee had to leave, too—my parents didn't want to
drive back twice to pick us up—and she stared away
from me, out the window, all the way home. The floor
of the car was littered with homemade necklaces, ugly
hot plates, lanyards and ties. My mother was dozing
in the front, fragile and pale, and my father drove like
a man doing penance at the wheel. I thought of the
spaghetti art left behind and about my bunkmates, and
by the time we reached Sea Haven the camp had begun
to seem fun again. All my life I've never been certain
where I should be.

"Dad," I said, "do you remember that summer
when I went to camp?"

"Vaguely." He picked up half a dozen pencils from
the floor of the car.

"Mom had just come back from the hospital. And
I built you a house out of twigs. It was supposed to
be our house. Do you remember? That was probably
the best thing I ever made."

He stopped on the landing. "You were seven or
eight," he said.

"Eight. I liked that house a lot." I was addressing

Mr. Denzer, who tried hard to look like he was following the conversation. He carefully lifted the philodendron from the ground and followed my father to the second floor. I could hear the screen door open.

"Move your deathly hide, Spunk," my father said, and the door slammed shut.

Just a block away from the water, on the opposite side of the street, the houses cost fifty or sixty thousand dollars less; they did have a view of the ocean, but the view included our house, with a slice of water on either side. Middle-class families could still afford to rent these homes for a week, which meant that the sidewalks across from ours were always teeming with kids, the smallest ones hunkered down on their knees among the pebbles, faces framed in the cups of their bonnets. Their older brothers and sisters bossed them around. Because Sea Haven was their temporary home, the renters' kids were wild; they took risks. They stole candy and comic books from the stores, threw chunks of jellyfish at strangers, and grappled with one another beneath the pier. They made up lies about themselves and no one knew.

Although we'd been told how lucky we were to live by the ocean, Bee and I had always lied, too, because we had no other houses, no other lives. "Where are you from?" the summer kids would ask, kicking up the smooth white pebbles of the empty lot with their colored sneakers. (Bee and I walked barefoot on the stones; our feet were immune.) "Alaska," Bee said once, to quiet them down. "Juneau, Alaska." They would have believed her but I'd interfered, wanting to describe the polar bears that ate from our hands, the igloos we built, the Eskimo neighbors whose subtle language we knew by heart. "Let's hear you say something Eskimo," a little boy said. I blushed and stuttered out a sentence we had learned in school: *"Como te llamas?"* Their shrieks of laughter could be heard all the way down the block.

I chewed the juice from my Popsicle stick and set it down. A boy across the street flipped his middle finger in my direction to impress a friend. I flipped mine back. Never let children take you by surprise.

When people ask me how I can stand to teach grammar to twelve- and thirteen-year-olds, I answer that this is the stage of life when people are clearly most alive. This is when everything happens: violence, love, sex, betrayal, friendship, fear, generosity, hatred, greed. Everything that will later become refined into boredom and rudeness remains on the surface. In the presence of my students I feel I'm watching volcanoes erupt and glaciers form; I am a witness to magic rites and uncover the secrets of primal things. In adults I see the seeds of what they were: the petty thief, the liar, the goody-goody, the zealot, the brain.

Even so, I'm not always good with children. Some of them like me because I'm young, but they're seldom interested in what I have to offer because my job is to provide them with guidelines and rules at a stage of life during which they've resolved to reject the arbitrary regulations of adults. I can sympathize. They're bleary-eyed, stunned and angry with new knowledge: their parents are loud and ungainly and have sex; the world is running out of trees; God, if alive at all, has

an unusual sense of humor; and no true consolation is
forthcoming—only this crazed bunching together of
fellow sufferers. And even this short-lived comfort
will disappear when everyone graduates or reaches the
age of twenty-one. Every September we begin with
high hopes, disappointing each other every time.

After the last week of school in June I'd sat down
to a thick stack of final essays—pages of hand-
scrawled work, some of it looking as if it had been
kept in a pants pocket for many hours. I began to work.
I graded generously, trying to round the grades up
whenever I could. I took breaks every hour or so, pacing behind my desk and wondering whether one day,
on a charming corner in a foreign city, one of my
students would recognize me and tell me over coffee
what a meaningful year it had been. I was restless and
felt like setting the essays on fire. When there were
only a dozen left I went to the store. I came back, used
the bathroom, and sat at my desk again, setting in front
of me, on the windowsill, two vials filled with solution. I opened a box of saltines and ate two at a time
while checking the timer on my watch. I returned to
the essays. "Even if this was the worst paper I ever
did," a student wrote, "and anyway its not, I know a
lot about the author of this book and his ideas." I gave
him a B. "Try to be more specific. Well done." Another student argued, "What a writer does is his own
personal business. Even if he doesn't believe in God,
which I do. In many respects therefore the ideas in this
book should offend everyone." B+. "Sheryl," I
wrote, "try to be more specific." The liquid in one of
the vials was getting smoky; the other was clear. "For

example, have you tried to define God? What sort of deity are you referring to? Do you believe in the existence of a divine plan?'' I crossed these comments out. ''Well done. Have a nice summer.''

I corrected the last few essays and got out my grade sheet to enter the grades. All the drawers of my dresser were open wide, and my suitcase, held together with masking tape, lay like an open mouth on the floor. As soon as I finished I knew I had to go somewhere, had to be gone. I reread the instructions on the different vials. One said, ''The liquid will remain pink if the test is *negative*.'' The other said that the liquid would turn gray if the test was *positive*. I felt a momentary wave of nausea, popped the lid of a can of seltzer, and went down my list. Albert, Michael. Ayers, Carl. Bettler, Sue. I thought of driving all night and day to get to Bee's house in Atlanta but knew when I arrived unexpectedly my sister would meet me at the door with an expression of virtuous and unsurprised suffering, like a seal. I didn't want to go to Bee's; there was only one place I knew I had to go. Bezinsky, Jay. Castler, Harriet. One of the liquids now looked blue. Was there a separate color indicating that the test-taker was making a mistake? Was there a color that said, ''Warning: you are not fit to assume the responsibilities that this test may place on you?''

Grayson, Will. Letchler, Kareen. Kareen was tiny; she had wrists as fragile as chalk. I always found it difficult to think of the delicate, shy students as potential adults; they seemed to lack experience even as children, and it was hard to let them go. Pearson, Sheryl. Tiffordson, Wynn. Wynnie had skipped a grade and seemed almost too young to be fully human; yet I'd seen carved on the lavatory door WYNN T. TONGS (I assumed this meant "tongues") MICHAEL Z. The second liquid was now distinctly gray. I stared at it, expecting a fuller fortune: "The series of random events that is your life will coalesce." Yalisove, Pam. Zinzer, Stephanie. I had given twenty-nine As, far too many, and a good number of Bs. Only a handful of hopeless cases ended up with less. I folded the grade sheet, signed it, and threw both vials into the toilet. An hour later I was driving to my father's house.

Over the phone my sister had tried to sound patient. "How can you have no idea where you are? It's three in the morning; if you're at a toll booth, there are signs. Or ask someone for directions."

"I can't, Bee," I said. I was standing in the fog on the interstate in the dark, clutching a fly-specked receiver in the open air. Drug deals were being made from the other phones. "The booths are all automatic. No one's there."

"Are you far from I-95?"

"I don't know. I've gone over a lot of bridges. One of them twice."

"You're still outside Philadelphia, then. You haven't gone anywhere. Why do you want to drive to Dad's right now? Last time you went home you spent half your time in a hotel."

"Thank you, Bee. Can you tell me how to get there?" Bee had maps engraved on her memory. She knew the exact location of rivers and railway lines, interstates and winding back roads where trailers rotted into compost on the ground.

"Jane," she said, "you didn't give up your job again."

I swatted a moth, its body an ugly gray cylinder.

"I think you'll regret it," she said.

I pictured her putting another demerit mark next to my name on her list of numbers by the phone.

"If you ever lived somewhere for more than a year, you wouldn't get lost so often. I've lived here in Atlanta for seven years."

"You're a real beacon, Bee," I said. "Will you help me or not?"

"All right, listen." She sighed. "It's 3 A.M. Is it cloudy there?"

I clicked my pen. "What do you mean, cloudy?"

"Look up," she said. "Are there clouds?"

I looked. "One or two."

"It's clear, then," she said. "Find the Big Dipper. Follow the two pointer stars to the North Star, then turn around; you're facing south. That's where you need to go. When you get closer, you'll recognize the roads and know the way."

"Bee, I'm not in a goddamn boat. I'm in a car."

"Just look through the windshield and steer. I thought the principal wanted to rehire you. Do you understand what you're doing? You're throwing an opportunity away."

The prerecorded operator asked for more money.

"Oh Christ," I said. "I'm going to spend my life on a highway."

"Calm down." Bee started talking slowly, as if my

English had gotten poor. "Get in the car. Ignore the map. Just throw it away. Get in the car and drive south, toward the ocean. No more bridges. Think about the globe. The ocean is east of you; home is south."

"Tierra del Fuego is south. Call me back, Bee. I'll read you the number."

"No," she said. "Hang up the phone, get in the car, and you'll get there. It will take you about two hours. If you stop for coffee and breakfast and wash your face, you'll arrive at sunrise. The sun rises in the east. That's over the ocean."

"Wait," I said.

"You'd better look for another job soon if you want to work next year. It's getting late in more ways than one." She hung up before our call was disconnected. I held onto the receiver in the dark, watching the occasional headlights come and go; the cars rushing along behind me seemed to mimic the sound of the ocean. I stood and listened and heard water—the salty blood in my veins, the buoyant amniotic fluid; when I closed my eyes I was floating in water, composed of water. Several minutes later, I was back on the road.

When I was small I used to sleep in different hideaways in the house. My parents would send me to bed but I'd sneak out of my room and find a place beneath a chair or in a closet: somewhere small. My favorite place, though, was the couch, where the sound of the ocean was loudest and the spray, when the water was rough, could lick the screens. My father would find me there late at night and pretend to believe that I didn't wake when he scooped me up in his arms. He carried me back to my bedroom, which faced east and in several hours would be pink with dawn. With the swaying of his gait, I always fell back to sleep again. But in the seconds before he lay me in my bed, sometimes brushing his unshaven face against my cheek, I could still hear him—as if from a distance—saying: "Here's the place for Jane, here's Janey's place; now stay awhile."

"Dad," I said. I had awakened from my second nap of the day. My father was sitting with his feet on the windowsill, looking out in the direction of the ocean, except that the shades on the porch were drawn. Enormous windows filled the room, but my father disliked the idea of drifters and tourists on the beach looking in, so he always shut the shades at dusk. He sat on the narrow porch, staring out at nothing, at the lack of view. When I came closer I saw that on the maple table at his side stood the tiny house of twigs that I had built. I'd peeled off all the bark before gluing it together so that the house was light and pretty. To the back I'd glued three feathers, one for each of the rusted seagulls on our real-life house.

"Where did you find it?" I asked.

"I didn't have to find it—I knew where it was."

I picked up the house and held it. I was standing where my mother had stood when she was pregnant, and where my father's mother, at forty-eight, had carried the fetus that didn't live.

"I notice you didn't unpack. I suppose you're thinking of stealing off in the middle of the night," my father said.

"Not tonight. I'm much too tired."

"Wherever the wind takes you. A free spirit. All night last night I wondered if you'd get here at all or keep driving until you reached the Florida Keys."

"Bee must have called you." I sat down.

"Three-thirty this morning she was yammering in my ear: 'Jane's on the road. Jane's lost.' She told me to turn the porch light on."

"The light was off when I got here."

"That's because I knew you didn't need it. And it wastes electricity. Bee didn't tell me, of course, that you were pregnant. Maybe you spared her that detail."

Gently I put the house of twigs back down. "How do you know I'm pregnant?"

"It's amazing." He cracked his knuckles. "Children always take their own parents for idiots. They come in reeling drunk at 1 A.M., smelling of cherry brandy and cigarettes, and think the old man's a detective for finding out they weren't studying with a friend. Christ, you've been eating and upchucking all day. And the top button of your pants has been undone. I'm a father twice, you know. I'm more experienced than you are."

We sat in silence for a while. "I was going to tell you," I said. "I think that's what I came for."

He waited.

I hadn't pictured our conversation going like this. "I wanted," I said, "I think I wanted to find out what it would be like to be pregnant here. Where Mom was. I won't stay long. I'll sleep in the attic." Again the wave of nausea and fatigue like a sudden increase in gravity. "It's not exactly a planned pregnancy," I said. "And it probably isn't very good timing."

He nodded.

"Was Mom happy to be pregnant?"

He got up and went into the kitchen for a beer, so I wondered if he had heard me or if I had asked the question at all. "I never use a glass," he said. "Beer tastes much better in the can."

Spunk was dreaming under the window at my feet. The black tip of his nose flared in and out as if he were still capable of smelling a dead blue crab, a nest of toads, a seagull's dung. "I guess I should tell you that I'm not getting married, Dad."

My father laughed. "That bad, is he? Why did you bother to sleep with him, then?" He tipped his head back so that the beer poured down his throat. "I assume this fellow knows that he'll be a father?"

"He won't be a father, not in that way. Just biologically, that's all."

"Biology." He nodded. "Is that one of the subjects you failed in high school?"

"Probably," I said. "I'm going to have the baby by myself."

"*Have* it? Well, of course you're going to have it. It's probably too late to do anything else, or I assume you would have done it. Having it is the easy part. You can get painkillers of all kinds. What are you going to do with it when it's born?"

"I figured you'd raise it for me." I couldn't resist this little joke; I was disoriented and punchy, and so far he was taking it fairly well.

"Humor me some more," my father said. "Tell me about the man who's going to marry you and raise your kid. Bill Denzer wouldn't marry you in a state like that.''

''Bill Denzer wasn't going to marry me anyway. And I just said I don't want to get married. I thought, on some level, you might be happy to have a grandchild. Even under unusual conditions.''

He stood up and finished his beer. ''You don't have any idea. You don't have a hint about what you're getting into. Plenty of people can't hack it. They give up. Their kids run around wild, they're uncontrollable, like—''

''Me,'' I said, and watched his face change. ''There aren't rules for this, Dad.''

He turned around, the windows black behind him. ''Just because you're playing without the rules doesn't mean they don't exist. If I could have given you anything, I would have given you caution and common sense.''

''Bullshit,'' I said. ''Those two were never in your repertoire.''

I thought he was going to start shouting, but again he didn't seem to have heard me. ''You know what I like about old Spunk?''

''What?'' I asked.

''He's a dog. A simple, ordinary dog, and he knows that he's a dog and doesn't fight it. That's what he is.''

''I don't get it. What else could he be?''

''That's the point. Nothing. He couldn't be anything more.''

I shook my head. ''I didn't ask you to judge me, Dad.''

He walked past me into the kitchen. ''You came home. What were you asking for, then?''

2

Lies

He creeps into my room at night before I fall asleep, shoes off so he won't make noise, and plucks the night-light from its socket on the wall. By the crack of light from the door I can see his face: oddly handsome, unlined, with eyebrows thick and dark as if they were painted above his eyes with a giant brush. He rubs his hands through his uncombed hair and paces between the dresser and the bed. Finally he draws a chair up to my side.

He begins to lie.

I don't know why he does it.

Bee and my mother sit downstairs with the TV on, although neither one of them watches. Bee works on a science project for school. She has been permanently excused from regular bedtimes because, my mother says, she isn't like other children and requires only four or five hours of sleep in twenty-four. My mother knits, counting the stitches, losing count, and counting again, while Bee sits on the carpet, legs splayed, a hundred tiny metal pieces between her knees.

Bee is smarter than the rest of us. She uses words that we haven't heard of; we have to look them up in the giant dictionary in the hall. Sometimes I ask her what it's like to be smart. She says it's relative, but I'm not sure what she means.

I ask her this, too: "Does he come into your room at night?"

"Who?" she says, so I don't press it. Bee is twelve years old; I'm eight.

Our mother has taken up knitting since she got sick but doesn't knit well. We keep waiting to see a sweater, even a glove, but she knits without projects in mind, tearing things out to begin again. Sometimes she puts the knitting down and looks out the window, as if there were something in the dark to see.

Upstairs he whispers, leaning toward me, the extinguished night-light shaped like the earth and moon in his hand. His knuckles are white from their hold on our planet. "Listen," he says, "listen. Benjamin Franklin was the first president of the United States. The Nile is located in Yellowstone Park. The Pilgrims came from California; they forged the Santa Fe Trail."

Some of these facts I already understand. In school I am flunking social studies and math, but I do well in reading. I am in the Bluebird group, which everyone knows is the highest, even though the teachers refuse to say.

"Albert Einstein wrote the Psalms. *T* was the first letter of the alphabet until a year ago . . ." Bee has told me that my parents are preoccupied and that if I need help with my homework, I should ask her. She hasn't said how I should keep my father from helping. I try to stay awake but keep my eyes shut just the same because I know this is a rule, even though no one has talked about rules or about this game. I look at him through the tangles of my lashes; he seems to fold in on himself, as if protecting a painful place inside his chest. The lies come out of him slowly. "Are you still listening?" he asks, leaning forward on the chair. "Jellyfish are the larvae of turtles."

Bee says, "Don't ask them how Mom's doing; she'll be fine."

"Gregory?" My mother's voice drifts down the hall.

Even in the dark I can see him change. He looks relieved, loosened. He stands up and pats my arm, plugging the night-light in again, then whistling as he joins my mother in the hall. "Nightmare," he says, a good excuse. Bee has just gotten a room of her own, and since she left I have terrible dreams almost every night. Sometimes when I shout or cry she will cross the hall in the dark and sit on my floor for an hour or two. She'll bring one of her projects and spread the pieces out on the rug, assembling things or disassembling them, understanding how they work. Once she took apart the clock. I try to follow her explanations, but gradually I drift back into sleep. I can't stay awake the way Bee does.

"Is she all right?" my mother asks, opening the door. I sit up so I can see her face, which has gotten thinner, much too pale, but is somehow prettier than it was. I have missed her, though she's been home. My mother has light red hair and freckled skin with

very delicate fragile features; Bee looks like her. My
father and I, on the other hand, are thick and brown.
"What were you dreaming of?" she asks. I would like
to confess things to her, to throw myself in her lap, to
open the cage of my chest and show her the bones.
"Lie down again," she says, and I think that her voice
will be the last thing in this world; if I'm unable to
reclaim it, I'll be lost. Her fingers comb the hair at the
back of my neck. "Sleep shouldn't be frightening."
When I look up to find my father in the doorway, he's
always gone.

In Mrs. McMurtry's class we are studying the ocean
floor. We learn about the earthquakes underwater that
cause tidal waves called tsunami. We learn the differ-
ences between octopus and squid. At a lull in the class
discussion I tell Freddy Hansen on my right about the
giant clams and about the cities underwater, the people
like stick figures made of coral who hunt the clams
with cocktail spears. Mrs. McMurtry asks me where I
got my information. I can afford to take a superior
tone, first because she was eavesdropping, which is
impolite, and second because she knows nothing about
the tiny salmon-colored hunters and their ways. I
quickly explain their physiology, their habits and rituals, their plans. Mrs. McMurtry says that it's fine to
pretend sometimes but that we should recognize the
difference between true and false, and that sitting alone
in the corner for a while might help me reconsider
what I've said.

"Don't worry," Bee says later. "Mrs. McMurtry's
a termagant. She doesn't like independent thinkers or

people who challenge her ideas.'' We are walking home the long way so that I can get an ice cream and Bee can stop at the hardware store for some rubber hose. When we get within sight of the house we see Mrs. Floot, the baby-sitter, standing in the doorway with her thinning hair and her orange lipstick, wearing a sympathetic smile. ''Mom probably has an appointment today,'' Bee says, quickly looking at me to see what I might know. But I know nothing, though I do suspect that there are questions I should ask. Now Bee holds my sweaty hand. ''We'll probably have burned pork chops for dinner.''

If I knew what questions to ask, no one would answer them anyway.

Three days later, during a discussion of the planets, I raise my hand. Mrs. McMurtry looks confused when I mention Yipton, the eleventh planet, which threatens every day to collide with the sun. It carves a wide ellipse and passes the earth only late at night, which is why most people don't know that it exists. It isn't even listed in the *World Book Encyclopedia* under *Y*. For my description I spend the afternoon in the principal's office, where Bee comes to find me after school. She writes the principal a note, explaining that I'm needed at home, then leads me through the hallway past the line of kids waiting for buses, who make cuckoo signs with their fingers to their heads when I walk past. By the time we reach the dust of the playground and the sidewalk that leads home, I am slack-mouthed and wailing, having dropped my notebook and pencils on the ground.

Bee pulls a tissue from her zippered schoolbag and picks up my things. "Jane," she says, "I won't tell you not to lie because I don't think you understand that you're lying. But you need to be careful what you say. At our age, we're made fun of if we don't reflect the norm—if we don't act the way that everyone else thinks we should." She tucks in my shirt, which is dangling out. "Where do you hear these things? One of the other kids?"

I am sniffling too much to answer; she goes on. "Be more cautious. Don't believe everything you hear. Lots of people say things that aren't true; you can't trust everyone. Learn to discriminate. Avoid the people who aren't trustworthy next time."

I look at her in amazement. "Are you trustworthy?"

"I'm your sister," Bee says. She hands me my books. "Use your common sense. Think about what sounds true and what doesn't. Trust yourself."

"But I don't *know* anything," I tell her. "I'm in third grade."

"Pay more attention," Bee says. "Stop convincing yourself of all your limitations." This is easy for Bee to say.

Everyone knows that Bee is a bookworm and a brain— she wears a white oxford shirt buttoned up to her neck to keep out the sun. Although I admire her as my older sister, I am sometimes embarrassed to be seen with her. Now, though, I'm a popular target because of the things I said at school, so there's nothing to be lost in going with Bee to the library, even though it's Saturday and everyone else will be outdoors.

Two Brznewski girls spot us waiting for the bus.

I give Bee the elbow. "Look."

"Ignore them," she says. Bee is good at ignoring others; she knows how to shut things out. Marie Brznewski is running toward me and singing "duh-WEE-duh" in a voice loud enough to attract other kids. If Bee weren't here, I would grind Marie's face into the cement. Bee hates violence, which seems unfair when it's the one thing I do better than she does; Bee never fights. "Here's the bus," she says. Before I get on, I pick up a stone and get off a good, quick shot, hitting Marie Brznewski in the chest. The doors close behind us and we pull away.

Although I'm not allowed on the bus alone, I can go with Bee, and because I love buses I'm willing to visit the library, even though I'll be bored soon after we arrive. Bee reads while we bounce along but I look out the window. First we pass through the section of town where the rooming houses clutter up entire blocks: they are huge, chaotic structures, hung with balconies, outer stairs, triangular windows and peepholes, widows' walks, and round little turrets that on the inside I imagine to be as smooth and inescapable as tin cans. Students live here in the summer, along with lifeguards and immigrant ladies who wear dark dresses and heavy stockings and never go near the water. The neighborhood changes as we near the bay. The houses are just as big, but here they're new, surrounded with fences and dogs and stunted pines and, in the summer, peopled with au pair girls pushing strollers toward the pier; they walk by the yachts, homesick and mumbling to themselves in German or

French. Finally we reach the tip of the island, which oddly enough *does* look like a tip: Sea Haven is shaped like a cigar, with bridges holding it to the mainland north, center, and south. The houses start to look pinched, the streets converge, and then you're up over the water, lifted off the ground as if with wings.

Fishermen slouch over the railing on the bridge or cast their lines from boats on the water below. They lift crabs and sand sharks, sometimes flounder and bluefish, from the bay. Beneath the bridge, tied to its metal supports, are the floating bait shops and hot dog stands, their owners bouncing in the wake of speed-boats ignoring the SLOW and DANGER signs.

After the bridge, away from the ocean, the land is flat and windless, specked with flies. Near a marsh in an impossibly damp town named Peery by the people who live there, we get off the bus and follow a side-walk lined with cattails to the library's blue front door. A lot of the library's books are used donations: sandy paperbacks left by vacationers—mysteries and how-to books and novels picturing women in torn dresses un-der willow trees. Bee ignores the regular shelves and heads for the desk, where she fills out circulation cards to collect what she ordered last time from the Atlantic City Library forty miles away. The librarians roll their eyes when she walks in.

"I don't think this is appropriate reading for a girl your age," one of them says, handing her the books.

Bee looks up, steady. "Is there anything on the jacket prohibiting minors from reading it?"

"There are quite a few illustrations—"

"Nudity isn't pornography." Bee returns to the loan

cards, signs them, and turns the books around so that they can be stamped. "You might help my sister find something to read. She likes animal books."

While Bee lugs the oversized tomes to a corner table and starts to read, one of the library ladies takes my hand. She finds me a stack of picture books about dogs and sits me down not far from Bee. The books look interesting; I am interested in knowing about dogs and feel sure that there are things here that I should learn. But when I look at the pictures they seem flat and stupid, and I don't care about dogs at all. Who cares about muzzle and brisket, pastern and paw? Without realizing how it happens, I am standing at Bee's side asking when we can go. "Soon," she says, her answer every time. She's reading a thick black volume that includes pictures of men and women without any skin. Whenever I ask her what she's looking for, she says never mind, but I think there are things Bee knows that she doesn't tell.

I lean against the table, swinging my legs up in the air. "Don't," she says. I wonder why Bee never gets bored the way I do. Even when we do things I enjoy, like Skee-Ball and miniature golf, I'm already thinking ahead to what we'll do next, wondering whether it will be fun and how much time we have left until it starts.

"Here," Bee says, "I brought a yo-yo." I hate it when she tries to get rid of me but I have had my eye on this particular lemon-colored model for quite a while, so I take it outside. I stand in the glare of the sidewalk near the weeds and move the yellow plastic up and down. I count to one hundred, then sing "The Ants Go Marching" until I can't remember any more of the words. When I go back into the library, Bee is composed, reading, but with tears spilling steadily out of her eyes.

"What's the matter?" I have rarely seen my sister cry.

"Nothing," she says. "These books are sad. But now I'm fine."

"What are they about?" I ask. "Why do you read them?"

Bee refuses to say.

Every night I think to myself: I will ask him why he does this, I will make him explain. He used to sit downstairs after dinner with the paper and a beer and leave me alone. "Noodles are harvested in spring," he says. "You need a small sharp knife and a woven bag." I don't ask him anything; I lie still. Sometimes he gets angry, pacing the room in his socks and pulling his hair. He is probably angry because I don't understand him; he must be sending messages in code. "In the Southern Hemisphere the sky is green," he says. It's like listening to another language; I think that if I listen long enough, I will suddenly *know*.

By morning I don't think about it anymore. There are the cornflakes and the plastic bowl, the cup with my name on it, the red and white tablecloth and the milk. There is my father in his plaid bathrobe—garters and black socks grip his muscled calves—eating a grapefruit over the kitchen sink with a serrated spoon. "Hustle up," he says, "move it along." Every morning he drives us to school on his way to work at Linders, where he has an office of his own. Until Bee explained what department store managers do, I thought of my father as a kind of president of Sea Haven, controlling what everyone wore to school. "Janey, take your vitamin," he says. He is two different fathers, I think. There is no use talking about the night-man when he isn't here.

My mother, who used to get up early, wash her hair, make our breakfasts, and put notes into the lunch bags we took to school, now sleeps late and appears in the kitchen wearing only a thin white nightgown, cradling a cup of coffee in her hands. Bee and I continue what we're doing, but we do it more quietly, pretending we don't know that she's there but making room for her all the same. My father gives her a businesslike kiss on the cheek. While we finish our breakfasts, put the dishes in the sink, and lace up our shoes, she stands in the middle of the kitchen holding her cup. I don't know how long she'll stand there, once we go.

"Do well, today, scholars," she says. She doesn't sound serious. When we get home she'll probably be opening and closing the cabinets, or looking at books without reading them, or gone. She doesn't go out much anymore. Only occasionally, on an afternoon that's barely warm, she'll put on her royal blue suit and go for a swim: the suit is the ladies' kind that's stiff up top, with a panel stretched across the thighs. Too big for her now, it's shaped the way she used to look, so that she's surrounded by the size she used to be.

Sometimes she swims alone at night, which isn't safe. I found this out one night when I woke up hearing Bee close the bedroom door—softly, as if there were something secret going on. When I joined her on the back porch and looked out the window, I saw my father standing in his bathrobe on the bulkhead, under a streetlamp of a moon, staring out to sea. I didn't see my mother until I followed his gaze and saw an arm emerge from the water like a blade. She was swimming just beyond the waves, in the calmest part, turning and swimming back, turning again.

I tried to imagine what surrounded her as she swam: fragments of seaweed like lace, shells mutely clacking against each other, the brown humped backs of sleeping crabs. She was swimming alongside millions of living things, some that stopped and watched as she flowed by and some that didn't notice her at all. My father didn't call to her or wave but just stood on the bulkhead in the dark, a towel folded in his hands. Bee and I did the same. We stood in our cotton nightgowns by the windows overlooking the beach, wondering what our mother was looking for and whether, once she found it, she would come in.

"Bee," I ask, "is Columbus still alive?"

"No," she says.

I hate for my sister to think I'm stupid. "I knew that," I say. "I was just checking. What about the Pilgrims?"

"What about them?" Bee looks up from her book.

"Well, you know."

"You want to know if they're still alive? No, they're not. Their descendants are."

"I knew that, too. . . . Bee?"

"Jane, I'm reading."

"Bee?" I want to ask her why he's picked *me* when I'm the one who's behind; it isn't fair. She sits in front of me learning and learning; I can almost see the information lodge in her brain. As I sit watching her, time clicks by and I don't learn anything at all. I forget things instead. I can feel them slipping out of me, and I want to put corks in my ears and nose and mouth and remove them only when I need to hear or breathe or speak. I have already forgotten how the telephone works, although Bee explained it to me only yesterday. I think of the world as a list of facts: how many feet in a mile, how many digits in a million, how many years before Jim is twice as old as Mary, who is now a third of his age, at eight and a half. To grow up I will need to have memorized all these things, and so far I remember almost none.

Bee wears a new pair of glasses, white with sparkles embedded on the sides; they make her look like a rat but she doesn't care. They were probably the first ones she saw at the glasses shop. She sits among a pile of open books; her room, as always, is a mess, an over-stuffed museum of miscellaneous things. If you walk into Bee's room and ask her, "Where's the chestnut you picked up in Pennsylvania two years ago?" she'll lift up a bag of screws and some bicycle parts, and there it will be. My room, on the other hand, is always neat, but I can't feel good about it in comparison to Bee's. I have three plastic horses on a shelf, a collection of teddy bears, and an all-day sucker in a jar. It looks like a motel room for kids.

"Bee, how much longer are we going to be like this?" I ask.

"Like what?"

"Me being the way that I am, and you like that."

"Probably forever." She turns a page. "At least, as long as we aren't subjected to some kind of life-changing experience. We might change a little bit but not completely. Our personalities have already been formed."

I feel I have always known this. Someone has drawn up the rules in advance and thrown the dice, and because there is nothing I can do, I reach out slowly, very gradually, to make sure that it won't look like an accident, and tear the corner off one of the pages in one of Bee's books. A library book. It's only an inch or so, a triangular corner, and there's no writing on the piece I tore, just two numbers, one on each side. Then I hand the piece to Bee. She looks at me through her glasses, which have slipped down her skinny nose, and she seems to understand. She doesn't get angry but accepts the piece of paper, her fingers, just for an instant, brushing mine. "Please find the tape," she says, and I find it right away despite the mess, which does have an order all its own. She tapes the corner back to the page, smoothing it carefully with her fingers, their nails bitten down to little stumps, and continues to read.

Mrs. McMurtry says that once a week for half an hour I will be excused from class to spend some time with Mr. Dell. He would like to get to know me. She will give me a pass every Wednesday at ten so that I can walk to his office down the hall.

Mr. Dell is an enormous man with a forehead hanging over his eyes like a cliff. He is eight feet tall or close, with hands the size of cinder blocks. The first time I am sent to meet him, I walk in the opposite direction, sweating from the neck down, and hide in the entrance to the cafeteria with my nose against the wall. One of the lunch-line ladies finds me and delivers me straight to his office: we see him looming in the distance as we round the turn.

"She was lost." I can tell from her voice that the cafeteria lady is also afraid of Mr. Dell. She pats me on the back and leaves me, squeaking away in her nurse's shoes.

On his orange sofa Mr. Dell and I discuss my grades, which are going down. Last period I got a D in "consideration to others" and an F in math. He rests his hands on his knees. "Do you enjoy learning?" he asks.

I say no because I am nervous and have misinterpreted the question.

"Why not?"

Now I'm bound to invent a reason. I look for guidance to the floor.

"Mrs. McMurtry says that sometimes you get confused. Is there a reason why?"

I continue looking at my feet. Next to Mr. Dell's they look like toys.

"I want you to understand that you're not being punished. Our talks will be opportunities. Other students might even be jealous that you're coming here." Mr. Dell has probably forgotten that the hall outside his door is always lined with kids who sway back and forth in their chairs and stab each other in the ear with pencils. "I'd like you to feel comfortable so that we can talk. Now, will you take this note home to your mother?" He scribbles quickly on a sheet of paper and folds it up, actually entrusting it to me.

The note is written in cursive, which I don't read well. "Thank you," I say, putting it carefully into my pocket, where it will remain until the long walk home with Bee. "Is everything all right at home with your family?" Mr. Dell asks.

"Great," I say, smiling, relieved that our time is over. He pats me on the head when I stand up to go.

Just beyond the school property line I watch my sister unfold the evidence and read. She mumbles to herself for a little while. "Not to be construed as formal therapy . . . lack of distinction between true and false . . ." Bee folds up the note again. "Bureaucrats," she says. "Sticking their noses into everything. Now what should we do?"

"Tear it up?" I ask hopefully.

Bee shrugs. "They need a reply. Let's give them one. But you'll have to go back, at least for a while." Bee types her response and seals it, delivering it herself to Mr. Dell. "From my mother," she says. She doesn't flinch.

In our next session Mr. Dell and I talk about zoos, about why the animals live there, who feeds them and grooms them, and why it's not right to hunt elephants for ivory or kill giant turtles for turtle soup. I almost forget myself and tell him about the koalas, how they sleep hanging onto branches high in the eucalyptus trees, but at the last minute I catch myself. And I tell him something true instead.

*   *   *

My mother continues swimming, even though it's too cold. She comes up from the beach with her lips and fingernails turning blue. She is always doing something with her hands, stringing paper clips together or winding yarn.

Bee has shut herself up in her room. She's taking algebra and geometry at the same time, over her teachers' objections, as well as studying chemistry on her own.

"Jane," my mother calls. "I need your help with something here." My mother seldom asks for help, so I run in. She's sitting at her dressing table, the one with the white flounced skirt and the matching stool, a hairbrush and a scissors in her hands. "This is harder than I thought it would be," she says. "I'm making a mess." Six inches of her hair, the color of peaches, lies in shards across her knee; it's cut on one side up to the level of her ear.

"I like it better long," I tell her. "I don't want it cut."

"It's already done," she says, petulant, matching my tone. "It's not a matter of what we want or don't want anymore."

I shake my head.

She holds out the scissors. "This is a small favor I'm asking." We aren't talking face-to-face but through the big oval mirror on the wall, which makes me think of fairy tales and people stuck in magic coffins under glass. Lately, talking to my mother is always like this. I don't want a mother from a book; I want the real thing.

"I don't want it cut," I repeat, aware that my father will blame me for this and that maybe he's been blaming me all along.

She takes my wrist and pulls me gently toward her, reeling me in. She puts the scissors in my hand. "This is the only mother you will ever have," she says. "Good or bad."

I brush her hair quickly, just the back, and a few strands get tangled and fall out. Then I pull all the hair over her shoulder, the way it glows, and cut with two hands; the scissors are dull.

"Keep going," she says, looking at herself in the mirror, and I do, the hair cascading onto my shoes and the floor. By the time I'm done, the threads of her hair have spread like fine tinsel on my sweater and shoes and socks. I let the scissors dangle in my hand.

"Now it's done, Jane," she says. Her hair stands out like a ragged bush. She hugs me but I can tell that she doesn't see me. She's looking over my shoulder into the mirror at what I have done and at the ordinary hair, brown and undeserving, on my head.

I go to my room and stay there, bright strands of hair leaving a trail of guilt to my door. I skip dinner, put on my pajamas, and go to bed.

I wait. The floorboards creak periodically in the hall; doors open and close. I hear dishes in the sink, I hear the TV and the shower, I hear Bee shut her bedroom door and turn out the light. I close my eyes for a while and lose track of time, and when I open them again, my father is sitting in his place in the bedside chair.

And it occurs to me that this time I can refuse his information, tell him that I'm too old for this kind of game and don't trust people anymore. I'm not the daughter he once knew. My father shifts in the chair but doesn't talk. He folds his hands and unfolds them. "Listen," he says. I steel myself to interrupt him, but he stops. I begin to drift off to sleep again. "Listen," he says, louder, insisting now, but there is nothing to listen to. I open my eyes and see my father clutching himself, leaning over the wastebasket as if he wants to be sick. But he makes no noise. He sits doubled up beside the bed as if in pain.

In the next room my mother is hanging things in the closet; the wire hangers clang against the wood. Maybe nothing is what it seems. I sit up in bed. It feels difficult at first, but all it will take is imagination and a little care. I fold the pillow behind me as my father lifts his head from his knees. He's ready now. I take a breath and begin to tell him what I know.

3

July

After my mother died, my father loved clocks. He turned my old bedroom into a study and filled it with ticking, a muffled back-and-forth we could sometimes hear through the closed door. One by one in the months after her death he came home with small, very ordinary timepieces, not saying anything about their proliferation but carrying them directly to the study, snapping the batteries in back and, as far as I knew, never paying attention to them again. Thirty or forty clocks of different sizes hung on the wall; a huge black desk and a set of fiberboard shelves above it held forty or fifty more.

Bee and I worried at first—Should he be in the presence of so much time passing all at once? Was he gauging its enormity, now that he had to spend it all alone?—but the ticking, like a constant, faint applause, seemed to do him good. No other room in the house contained a clock of any kind; once out of his study, my father didn't wear a watch on his gray-haired arm.

Aside from clocks, the study held a file cabinet stuffed with tax and retirement forms, two gold wing chairs, and the ingredients of my father's only hobby— seashell lamps. To pass the hours and to make a little money, he filled the wide empty glass bases of table lamps with driftwood, sand, seaweed, and shells. He took this activity seriously and worked with an artist's patience and an artist's eye, often laboring over sophisticated patterns with rows of sea urchins, fishing hooks, and sand dollars of increasing size. He sold the finished lamps to gift shops downtown and sometimes got orders from hotels. Occasionally a loyal customer would assume that he knew how to fix lamps, too, and would leave one on the porch when he wasn't home; these usually ended up permanently disassembled, lying in pieces across the desk and the two wing chairs.

During the second week of my visit, I knocked on the study door and went in, finding him opening a tube of clear cement with his teeth. "Stuck," he slurred, as the tube finally loosened in his mouth. "What's going on?" In front of him on the desk was a tiny starfish with a broken arm. The clicking, tocking, snapping of the clocks was like a constant conversation; it was hard to interrupt.

"Nothing." I sat behind him and looked out the window, where pigeons were building a nest under the eaves. "We'll need some cherry bombs for those," my father said. "I know a place where you can buy them through the mail." He worked on the starfish like a jeweler cutting a stone. "The moron who delivers these must have kicked them up the highway from Miami. I had to glue a couple of dozen." Fifteen or twenty starfish lay on a piece of cardboard at his feet.

"Can't you send them back?"

"It's not worth it. Somebody gets the axe if I complain."

I thought he probably had an inflated idea of his own power, but I didn't say so. We'd been getting along fairly well by not confronting each other: I'd been sleeping in the attic and rarely came downstairs before noon; entire days went by when our paths barely intersected. We greeted each other politely, like hotel guests meeting in the hall, and didn't discuss my pregnancy. I suppose each of us was waiting for the other to bring it up. "It's nice in here," I said. The room was painted a soothing sea green. My mother had painted every room in the house an ocean color. "I think it's good that you have a hobby—you've got something worthwhile to do."

"Worthwhile?" He fitted a seahorse into the half-filled lamp base on the desk. "This isn't worthwhile, it's an absolute waste of time."

"But you like making lamps," I said.

He let a gust of air out his nose. "You know what I'd like to make? I'd like to make a lamp out of garbage. Fill one of these up with some dented beer cans, a plastic shovel, and twenty legs from Barbie dolls. And a piece of dog dung. That would be art. I could sell them to museums. Any idiot could make one of these in half an hour."

"Why do you do it, then?" I asked.

He opened the desk drawer, scanning the small, perfectly arranged white boxes that held angel wings, bonnets, arks, conchs, cockles, Venus clams, helmets,

virgin nerites, livid naticas, whelks, turrets and spin-
dles, and half a dozen types of babies' ears, none of
which he had found in Sea Haven. "What else does a
man my age do with all his time? It's one activity or
another. Some people weave baskets. I make lamps."
He filled the wide interior of the base with pink and
white Styrofoam and carefully pressed a cowrie-helmet
to the glass. "Anyway, this keeps the old geezer off
the streets. You wouldn't believe what people will pay
for a set of these things."

"Dad, I want to ask you something about money."

He looked into a white plastic tub filled with shovels
and funnels and sand. "How much do you need?"

"None," I said. "I want to pay rent."

He turned around. "I've got a tenant downstairs.
You want him out?"

"No, I mean rent for up here. For the attic. So that
I won't feel guilty about eating your food. I can pay
you around a hundred dollars a month."

"Out of what? You're planning to sell your blood
at the blood bank?"

"I have money."

"You have several thousand dollars in savings that
I gave you when you turned eighteen, presuming that
you haven't squandered it, and at best a couple of
thousand more."

I shrugged. He overestimated my capacity to save.
I had spent most of the money he gave me several
months after I got it.

My father put his hands in his pockets as if searching for cash. "How many months are we talking
about?"

Over the last ten days, I had had time to think things through. I didn't want to teach in my condition, then waddle off to the hospital with my hand over my stomach at midyear, and there seemed no real reason yet to abandon my father's house. I was comfortable upstairs, I felt reassured among the things that I'd grown up with, and I would worry about what to do next year when next year rolled around. "A few months," I said. "A little while."

"Beg your pardon?" Half a dozen clocks behind him marked the hour. My father believed that adult children did not belong in their parents' homes.

"I don't know. Through fall. I can sublet my apartment in Philadelphia."

He raised his eyebrows, so gray and wiry that I wanted to smooth them with my thumb. "Don't you have a job, or something to do, that starts in September?"

"I'll get a part-time job here. Maybe something will come up."

He turned away, bending over the tub of fine white sand. "I don't want your ridiculous money."

"I'll pay for my groceries," I said. "I'm eating for two." I picked up a mussel shell and stroked its pearly surface. "I've been wondering. When Mom was pregnant, did she feel sick? Sometimes I'm so hungry, I feel like—"

"How can I concentrate," he snapped, "when you're in here yakking all the time?"

When I left I heard him kicking the bucket of sand across the room.

*   *   *

I loved staying in the attic. Every morning when I woke up, I could tell both the time and the weather from the level of noise on the beach. I slept with my head near the attic's porch door so that at night I could hear the ocean, the quiet crash of the waves, the hiss and draw of the shallow water sucked back from shore. Growing up next to the sea was like being constantly accustomed to hearing heartbeats and respiration from inside the womb. Once you left, the silence was always with you.

The other side of the long, rectangular attic had two triangular windows overlooking the street. The attic had low, unfinished, sloping ceilings, with the rusted tips of nails sticking through from the roof; it looked like the inside of a pine coffin except for the hole in the floor for the stairs, the two small windows, knee height, at the far west end, the square porch door, and a series of lightbulbs on the ceiling that could be lit by pulling a string. Near the porch side my father had set up a makeshift room, clearing a space for the old mahogany bed with pineapples carved in the headboard and on all four posts; for the antique dressing table with its silvery mirror; for the threadbare Oriental rug and the cane-seated rocking chair. It looked like a room roped off in a museum or an open-faced bedroom on a stage. On the other side of the stairs, the larger part of the attic remained an attic: full of the junk of my parents and father's parents—old clothes and scrapbooks, moth-eaten linen, and over a hundred cardboard boxes, taped shut and labeled with a handwriting no one could read. I slept with a single dim bulb lit to scare the silverfish away.

The only problem with the attic was that it heated up like an oven, and I liked to sleep late, with the blankets on. On one particularly steamy morning I woke with a headache, peeled the wet hair from my forehead and my neck, and stumbled through the brilliant square of sunlight outlined by the attic's porch door. The door was short—about four and a half feet high by three feet wide—so that I stooped as I emerged in my sweaty T-shirt, squinting and limping foot to foot on the floorboards, which were splintery and as hot as asphalt. I gripped the guardrail at the edge of the tiny deck, still blinking and rubbing my eyes, and saw—looking up at me from the bulkhead down below—my sister, Bee. She didn't wave or call my name but stood on the red-stained boards and studied me, the collar of her starched blue workshirt turned up as a defense against the sun. She also wore sneakers, the white girl's kind she had worn since the day she learned to walk, and a pair of long tan shorts so wide that her legs looked as skinny as a hen's. In spite of her lack of care Bee always looked good, or at least deliberate. She cut her short blond hair herself, in a jagged way, but it always looked daring instead of ridiculous, as it would have looked on me.

"Why are you staring at me?" I called. In the driveway to the right I could just see the hood of her well-built expensive German car, a new model she probably dismantled and reassembled on weekends for fun.

"I was looking," Bee said. "Not staring. Come down."

"You come up. I have to get dressed."

Bee looked away from me, toward the beach, which

was spotted with brightly colored things: bathing suits and umbrellas and folding chairs. "I'll get dressed," I said again, but I wasn't sure if Bee heard me because of the wind.

By the time I'd taken off my nightshirt and wiped my eyes, she stood behind me on the attic stairs. Bee was modest on her own behalf but didn't care about the nakedness of others: she appraised me, looking at my stomach and my breasts, then my face.

I pulled a shirt over my head and lifted my shorts from the nail. Before I could put them on Bee took a step forward and lay a hand against my stomach. Her palm was flat, utilitarian and cool.

"Dad told you," I said.

She nodded, businesslike, and put her hands back in her pockets.

"Not a very good way to learn about your sister's condition. Is that why you're here?"

"Why are *you* here?" she asked.

I put on my shorts, which were getting tight, and zipped them up most of the way. Next to Bee I was fleshy, thick, ungirded. "I'm sorry," I said. "I was going to tell you. I didn't want to do it on the phone."

"No, of course not." She picked an invisible speck off the front of her shirt.

"I didn't think you'd be happy to hear it." I looked for my comb. "In general, you know, we don't talk about these things. We don't even mention them."

Bee shrugged.

"How did Dad tell you? Did he say I'd been 'compromised'?"

"No, I think he used the term 'knocked up.' 'Your

sister seems to have gotten herself knocked up.' I'm supposed to find out what your plans are."

"That won't be easy. I don't have any yet. I haven't gotten any farther than coming home."

"Not exactly a step in the right direction," Bee said.

Clearly she'd come to cast a long, disapproving shadow. I had come for less certain reasons: the creature in my womb was a tiny compass, my father's house the pole.

"How long are you staying?" I asked. "How did you get the vacation time?"

Bee shook her hair away from her eyes. "I have a lot of days coming to me. I haven't taken much time away from the job."

I doubted she had taken any. Bee was a computer systems expert. When local companies discovered problems with their computers, they called her at any time of night or day. She wore a beeper on her belt. My father had always wanted her to be a doctor; now she had responded to his emergency call about me.

"Great," I said. "You can relax for a little while."

Bee sat on the edge of my bed, straight as a rod. It had been almost a year since I'd seen her. The last time I'd visited her in Atlanta I'd spent most of my time alone in her apartment—she was always being called to work. She seemed to like her job, which I found depressing—she dealt with humans seldom or not at all.

"When is it due?" she asked, so quietly that at first I wasn't sure she'd spoken.

"December or January, I think."

"Have you seen a doctor?"

"Actually I found one through the phone book. I have an appointment Monday afternoon."

"Name?" Bee was always officious.

"Subramanian. He's supposed to be very good. Anyway, he was one of four doctors listed in Sea Haven. And I can't go to Dr. Crown."

"Crown must be dead." Bee fingered the bedpost. "He was dead when he was our doctor. Why are you sleeping up here?"

"I like it," I said. "I like to be alone. I might make a bed out on the porch like we used to do."

"We did that *once*. We ended up covered with bites. I think you romanticize our childhood."

"No I don't. I think, for the most part, it was hell."

Bee smiled. She handed me a brown grocery bag that she'd brought upstairs. "A present," she said. "Open it."

I shook the contents out on the bed. Two pair of white sweatpants with elastic waists and three red T-shirts, one of them long-sleeved, men's large.

"Your new wardrobe."

I didn't ask about the lack of variety; when Bee found a color she liked, that's what she bought. "Thanks," I said.

Bee turned away and walked toward the cluttered end of the attic, her hair a quick gold flash in the clouded light. "You used to be afraid to come up here. I used to read in this chair sometimes to get away from you. You would come halfway up the steps a dozen times but never far enough to see me."

I didn't remember that at all, although I remembered being scared of the attic. The standing birdcage, in particular, terrified me. Bee walked past it, toward the old baby buggy, the treadle sewing machine, the claw-foot bathtub filled with deflated rubber rafts, the stack of hospital bedpans, the porcelain floor lamps, each in the shape of a fox jumping for grapes, the barrel-stave skis.

She disappeared behind some steamer trunks, making my "bedroom" seem like a small independent republic bordering on an empire out of control. "Dad says you're going to keep the child?" Back in view, she picked up a broken tape recorder and pressed the button that said ON.

"Do you think I won't be good at it?"

"I think you'll get used to it," she said. "Whatever 'it' is." The button popped up again, and Bee unfastened a tiny screwdriver from her key ring. "You're following a precedent, I guess. Mom was in the same situation."

"What do you mean?"

"I mean she was pregnant and not married. I was one of those full-sized premature babies you hear about."

"Why didn't I know that? Did she tell you that?"

"Nobody told me," Bee said. "It's easy enough to figure out if you compare my birthday to their anniversary."

"I can't believe nobody ever told me that," I said.

Bee popped the back off the tape recorder. "Why? What difference does it make? Are you so forthcoming with others?"

"No," I said. "I guess not."

We heard the door downstairs bang closed.

"Was it a boyfriend?" Bee didn't look at me. She and I didn't discuss the romantic aspects of our lives; her last relationship, as far as I knew, had involved a scrawny, unsocialized physical chemist and ended five years before. "Are there any fugitives that need to be brought to justice?"

"Not really," I said. "I didn't tell him. He wasn't important. Now he's gone."

Bee nodded as if satisfied. "I think I'll go down and make lunch. Or in your case, breakfast." She picked up the pieces of the tape recorder. "You should sleep in my room. We'll buy a portable fan. It's too hot up here for you." Bee always offered kindness in a bossy way.

I shook my head. "I'm fine."

Soon I heard her rattling the kitchen dishes—not the paper plates—and my father objecting futilely in the background.

I put on my sandals, which barely fit my swollen feet, and made the bed. I had thought that after I broke the news to my father, I might feel I was ready to leave. I wasn't. My mother had married my father because she was pregnant. She was fragile and distant when alive. As little as I thought I knew her, now I was sure I knew her less. Instead of dying, it was as if she had dissolved.

The three of us hadn't been home together during the summer for a dozen years and the house, as always, seemed smaller in the summer. Paradoxically, during the best weather of the year we were thrown together indoors or on the porch because of our common desire to avoid the volume and brilliance of the vacationers out in the open. I had always felt desperate in this season. I remembered one summer evening when I'd run to Bee crying, saying that our father loved her more. She'd tucked my hair behind my ear and reluctantly agreed. "He can't help it," she said. "Most of the time he tries not to let it show."

Now together again, Bee and I often sat on the front porch, reading the paper; finding us there, my father would rub his hands together, saying, "Well, if it isn't the two daughters of Torquemada." He used to call my mother Mrs. Torquemada when they were tipsy and in a good mood. Although I think he was glad to have us, he wasn't used to all the companionship and sometimes got crabby without warning: he shouted at Bee for invading his workroom, fixing the broken lamps and a closet hinge, and told me that if I didn't keep my paws out of the mint chocolate chip ice cream he would remind me to keep them out by cracking me over the head with a broom. We all crisscrossed the house, restless and uncommunicative.

At night we usually played Scrabble, though it put all of us in a foul mood. My father and I were sore losers and Bee always won, harassed and challenged every step of the way. She would leave the room when it wasn't her turn, come back to the board and choose her letters, then almost immediately lay all of them down in some combination we'd never seen. When we challenged her and lost, she was a stickler about our forfeiting our turns. My father kept score, though, and sometimes didn't count Bee's doubles or triples or bonus points. While he was monkeying with the numbers, I returned the letters I didn't like to the canvas bag and chose some more.

Finally, late one night, my father spelled *zebra* in a triple word space. "Get back here, you hopeless loser," he called to Bee, "you're going down."

She came back with the tape recorder she'd found in the attic, spelled *zaibatsu* off the *z* with all seven letters, and pulled a screwdriver from her pocket. "I've almost got this thing working."

My father and I looked at each other. "What the hell is *zaibatsu*?" he asked.

"Are you issuing a formal challenge?" Bee didn't look up.

"I'm just asking what the hell a *zaibatsu* is."

I said I was going to look it up.

"After the game," Bee said. "Look it up now, and your turn is over." She closed the back of the machine, screwed it in place, and rethreaded the tape.

"Do you have to do that now?" my father asked.

Bee spun the tape and switched it on. "Jane, your turn."

I studied my collection of *fs* and *bs*, wondering why I was spending so much time with people who lowered my self-esteem. I could spell *fib, dim, flab*. Suddenly the tape on the recorder started to spin. We heard static, then childish laughter followed by a shy rendition of "Mary Had a Little Lamb," sung by myself at around age three. Clapping; then the sound of the machine being turned on and off. Bee, age seven, recited a medieval sonnet full of sexual puns.

"Is that Spenser?" I asked. "I can't believe it."

"Shh," Bee said. "I want to hear the rest."

The machine clicked on and off again: chaos and more laughter. And then in the background we heard my mother's voice, perfectly preserved and wonderfully clear: "No, of course it's not enough. It's never enough. I don't think that's possible."

She had a smooth, low voice, liquid and intelligent; hearing it again was like stepping out into thin air and being held up, floating unsupported above the ground. "What are you doing?" she asked. "I don't want to be recorded. No, it's not. I won't say another word until you stop." The tape ran on for another minute, but she didn't talk again.

Each of us looked at the machine.

"Erase it," my father said.

I told Bee to check if there was any more.

"I said, erase it."

Bee played it back and we heard the same phrases. The rest of the tape was empty, gone.

My father shut himself in his room. Bee and I put the game away.

I said, "What was she talking about? What do you think wasn't enough for her?"

We gave Spunk his pill in butter and listened to Mr. Denzer shutting the windows down below.

Dr. Subramanian, according to the framed certificates on the wall, graduated from high school in New Delhi, from college in London, and from medical school in Cincinnati, Ohio. He also had a master's degree in English from a school in Florida I didn't know. He had a small, damp office downtown on top of a jewelry store whose window boasted a red velvet raft of wedding rings. Through the venetian blinds (he didn't close them) I could see the water slide and the Ferris wheel, its tiny colored boxes circling around.

"You are probably twelve to fourteen weeks pregnant." Dr. Subramanian examined me while staring at some imaginary point above my eyes; I in turn looked at the ceiling above. There is an etiquette to these things.

"In other words, you are entering the second trimester. And this is your first prenatal examination?" He spoke with a beautiful distinctness. He was slight and dark; there was something of the baby about him: his hair was matted, low on the forehead, and his nose was undeveloped, a delicate thing.

"I was preoccupied," I said.

He scratched his head. "If you are uncertain of the date of conception, we can order an ultrasonogram. They're really quite nice: you can see an image of the fetus on a screen. Your due date is probably around Christmas. A holiday child."

For some reason I pictured a turkey, waxed and fleshy and curled in a ball.

"Do you have any questions?" He was fiddling with a circular chart printed with dates; he turned it around and around and then looked up.

"What do most people ask?" I said.

"Anything." He looked surprised. "Ask me anything you like."

"How big is it now?"

Dr. Subramanian looked sympathetic. "About the size of a bar of soap. Would you like any information on diet and exercise?"

"I guess that would be appropriate," I said. Neither one of us moved.

"I hesitate"— Dr. Subramanian actually paused when he spoke the word.—"to counsel patients who indicate on their charts that they don't want counsel."

"I didn't want to end up in a room with a bunch of sixteen-year-olds and their friends. And I guess the whole idea still seems abstract. I don't imagine myself as anyone's mother."

"I do not perform abortions." Dr. Subramanian straightened some papers on his desk. "But I can refer you to people who do. Also, I can put you into contact with adoption agencies."

"What about a dating service?"

"No, my practice doesn't extend that far." It took a moment, but he smiled. "I'm sure you'll think of questions, and I hope you'll feel free to call me when you do. I'll give you some literature, meanwhile." He handed me several glossy pamphlets, one of which pictured a woman, hand on her stomach, conferring with a white-haired, white-skinned doctor actually wearing a shiny white disk on his head, as though he were playing at his role.

"I'm keeping the baby," I said. "The fetus. Right now I'm staying at my father's house. I mean, I'm living there, but just for a little while. I grew up in Sea Haven."

Dr. Subramanian's face was unchanged. "Anything else?"

"No," I said. "Yes. Why did you get a degree in English?"

"General interest." He folded his arms. "I'm a student of the human condition. Make a second appointment and we'll talk.''

I tucked the pamphlets under my arm and left the room.

"This dog," Bee said, "needs to go back to the vet today. He hasn't eaten anything.''

My father was on the phone, scheduling a starting time for golf for the three of us, even though Bee and I didn't want to play.

It was a Wednesday; in three more days Bee would be going home. Although ostensibly she'd come to keep an eye on me, we hadn't spent much time together. In a crisis, other families probably rush to hold the ailing person's hand; our family rushes to the general vicinity of the crisis and putters around, hoping the patient will spontaneously recover on her own.

"The pair of you are as energetic as a rug," my father said, hand covering the mouthpiece. "And the dog doesn't look any different than he did last week. Why in the world should he be hungry when he ate half my hamburger last night?''

"I think he's got a lump," Bee said, low-voiced, to me.

"Two-fifteen." My father triumphantly hung up. "Hell, of course he's got a lump. The dog is old. You should see the lumps I've got. Enormous things. You don't see me running off to check every goiter and bunion.''

"Goiters and bunions aren't in the stomach. I'm going to take him in.''

Slowly, my father put down his pencil. I could see

something starting in his face. "Two girls," he said. "Two daughters. After Jane was born I thought, 'Great. Now I'll teach them to play chess. I'll take them fishing. We'll play catch in the backyard. I don't mind having girls.' That's what I thought. 'We can still do all of those things.' "

"We never did any of those things, Dad," Bee said.

He ignored her. "If somebody pointed out to me, 'Girls don't stick by the old man the way boys do,' I'd tell them they were talking about someone else. I'd say, 'How do you know my girls won't stick around? How do you know they won't be loyal and come back to me when they're grown and keep me company, hanging around the house, eating and breaking things, and getting fatter, and agree to play nine lousy goddamn holes of golf and leave the goddamn dog alone?' "

Two hours later, we were on our way.

Bee drove. She was a terrible driver: no one in the Haus family drove very well, though some demonstrated more confidence in their lack of ability than others. My mother had driven recklessly and fast, searching for things that had fallen beneath her feet as she sped along or opening her purse to find a tissue or a pen; she often wrote lists or short letters at the wheel by leaning a scrap of paper on the horn. My father drove too slowly and tended to drift toward bicyclists or objects at the side of the road, as if drawn by a magnet. Sometimes he still reached for a shift that wasn't there. My habit was to get lost, entire highways disappearing at my approach, while Bee's was to follow much too closely on the bumpers of other cars, whether they were driving ten miles an hour or sixty-five. Her back never touched the seat; her chest nearly grazed the wheel, and she accelerated rapidly only to brake when she was about to hit someone. Now she was nosing up to a Buick.

I sat in back, fastened my seat belt, and closed my eyes.

"You two," my father said, "may run into some of your buddies on the greens. Don't let me stop you from yakking if you do."

"Who in the world would we run into?" Bee asked. She'd had few real friends in high school and certainly wasn't buddies with them now.

My father braced his hands against the dashboard. We were four or five feet from the Buick. "Well, Jane's probably still in touch with what's-his-name, Sandy or Dirty, whoever it was."

"Dusty," I said. "I'm not. I don't keep track of my high school boyfriends anymore."

"Plural?" he said. "Your memory's generous. I remember only the one."

The Buick pulled to the side of the road. A man and a woman in the front seat craned their necks as we drove by. "Dusty," I said, "and then Bert. Maybe I didn't bring the others home."

"Obviously not," my father said. "You were embarrassed about your family."

"Everyone's embarrassed about their family at that age."

Bee turned left, not using her blinker.

"In the old days," my father said, "we had a lot of quaint customs. People dated, brought the guy home to meet their families; sometimes they married. Simple stuff.''

I could hear the engine straining. ''You mean to tell me that you weren't embarrassed to bring friends to meet Grandma and Papa? Papa was crazy.''

''Bee, slow down.'' My father gripped the dash. ''This isn't an ambulance. My father, you know, was orphaned in his teens. He didn't have an easy time.''

''I heard he tried to murder Aunt Clara once,'' Bee said.

''*Only* once. Some people thought he should have tried at least once more.''

I remembered my mother saying that every Christmas my father's father would wrap up a small teak box and put it under the tree. She would open it—this was a gift—and find inside a collection of fingernail clippings. ''Thank you,'' she said, every year. ''I don't regret that you never knew him,'' she used to say.

My father rolled down the window. ''People were more interesting back then. What you see now, most of the people you see today, they're watered-down versions of their parents and grandparents. There's very little strength of character anymore.''

We passed the high school, which all three of us had attended. Only my mother had grown up outside of Sea Haven. She was from Maryland, which seemed mysterious and far. She didn't talk about her family or about growing up: her parents were dead, and all she ever said about them was, ''We didn't get along.''

''What are these?'' Between the bucket seats Bee found the shiny pamphlets I'd left by accident in the car: ''Breast-feeding—The Natural Way,'' ''Birth and

Recovery," "Caesarean Section," and so on.

"Let me see those," my father said, grabbing them from Bee before I understood what they had found. He brushed my arm away when I tried to take them back. "Oh," he said. "Hm." He raised his eyebrows, reading silently to himself.

"Good information, Dad?" Bee asked.

He continued browsing. "Listen to this. 'Fatigue is common during the first trimester. The mother should rest as often as possible when she is tired.' This is new? Hold your horses," he said to me, chasing my hand away again. "We didn't have guides like this when you two were born. Your mother and I had to do a lot of guessing." He flipped the pages. "I used to mark the tub once or twice a month and fill it up with water to the mark; then she'd get in so that we could see how much water she displaced. That way we could tell if the baby had grown."

"That doesn't measure the fetus," Bee said. "It measures the woman."

"Mom went along with that?" I asked.

"Sure she did. Your mother trusted me completely. Anyway I didn't give her a choice."

The image of my father coercing my naked, pregnant mother into a tub was entirely obscene. I could imagine her fending him off for a little while, then giving in: "All right, Gregory, I'm going in, just give me a minute, please, alone." He always won.

" 'If you plan to breast-feed,' " my father read aloud, " 'the nipples should be toughened in preparation.' "

Bee and I stared at the road.

" 'Hemorrhoids,' " he continued, " 'are common in the second and third trimesters.' That we can fix."

Bee made a U-turn into the parking lot. "We're here."

I opened my door while the car was still running.

My father didn't stop reading the pamphlets until I took them from his hand. Then he stepped smiling from the car. "Ready for defeat?" He waved to a man in a blue and white striped shirt, cupped his hands around his mouth, and shouted, "I taught these two kids everything they know. And they're still ungrateful."

Bee rolled her eyes and walked off to rent a cart.

The other man smiled but didn't wave.

"Bastard," my father said. We started for the first tee.

I always enjoyed Bee's comparative clumsiness. She couldn't hit a ball with a bat, could seldom catch an object thrown directly into her arms, and she looked like a stork when she ran. I didn't putt with the concentration that I used to have, but Bee was hopeless on the course in every way, which made the game much more worthwhile. We were an odd-looking threesome. Bee wore slick-bottomed sneakers, I wore my brand-new, bleach-white sweats, and my father carried a patchwork leather golf bag sewn together by handicapped veterans sixty years before.

At the tee we waited while the man who had snubbed my father chose a nine-iron. He pretended not to notice us when his ball veered into the trees.

"Too bad," my father said with a broad smile.

"Awful slice." The man didn't turn around but took a second shot, following it down the fairway guiltlessly.

"Isn't that cheating?" Bee asked. "Dad, you're up."

He waved her away. "Tee off. I'm going to stretch my legs awhile."

"You said you were going to play," I called, but he headed off in the direction of the lost ball.

"I thought he'd stopped doing that," Bee said.

For a while, my father had visited golf courses only to retrieve other golfers' balls. He had started when I was in high school and I didn't want him looking over my shoulder at every swing; I'd send him away and he'd come back with three or four balls, dented and stained. Then he discovered that the pro shops often bought good-condition used balls for a nickel each. His bag began to bristle with devices: long, telescoping rods with cups or sieves to rescue balls from water; metal pincers, rakes, and hooks to cull balls from thick brush. He could spend over an hour on his knees at the edge of a man-made pond, ignoring the stares of other golfers as the pile of balls beside him grew.

Bee pulled the driver from my father's bag. It was too long but she didn't notice; she squared her shoulders and, in one amazing motion, jerked her arms straight up without bending her elbows. The ball skittered ahead about thirty feet. "I was never good at this," she said. "Your turn."

I squared off, slightly unbalanced because of my changing shape; I felt like my hipbones were poised on two sides of a chasm. It felt good, though, to concentrate on the tension in my neck, to recognize the angle of my wrists, and physically to remember the automatic ideal placement of feet and knees. It was probably this sense of perfection that first drew me to the game and also drove me away: the sense of relaxed, ideal precision and the quickly following knowledge that no perfection is attainable and that near-perfection doesn't bring the benefits it should. On a good day, though, on a lucky day, there's something about the motion of a golfer's swing that is in harmony with the world. In the right palm's overlapping of the left thumb, in the shifting, muscular glide of elbows, wrists, hips, and knees, and in the pleasant stasis of the head and feet, you feel synchronized, whole, as if mimicking the motion of the planets, each with its own rotation fitting the rest. Though I hadn't touched a club all year, the ball cleared the sand trap nearest the green and landed thirty yards from the pin. My father emerged from the woods as the ball sailed past him and gave me the thumbs-up sign. Then he dove back into the trees. Bee picked up her ball. "Let's get this over with," she said, and we drove to the green. I took one putt for a birdie three. Going onto the fifth tee I was under par. We stopped the cart in the shade and waved a foursome on ahead. Bee was methodically putting the golf balls into the ball wash, pumping the handle up and down.

"You know it amazes me," I said, "how much you and Dad are alike. Ever since we were small. I felt like I was growing up with a miniature version of my father."

She looked surprised. "I'm not like Dad. I take after Mom."

"I'm not talking about looks," I said.

"Neither am I." She wiped the ball on her shorts. "You've always reminded me of Dad. I'm more like Mom. She was sure of herself and thoughtful—I don't mean considerate—but slow, in a way, like me. You and Dad are rash and sentimental. You jump to conclusions; you never think things through."

I watched Bee reorganize the tees in my old golf bag. "Mom always seemed to have a lot of secrets," I said. "I don't think anybody knew her very well."

We looked down at the fifth green, dotted with light gray seagulls taking a breather on their way to the boardwalk or the pier.

"Tell me why you're doing it," Bee said.

I knew what she wanted. Not the history—how accidentally it happened, and who, and when—but why I was adding to a life that had never been well arranged an obstacle larger than either of us could imagine.

"I can't explain it clearly yet." I sat on the edge of the golf cart and looked at my knees. There were moments when I felt full of myself and round, as smug as an egg, but there were others—more—when I began to sense how truly stupid I could be. "That's partly what I came home to figure out."

"This will only be vicarious for me," my sister said. "I'll be the spinster aunt. Odd aunt Bee."

"You'll be the only aunt," I said. "A third of the family." I turned around to look at the pine trees, which neatly shielded one hole from another. They had been scrawny, scrubby things when I learned to play. "Dad's disappeared," I said. "He probably fell down a rabbit hole."

"I have a friend," Bee said, "a man at work whose wife had a baby, but after it was born they got divorced. He said he looked in the crib one morning and knew he wasn't looking at his life."

I knew Bee was studying me through her perfect tortoiseshell sunglasses. She wasn't done. "You have lousy job prospects. You don't earn enough money for what you do. Your apartment is small. You have no support systems; you haven't lived in the city long enough. Your neighborhood isn't safe. I doubt, if you got your job back, that you'd get maternity leave."

"What about your friend?" I asked. "The one with the baby. Does he see it anymore?"

Bee sighed. "He left work a while ago. I didn't ask."

"Were you in love with him?"

She quickly looked up. "What you and Mom have in common is that you can't follow anything through. You do everything halfway and then come apart at the seams and need to be rescued: 'Jane's been caught stealing. Jane's dropping out of school; Jane's having a nervous breakdown.' "

"What was Mom unable to follow through on?"

"I don't know. Lots of things. The point is that Dad and I can't support you. Not for long."

"God forbid I should ask you to change old habits," I said. "You were my cheerleaders for failure, you and Dad. I think Mom would feel differently about this whole thing—my being pregnant. She went through it herself—she'd identify. Maybe part of the reason I'm doing it is because of her.''

Bee ran the tip of her sneaker through the grass. "Please don't use Mom as an excuse."

We stood only several feet apart, but I felt the miles stretch between us. In some ways I felt the decision to have a baby wasn't mine; it came from instinct, from some basement level of my psyche that shouted orders from below. I had a strange superstition that all the dead people in the world had cast their ballots and unanimously decided the question for me. I felt less like a person than a fruit, plump and irrevocable and dangling from a vine.

"An excuse is different from a reason, Bee," I said. "I mean, look at the coincidence. She and I were both pregnant and unmarried, and no one told me. Why wouldn't someone have told us? Why would they leave us out of everything? You remember more than I do. I wish I could remember more about the time when we were little and she was always home.''

"She was never 'always' home," Bee said.

"You know what I mean. Dad had to deal with us when she was sick, but she raised us and fed us and spent the time with us, at first. And I don't remember it very well. Dad was at work; most of the time when we were little, he was gone.''

"No, he wasn't." She looked surprised. "He worked part-time when you were small. I remember him changing diapers, feeding you in the high chair, giving you baths, everything. I used to wonder if he did as much for me.''

"That must have been only for a month or two," I said.

Bee smiled. "I just remembered seeing him strapping you into your high chair, pulling your legs through the plastic belt. You were incredibly chubby. I had to mash up the bananas for your lunch."

I tried to picture my father, all thumbs, and my five-year-old sister, skinny and dour, keeping up with my appetite and demands. "But Mom wasn't sick back then. She was diagnosed the first time when I was eight, and no one told me what was going on."

Bee was looking into the distance.

"That was the first time she was sick. Right, Bee?"

"I don't know," she said. "Isn't that strange? I can't remember." She twiddled the golf club in her hand. "Maybe it was earlier." She looked at me oddly. "I never considered that before."

"Considered what?"

She shook her head. "You have to stop blaming Dad for things that happened years ago. He may be eccentric, but that's his nature. What you need to do is come up with a plan for next year. What are you going to do with your apartment? How are you going to survive?"

Talking to Bee was like having a series of steel doors close in your face. I was about to explain to her that there was nothing wrong with taking a pause in the middle of your life to think about things when I suddenly remembered the wooden high chair she described, the feel of its grain against my legs, the hunger of sitting there, waiting, Bee staring at me in curiosity, in anger—angry about what?—the feeling that no one would bring me food, that I would starve while Bee ate in front of me, that I could never have enough. I remembered my mother's voice: "never enough."

Now the golf course, the trees, and even the weather—the three o'clock sun lighting a patch of my sister's hair—seemed unappealing, pointless and absurd.

"So eccentricity is in his nature," I said. "That's a real catchall. You can make almost any excuse with a term like that. I don't think other families operate like ours. Other people talk. They know each other. Nobody will talk about Mom to me."

"I was always the practical daughter," Bee said. "You'd be disappointed if I changed now. And Mom was a private person—you shouldn't nose into her business if she didn't want you to."

"Mom is dead," I said. "I don't think at this point she would mind at all."

My father was climbing the hill behind us, face shiny with exertion, the lumps of fifteen or twenty golf balls in his pants pockets. "You wouldn't believe," he said, "what people will walk away from. Look at this. A monogrammed ball. I must have found half a dozen from private clubs."

"That's great, Dad," Bee said.

"Look, here's one from Maui, with a little pineapple printed on its hide. I'll be damned." He looked up. "What's the matter with you two? I thought we came here to have fun." He looked back and forth between us.

"Jane and I were talking about nature," Bee said.

My father stared. I climbed into the cart and Bee followed. "Come on, Dad, we're ready to go."

"Oh, nature." He took off his hat, turned it inside out, and wiped his hands on the cloth inside. "Well, I guess I see what you're saying." He hoisted the clubs and himself in back. "We should let the dog out, anyway. He knows what you mean by nature. He has nature problems of his own."

"Spunk doesn't need a walk, he needs a vet," Bee said.

"Don't worry about Spunk. If he needs a vet, he'll go."

But Spunk was dead when we got home. He lay in the last patch of sunlight on the kitchen floor, eyes open, a pool of urine soaking his hind legs and his tail. "Poor ugly beast," my father said. He knelt by the dog while Bee and I stood, straight and compassionless and tall. We buried Spunk the next day at sunrise, just out of sight of the tourists, in the backyard.

4

Losing Ourselves in Trenton

We are here in west New Jersey for the funeral of my great-aunt Agnes, dead of heart disease at the age of eighty-one. She is—or was—one of my father's last relatives, and he's unusually depressed, considering her age and the fact that she was active, even lucid, until the end. Aunt Agnes was a massive, rectangular woman who always wore a hat and shoes to match her dress: Bee and I didn't know her well because she didn't like children and often made it a point to say so when we were around.

My mother spreads the curtains of the hotel window. Twenty yards from our room is a major highway; a barbed wire fence protects the half-empty, stagnant pool. "We probably came too early." She looks tired. Two police cars turn on their sirens down below.

My parents don't travel well. They accept the worst tables in restaurants and tip the wrong people in hotels. After arguing along the highway about the difference between motor lodges, bed-and-breakfasts, inns, and motels, we have ended up in this double room with an orange rug, two queen-sized beds, one of which vibrates when you drop a quarter in the metal headboard, and a tiny bathroom with unwashed towels.

Beatrice mutters to me in the hallway that Aunt Agnes isn't the real reason that we've come.

"What is it, then?" I ask. Having worried all morning about the funeral—whether we'll have to shake hands with the minister or even the corpse, whether the body will be sitting up in a chair or lying down—I hope that release is on its way: maybe we won't have to go to the funeral after all. "What *is* the reason?"

Bee won't answer. She eyes my father, standing sentry by the door. Of course, this is *his* aunt, *his* trip; I wonder if he has arranged Aunt Agnes's death in order to bring us—my sister and me reluctant, our mother distant, with yellow circles embossed around her lovely caramel eyes—here to Trenton on a voyage of his own design.

My father has told us that some of Aunt Agnes's jewelry will be Bee's and mine. Aunt Agnes mainly wore enormous pins: peacocks with emerald tails, clusters of flowers in topaz and garnet, horses' heads with ruby eyes. When I asked why Aunt Agnes ended up with so many jewels, my father said, "Because she didn't have children to pick her clean."

I take a quarter from my mother's purse and put it in the headboard's slot. The mattress becomes a motorboat.

"We should have left the house this afternoon," my mother says. "That would have been the better thing to do." My mother is pretty in an annoying, fragile way: lately I think she looks wispy on purpose, and I take personal offense at the way she presents herself as a vanishing species.

"We needed a cushion," my father says. "Things happen. Disasters. We could have had a flat tire."

Bee, on the bed next to me, manages to go completely limp on her side of the mattress, her skinny arms and legs jiggling flesh into rubber, her cat's-eye glasses walking by millimeters down her nose.

The mattress stops. My mother lets go of the curtain.

All of us sit or lie immobile on beds or chairs as if hurled into position from a distance.

"Christ," my father says, scratching his forehead, which every year looms larger than the year before. "How could Agnes live in this awful city?"

Of course we should have left in the afternoon. Instead, we woke to four separate alarm clocks at dawn and ate our prewrapped breakfasts in the car, arriving in Trenton at 9 A.M. The funeral is tomorrow. Now we have twelve or more hours to kill, and we are miles from stores or movie theaters or anything else to do.

"Settle down," my father says, even though we sit empty-handed and silent, not doing a thing. He is clearly as bored as we are and stares at his knees.

Bee gets up and ransacks the drawers. She finds two extra pillows, half a candy wrapper, a Bible, and a deck of cards. Clandestinely she shuffles and sets up a game of solitaire. The rest of us watch.

"Nine on the ten," my father says, pointing with the tip of a polished loafer.

"You need a king-space," adds my mother, fading

back against the chair like a feather settling.

Bee manipulates the rows.

"You're not going out in *this* game." My father reaches over her shoulder. "Look at those kings. Might as well pick them up and start again."

"Doesn't solitaire mean that you play alone?" Bee takes off her glasses to clean them. Her hair, white blond, looks dim in the filmy light of the hotel. "I think this deck is missing some cards."

"What do you expect?" Magnanimous, my father pulls out his wallet. "Buy a deck downstairs. Buy two. Bring back the change."

Bee folds the money, creasing it with her thumb. "Take Jane," my mother says. We live by an unspoken rule that insists we will travel only in twos: Never send an explorer out alone. We run downstairs to the gift shop and buy two bags of chips and a deck of cards for $14.50.

"That's expensive," Bee says to the bored-looking woman behind the counter.

"It's your money," the woman says.

Back in the lobby, Bee counts the change.

"You were going to tell me why we came here," I say. "You were going to explain what the reason was."

Bee looks blank. She has a way of washing all expression from her face, as if she's passed through a waterfall. "The reason keeps changing," she says. "You have to figure it out for yourself."

"Are we still going to the funeral?"

"Of course."

"Then what's the other reason that we've come?"

Bee seems to examine me for flaws, as if I am capable of leaking. "You probably know it already," she says. "You feel it inside."

Taking an inventory of my inner organs, the ones I know, I want to ask her, *"Feel it where?"* But Bee is wearing her mightier-sister-than-thou face, and I'm certain she won't tell. She straightens my hairband and pulls a kneesock to my knee. "Let's go."

My father opens the chips and sorts the cards, using two jokers from the new deck as replacement cards for those missing in the old. Because of the different patterns, they stand out clearly from the rest. They are the ace and king of spades.

"Now what we do," he says, cracking his knuckles, "is we teach you ignorant children how to play bridge."

"That's supposed to be complicated," Bee says, casting an obvious glance at me.

"That's why you should have learned earlier. You pick it up faster when you're young. Your mother and I used to play before you were born."

"We haven't played since," my mother says. "We fought too much."

"There are only two things you need to know"— he shuffles expertly—"to qualify as a member of the human species: how to putt uphill and how to make a bid in bridge. Without them you're a gorilla."

"A Neanderthal," Bee says.

"That too. Get me a scorepad and a pen."

"Were you good at bridge, Mom?" Bee asks.

"She was adequate," says my father. "She lacks all

the proper instincts. You need to have a killer's drive.''

"Do Bee and I have that?'' We sit around the nightstand, eating chips and wiping the salt from our sweaty palms.

"Is your name Haus?'' My father deals. "At least half of your genes are mine. And I know the game. *Caroline*.'' My mother, who has been looking out the window again at the brackish pool, drops the curtain, sighs, and picks up her cards.

I have played solitaire, spit, scrunch, fish, old maid, slapjack, and war, but I have never heard of trump and know nothing of bids or counting points. My father soon becomes impatient. "A ten of *hearts*? You're playing hearts? You didn't follow suit two tricks ago if you still have hearts—you can't possibly have that card.''

"I saved it,'' I tell him. He has been offering all sorts of tips and instructions to Beatrice, but none to me because I'm not his partner. Whenever I look to my mother for guidance she makes a halfhearted explanation, helplessly waves a pale hand, and says, "You'll see.''

"Hell,'' my father says. "Throw in the hand again.''

Ordinarily I would buckle and refuse to play, but the game has caught me with its orderliness and method, its way of making sense out of random luck, its potential for reward if only you can manage to remember a thousand different constantly changing bits of useless information. It's more of a ceremony than a game.

When Bee and my father have won three rubbers and my mother and I still haven't won a game, we decide to go out for sandwiches. My mother wants to stay in the room.

"Jane, you stay too," my father says.

I don't want to stay with my mother, who didn't play well enough to allow us to win even a single game. I throw my jacket on the floor.

"Don't open the door to *anyone*," he says, as if criminals and murderers have already selected us as their target. Once they're out of earshot, I unlock it, leaving the yellow chain links dangling down.

My mother lies motionless on the orange bedspread, shoes and stockings off, a dingy washcloth sheltering her eyes. I understand that she's sick, but I am tired of needing to be quiet and sympathetic. I know that I am a selfish, demanding, ordinary child, and because of that, I resent my mother more. She has a new hairstyle—a wig—that doesn't suit her: it's too blond, not the red wheat color of her old hair. She's always touching or adjusting it. She wears a cinched-at-the-waist blue dress that makes her look too thin.

For a while I sit in a chair and study a bruise on my left ankle, imagining that I live in Arizona on a pony ranch and that my parents cook up great vats of beef stew on an open fire while the hired hands gather around. My mother would laugh and wear spurs and flirt with the men, who all admired her; they would confide their crushes to me while squinting into the distance at the setting sun. When they rode away my mother would pull me up onto her horse and explain the secrets of animals and plants. Bee would have died of a childhood illness before I was born.

My mother peels off the washcloth and sits up. She runs her hands up and down her calves. "I'll have to borrow your father's razor," she says. "I never think about shaving anymore. It's strange what you can forget."

She isn't talking to me but to herself.

"You should see the hair on *my* legs," I say, feeling desolate and surly. I pull down my sock. "It's worse than yours. It's like a jungle. I should shave, probably, too."

"Let me see." She comes closer to the edge of the bed, balling up her dress between her thighs. She occasionally has a way of seeming amused by my ideas, and I hope that this isn't one of those occasions. My mother's skin is so white, it looks transparent: I've never admired a woman's upper legs before. "Come over here." I hate and love her for her clarinet of a voice, for the power of her loveliness over me. I pull my chair up toward her and gradually ease my way onto the bed, as if drawn there by magnets made of the blood in my own body. I want small internal implosions to return me to my infancy so that I can curl up in the cradle of her arms. "Well, your hair's darker than mine; I don't know. You're. . . ."

"Eleven," I tell her. "I was born eleven years ago."

She runs her hand over my shin. "Does your sister shave yet?" Sometimes she looks at me the way a doctor does: apparently curious about whatever the trouble is but not really listening very well. "I suppose Beatrice wouldn't bother."

I want to tell her that I'm still too young to shave, that none of my friends shave, and that she should keep up with these dates and landmarks like the other mothers do. She should have read books about how to raise us: You don't spend so much time staring out of windows, you don't talk about the hair falling out of your legs, and you don't let your children miss you when you aren't gone.

"Why don't you wait another year or two," she says, her hand still warm on my skin. "Did you know that I never liked Aunt Agnes? I don't know why."

"Mom," I say.

"What?"

I can't think of anything to ask her—I have no theories—and so I tell her my head hurts, and she moves her fingers through my hair for a little while.

I shut my eyes and let the pictures come. I imagine the campfires, the armadillos, the brilliant scorpions that try to creep into our sleeping bags. I see all the dangers, but the blessings, too: My mother will save me from the emptiness, from the nothing that surrounds us like a dry expanse of flat earth, without light and water, without end.

Our lunches are chicken or turkey on white bread, bought from a dusty machine in the lobby. The sandwiches are sliced into triangles, crusts against the cardboard in the back. They're stiff and smell somehow of Vaseline, one tiny slice of pressed meat inside of each.

"Revolting," my father says, eating his readily,

then finishing my mother's and half of Bee's. I get used to the unusual flavor and finish mine.

After watching half of a police show on TV and staring at the traffic on the highway for a while, we decide to return to bridge, which, my father explains, is good for the intellect as well as the soul. My mother files her nails and says "ha ha."

"It's a distraction, at least," Bee says, goody-goodying up to my parents. My mother kisses her for her trouble while my father and I each shuffle a deck of cards.

We play for hours. Bee develops a gift for the game, which is no surprise, and she begins pointing out the flaws in my father's play. "If you had finessed the king," she says, "you would have won an extra trick."

"I didn't need the extra trick. That's the end of the rubber, smarty-pants."

"I think you lost count, though, Dad. The five of clubs was good."

"There's no reason to keep count of fives."

"But the game demands it." Bee cuts the full deck. Her fingernails are chewed down to the nubbins, her glasses halfway down her needly nose. "You have to keep every card in your mind, all the time." She says this as though announcing that none of the rest of us is able to do what she easily does.

"I don't count any of them," I tell her.

"Well, you should try."

Her implied sympathy disgusts me. The way she patiently waits while I sort my cards (laying them face-up by suit across the bed while everyone tries to look away), her refusal to belittle my poor abilities, and her way of holding knowledge in her hand like an extra trump make me want to drive her to the edge. I don't want anyone's patience. I want to be the best at this game, or I want to ruin everyone's fun.

"I don't want to try," I say. "I don't need to store things in my brain. I have other things to think about. I'm not like you."

"What do you think about, Jane?" my mother asks. She's smiling but I know she wants a serious answer. Mainly, during the last half hour I have thought about dead people in their coffins: I've thought of them kissing me, putting their jewelry, mostly tiaras, on my head. I've thought of the man downstairs at the hotel desk coming up and killing every one of us with an axe and chopping the cord to the telephone just when I pick up the receiver to dial. I've thought of the reasons that we might have come to Trenton. I've thought of centipedes and leeches crawling up the bathtub drain.

"I'm not allowed to tell," I say, which in some way is very true.

"Do you want to keep playing?"

"Yes," I say, and the game goes on.

By six o'clock the score is thirteen rubbers to one. "That's it," my mother says. The yellow circles around her eyes have gotten deeper. She climbs into the nonvibrating bed and pulls the covers up to her chin.

"You nap a while. We'll wait," my father says.

"No, I'm not hungry. I want to stay here." She's

slipped into her pouting movie-star persona.

The three of us stare down at her on the bed. I don't want to have to stay if my father and Bee go out to dinner. I don't want to watch her twitch under the covers in her sleep, ignoring me.

"If we wait an hour, you might get hungry," my father says.

"I won't get hungry."

"You might."

She sits up in bed and looks at him as if she needs to put him together like a puzzle and try to make sense of what she sees. "Out," she says. "Go."

Downstairs, the three of us push through the metal door to the fumes of the parking lot outside and drive without speaking to the very first restaurant on the highway, a diner called Nathan's Grill.

We choose a red vinyl booth overlooking the road.

My father, now that we aren't playing cards, has resumed his bad mood. "Don't slouch," he says. "Try to sit up straight."

We are already straight. Bee hands out the menus, which are twelve pages long and include an endless variety of food, from Cajun shrimp to manicotti to potato pancakes to leg of lamb.

"We shouldn't have come so early," Bee says. "We could be eating dinner at home."

"And looking for a hotel room after dark? What a good idea." My father snorts.

"I have the impression that our room would still be available." Bee turns the page. "We could have stayed home. It wouldn't have mattered to Aunt Agnes."

"That's one theory," my father says.

The waitress appears. She doesn't ask for our order but stands silent by our booth, pen on a pad, more like a monument to waitresses than the real thing.

"We'd like to know if anything on this list is worth the trouble," my father says.

"The meat loaf is supposed to be good. I haven't tried it." She waggles her pen.

"All right, on that overwhelming recommendation we'll have four plates of meat loaf, mashed potatoes, and peas, one in a plastic container to go. Hold the gravy. The fourth plate has to stay hot, so bring it last."

"Nothing to drink?"

"Four glasses of milk, one to go. Keep it cold."

"I don't like peas," I tell him. "I was going to order fish."

"We'll eat the same thing," he says. "It'll make your sister happy. It'll be like home, where some of us evidently would rather be."

My sister twirls the salt and pepper shakers. Her freckles have disappeared; her face is flushed. In the last six months, she seems to have grown older by several years. "Even if the three of us had to come," she says, "Mom should have stayed home. That's just too much."

My father shuts his menu with a snap. "Too much for whom?"

"For all of us," Bee says. "For Mom. You know what I mean. I don't know why we made her do it."

"She was forced?" He shakes out a napkin that was knotted into some unidentifiable shape.

"She might as well have been. She should have been left to stay at home."

"There are four of us in this family."

The waitress arrives with the milk. Bee holds her glass in front of her but doesn't drink. The lamp above the table makes a crown on her bright blond hair. "Three of them aren't dying."

I watch my father's face. He has a calm, even pleasant expression. He looks Bee right in the eye.

She looks right back. Then she leans across the table, her pointed chin just like our mother's: "Slowly, I know. But did you think we wouldn't notice?"

"I don't give a sweet goddamn what you notice," my father says, still looking calm and even-tempered. He stands up and heads for the men's room.

"Stay here." Bee starts after him. "Don't move."

I don't. I sit in the booth hoping no one will notice that I'm alone. I pray that the food won't come, that food will never sicken my gaze again. I read the menu over and over until water rises in my eyes and floods the printed words away.

"Where'd your buddies go?" asks the waitress, arms laden with identical plates of food. The meat loaf looks like a brick, and the cook has forgotten to omit the gravy, which is thick, almost elastic, draped over the potatoes like a tarp. Just as I turn to her, thinking I will have to be taken into custody for an unpaid bill, my father and Bee reappear.

They sit down quietly, composed.

My father slices his meat loaf, then reaches for the salt and shakes it deliberately, five or six times, above his plate. The holes in the shaker are large and the salt streams onto his food, landing in damp, small piles. He looks at me briefly, then picks up my fork and puts it into my hand. He watches until I deposit the food in my mouth. "When I was Jane's age, here, my aunt Agnes caught me swearing. She heard me say 'bitch' or something like that, and she didn't like the way I said it. I thought she would tell your granddad, but she pulled me aside and said, 'Gregory, don't say "bitch" by itself that way; that's not a curse. Say "son of a bitch." ' Then I said it and she slapped me."

He hasn't tasted anything.

"You shouldn't use so much salt," Bee says. "It's bad for your heart."

The two of them simultaneously smile.

I have no idea what anyone is saying; I'm hearing a foreign language spoken for the first time. The potatoes on my plate are full of bumps, lurking and warm.

"Wipe your eyes, Jane," my father says; Bee hands me a napkin, and we continue with our meal.

In the morning my father wakes me and hands me my clothes: a brown dress I have never liked, a cotton undershirt, underpants, socks, and a new pair of lace-up shoes. He pushes me toward the bathroom, flips on the light, and shuts the door. I am washed and dressed before I begin wondering why Bee has been allowed to stay in bed, with the blinds drawn. I leave the fluorescence of the bathroom and head for the lump in the sheets where my sister lies. Lay. My mother's bed is empty too.

"They went out for breakfast." My father straightens his tie.

"When did they leave?"

He looks at his watch. "About an hour ago."

"They'll be finished by the time we get there," I say, just in time to catch sight of the glazed donut and cardboard carton of milk on the little table by the door.

"Bring them with you," my father says.

I look down at the donut for a while. "Will we meet them there?"

He doesn't answer, so there is nothing to do but follow him, the donut sticky in my hand as we walk down the hall, through the lobby, and under the brilliant sunshine toward the car.

The small white chapel holds thirty or forty people, all of them clustered in the back, away from the bier. My father looks rigid and nervous and poorly dressed: there is something wrong with the color of his jacket or his tie. I've never been in a church with him before; he refers to religion as "hocus-pocus" and to church-goers as "sheep." A stained-glass window with a picture of Jesus spills its multicolored shadow over his shoes and onto the floor.

We stand like wallflowers apart from everyone else until it's time to file into a pew. Organ music rolls out over our heads.

I want to ask questions about where we'll meet Bee and my mother later and about why I've been chosen, instead of Bee, for this meeting with death, but my father is stone-faced, staring at a purple hymnal in the pew. He opens it, leafs through it as he would a magazine, and shuts it just as a minister in a suit and collar approaches the bier.

"Friends," he says, letting the word hang in the air like a lost balloon. He nods along with himself, approving in advance what he plans to say. "Neighbors and relatives. Loved ones." My father turns his head toward the back of the church.

"We are here to remember Agnes Mary Vaughn. We are here to celebrate her life, her giving spirit, her generosity and kindness toward family and friends."

The minister is young; he pauses and smiles, probably used to being able to cheer people up. I doubt that he ever met Aunt Agnes. According to my father, she wasn't exactly generous or kind: he admired her for her crustiness and the way she held her liquor. Now my father turns around in his seat again, craning his neck toward the back of the chapel as if expecting to see a bride. Several people, heads bowed, try to turn stealthily and look. The minister talks about loss and somehow from there decides that all of us have gained something, even if we don't know what it is. He says that death is a river. He says that everyone walks toward and then wades into it on his own.

My father stands. For a moment I think he's going to offer a correction, to say that Aunt Agnes cheated at cards and kept a flask of whisky in her dress. But he grabs my wrist and walks out of the pew. We stumble over several sets of feet on our way to the aisle.

In front of the church the hearse waits, a gleaming thing.

"I don't think we were supposed to leave yet," I say.

My father crosses the street, opens the car door, and steps inside: for a moment I think that he'll abandon me, that I'll end up riding beside the flower-strewn coffin ambulance-fashion in the back of Aunt Agnes's hearse. At last he unlocks the passenger door.

"Where are we going, Dad?" I ask, climbing in.

He starts the motor and pulls out; the tires whine.

"To the graveyard? Do we know how to get there? Dad?"

"You have the map," he says.

I locate the sun-bleached map of Trenton, bought twenty years ago at a gas station that has since gone out of business. I might as well have a map of Mars.

"What's the name of it?" I ask.

"Name of what? Oh, Roselawn," he says.

Unbelievably, I find it in the index on the back, but we're already speeding down the highway, whether in the right or the wrong direction I can't tell.

"Maybe you should pull over for a while and help me figure out where we are."

"A good navigator, Jane," my father says, "finds East and West, and gets his bearings on the road." He looks determined in a reckless way, deliberately calm. I would rather be back at the funeral, hearing lies about Aunt Agnes.

"Why are we here? What if we're late for the rest of the service?"

"It's hard to be late to a burial," my father says.

We continue down the highway. As far as I can tell, if we keep going, we'll enter the orange blob of Staten Island and never get home. "Take this exit," I say. He obeys like a robot, changing lanes. As soon as we're off the exit I realize that I've made a mistake; we have missed the highway heading south and are instead on a fast-food strip crowded with local traffic, buses, and trucks.

"I think that might have been the wrong exit. We weren't supposed to end up here." I expect my father to grab the map in exasperation, but he doesn't seem to be listening. He cruises along, seeing the sights, as if we were shopping instead of on our way to Aunt Agnes's grave.

I let the map slide to the floor when we stop at a light.

"I'll be damned," my father says. Up ahead, off a dusty side road, there's a double-decker driving range. We've heard about these but have never seen one.

"Dad, I don't think we have time for golf right now." I'm taking my second year of lessons, and my father dreams of entering us in tournaments as a father-daughter team.

We're already pulling onto the shoulder.

"Help me figure out where we are, Dad, okay?"

He smiles. "You never know what you'll run into, do you, Jane? Every minute's a surprise, away from home."

The gravel lot is full of cars that are rusty and worn. The range does look funny: all the golfers in their tiny boxes, one row of ten on top of the other, and in almost every box someone swinging away. "I'll buy a small bucket," my father says. "Toot the horn when you want to go."

"Give me a hint at least, Dad."

He tosses the keys onto the seat. "I'll be back in a little while."

I wait until I see him climbing the steps to the second tier, and then I take the map inside the driving range office to ask for help. Maybe because I look young and lost, asking directions to a graveyard in my brown dress, several high school boys as well as the owner stop what they're doing to look at the map. We're thirty minutes from the cemetery by now, and each of them offers a different route. I'm afraid to change my mind and ask for directions to the motel. Finally they settle on the owner's way, and one of the boys—the handsomest—carefully writes the directions down. They fill half a page.

Back in the car, I wipe the dust from my shoes and toot the horn. My father sets another ball on the tee. I watch him swing. He relies too much on the shoulders, twisting to the left as he follows through. The ball lands short of one hundred yards. He tees up again. From a distance, the colored squares full of tiny golfers form a toy. I look at the clock: ten-fifteen. Check-out time at the motel is at noon. I picture Bee and my mother on chairs in the lobby, waiting and wondering where we are. "We were becoming more fully human," I'll explain, citing my father's belief in the powers of golf and bridge.

"Dad," I yell, sticking my head outside the window; several men in the boxes turn around. My father isn't one of them. He swings and this time the ball soars, better than two hundred yards.

This doesn't satisfy him, though, because he quickly tees up again. He doesn't appear to be watching the

ball: he tees up too quickly, ignoring his own advice—
"Never hurry your swing." The other golfers look like
they might be enjoying themselves, relaxing and
having fun; my father appears to be golfing at gun-
point, as if a madman had come up behind him and
told him he could save his family, his wallet, his soul,
in only this way.

I take off my shoes and socks, knowing it won't do
any good to call again. Eventually my father will come
down. He'll appear at the window, knocking, with blis-
tered palms. Seeing him through the glass, I'll know
that instead of being lost all by myself we are lost
together and that neither maps nor the help of others
will allow us to find our way.

5

~

August

Dr. Subramanian warned that I was gaining weight too fast. I had four more months to go and had put on enough to last until Christmas. As soon as my nausea stopped, an overwhelming hunger set in: I ate mixing-bowls full of cereal, loaves of Italian bread split down the middle with butter and jam, entire pizzas, ice cream by the half gallon; I drank quarts of milk. I felt I had never eaten before, never truly understood the satisfaction food could bring. Silverware seemed inadequate for my needs. He shook his head. "If the weather stays so hot, you will be uncomfortable." He palpated my ankles, which retained water and looked like semi-inflated balloons.

"This kind of heat never keeps up," I said, not telling him that I'd had to pause twice on the flight of stairs leading to his office.

He scheduled my ultrasound appointment for the end of the month, measured my stomach, and let me go. "Do you have an air conditioner at home?"

"No," I said. "We have the ocean."

"Make use of it," he said.

I did. When I got home I pulled a cobweb-covered beach chair into the surf and let my hands, swollen like mitts, drag the ocean floor.

It was in this posture that I met Ellie. She stood at the foot of my chair, blocking the sun. "Go away, shadow," I said, without opening my eyes. The shadow stayed.

"Ms. Haus?" She stood at the edge of the water, wearing boys' Hawaiian print trunks and a white bandeau. Her straw-colored hair hung limp to her shoulders, which were narrow and pointy and almost poked through her sunburned skin.

"Ellie Lund?"

"Yeah, it's me."

Ellie had been a student in my English class in Philadelphia. She looked more lost here on the beach than she had in school, where she'd affected a fair amount of nonchalance.

"I thought it was you," she said, lifting a scrap of dead skin from the tip of her nose. "I walked by yesterday and the day before. My parents have a place just up the block. The light blue one with the spiral stairs."

I knew that house well. My father said it cost half a million. "What does your father do?" I asked.

"Not a lot," Ellie said. "Ms. Haus, are you pregnant?"

I was wearing a size fourteen tank suit bought at a used-clothing store, and my breasts, newly large and ebullient, were lolling toward the sides of the stretched-out top. Sunning was a new experience for me. "Yes, I am."

Ellie nodded. "I liked our class. I thought you were fairly cool for a teacher. For English the year before I had Mr. Kline. He was a jerk." Ellie was standing on the balls of her feet, looking down. "What are you going to name the baby?"

"I don't know." I felt lazy with Ellie there. I had noticed in the last few weeks that many people feel ill at ease around pregnant women. They don't want to look at your stomach or your eyes.

"You haven't thought about it?" she asked.

"No, it's too early. There are a lot of things that I haven't thought about."

"It could be born premature."

"If it were born tomorrow, Ellie"—I looked at her over my sunglasses—"it wouldn't need a name at all."

I saw her shiver. "That's disgusting. A name's important. Ms. Haus, do you mind if I smoke?"

"Go ahead." She wasn't my student anymore. I moved my feet and she sat on the edge of my chair, taking two cigarettes from a baggy tucked in her shorts. The bandeau slipped every time she moved— she tugged at it now and then and tried to hold it in place by keeping her arms clamped down.

"Ms. Haus?"

I had let my eyes close again. "Yes, Ellie?"

"Does this mean that you won't be teaching in the fall?"

"Yes, it does. Technically I'll be taking a leave of absence, but I didn't tell anyone why. In fact, if you see Mr. Cole or the superintendent, don't tell them you saw me.''

"Why not?''

I sat up, dimly aware of how I looked: salty ropes of brown hair, pallid waterlogged skin. I was undergoing great change without grace or style. "Well, Ellie, it doesn't look good for an unmarried teacher to have a baby. I might turn into one of those women you've been warned about. They end up yelling at their kids and wishing they had washers and dryers and better cars. I'm probably someone your mother wouldn't want you to talk to again.''

"A role model.'' Ellie smiled. "My mother doesn't care who I talk to. She spends all her time on the phone.''

"What does she do?''

"She raises money for people. They pay her because she's pretty and she can talk people out of their wallets. She's really good.''

"That's impressive.''

"Yeah, I know.'' Ellie puffed on her cigarette, then put it out underneath my chair. "My aunt just had a baby. She read studies. She heard that if you sing to the baby when it's inside you, it'll learn to be good at music when it's grown.''

"What if you have a lousy singing voice?''

Ellie looked thoughtful. "You could read to it,'' she said. "If it was me, I'd probably hum to it—that way you don't have to remember any words.''

"You'd probably be better at this than I am,'' I said. "But don't try it soon. *Do not attempt this experiment at home.*''

"Why aren't you good at it?"

I thought up a number of flippant answers and discarded them all. "I don't think it's possible to really comprehend the outcome or understand all the ramifications, so I guess I've chosen not to consider any of them," I said. "Yet."

"That sounds really stupid," Ellie said. She chewed at her nails, which were short and chipped, painted the color of a ripe plum. "I think it would be lousy if you gave up teaching. I told a couple kids to take your class."

"Would I like these kids?"

"Probably not. I didn't think about it from your side. They're probably a lot like me."

"I liked you, Ellie. *Like* you."

"You think I'm okay." Ellie stood up. "I'm less of a pain than some other kids. I'm not like Don, anyway."

Don was a hoodlum-in-training. He had seemed to be Ellie's best friend. "Why did you sit next to him all year if you felt like that?"

"Don and I are lovers," Ellie said. "Ms. Haus, will you be here tomorrow?"

"Sure. Come see me again."

"Don't tell anyone you saw me, either," Ellie said. Her shadow bobbed behind her down the sand.

When Bee went home to Atlanta at the end of July, I assumed that we wouldn't see her until Thanksgiving. She had left after giving me a series of presents: first a baby name book with a smiling generic child, holding out its hands in greeting, on the front; then a tiny white stretch suit, probably half the length of my arm, with a yellow bow; a sweatshirt, even smaller, with a row of ducks across the chest; a squeaky plastic bird; a stuffed polar bear wearing a sweater; a small box of diaper pins; and a copy of Dr. Spock's *Baby and Child Care*.

"A dose of reality," she said, when I opened them up. The clothes she bought were elaborately cute, with baby animals and curlicues and bows, but she offered them in the spirit of stocking a larder for famine and war.

Now, less than two weeks after she went away, here was Bee again, getting out of a cab in front of the house with the same square brown suitcase she'd taken home. My father and I were rocking on the front porch, the runners thundering unevenly on the warped wood floor; we watched her struggle up the stairs in the stifling heat, thunking the bag against every step along the way.

"Well, push me over with a feather," my father said when she reached the top.

Bee, out of breath, put down her suitcase. "What's new?" Typically, this was the way Haus family members greeted each other: stoically, unsmiling, sitting down.

"Good to see you again, Bee," I said.

"Likewise. I need to take a shower. Are there any towels?"

"About a million of them," said my father. "Jane has to wash them every time they're touched. You just glance at a towel and it goes in the machine."

He and I rocked back and forth in our chairs, studying Bee. She looked almost nervous; there was a small blue stain on the collar of her oxford shirt.

"What about my bedroom? Is it still free?"

"Last time I looked," my father said. "Unless Jane went and rented it to some hobos."

"Good." Bee picked up her suitcase and walked to the door. "I'll make dinner. Seven o'clock."

When the screen slammed shut, my father picked up the paper. "I wonder what all that's about," he said.

Dinner was a roast turkey breast without the skin, baked potatoes with low-fat cheese (no butter), miniature onions, and fresh broccoli, steamed just long enough to be cut with a good steak knife. Bee had taken a quick tour through the freezer and cabinets and driven off post-haste to the grocery store. At seven o'clock the thermometer outside the house said eighty-two. Inside the house it must have been well into the nineties. Steam condensed on the windows by the stove. While my father ate, sweat dripped from his mismatched earlobes and from the tip of his nose into his food. My hands were so swollen, I was holding my fork in my fist like a two-year-old. Bee carefully speared a bite of turkey, then onion, then potato, creating a private shish kebab.

"Is it cold down there where you come from?" My father chased an onion around his plate with a serving spoon. "Do they live in igloos in Atlanta?"

"No, it's hot. I'd say it's probably the same as here." She didn't look warm. Her long-sleeved shirt was barely open at the neck.

"Anyone who works in a city like that deserves a

raise, in my worthless opinion. You should tell them you need more money; you're probably due.''

''What do you mean 'in a city like that'? You've never been there. And last time I asked for a raise, I got a lecture.''

''Hell.'' My father mopped his forehead with a tissue, which left small white shreds all over his skin. ''You don't need it. Who cares? Tell them to keep their ugly money.''

Bee sliced her turkey with the precision of a surgeon. ''Actually, this time Jerry offered *me* the raise. I didn't think he would do it. Budgets are tight.''

Jerry was Bee's boss, a superhero in her eyes, even though he'd overworked and underpaid her for five years.

''The man's a genius all of a sudden,'' my father said. ''Why'd he change his mind?''

''Because I'd just told him that not only could he keep his ugly money.'' We watched as Bee took another bite, chewed slowly, and lifted her glass of water: warm, without ice. ''He could also keep his ugly job.''

My father looked at me, his face prepared to take a hit, like a baseball glove.

''I don't have anything to do with this,'' I said.

''You told them you found another job?''

''No,'' said Bee.

''You told them you were going into business on your own?''

''No.''

My father took the fork from Bee's hand and set it down. ''Then what? Let's hear it.''

Bee smiled on one side of her mouth. "Time off."

"Time off for what?" I felt the turkey and onions revolving in my stomach.

Bee looked at my father. "You wanted me to find out about Jane's plans. Jane doesn't have plans. She's staying here, and so far she doesn't show signs of leaving. And I can't help if I'm in Atlanta. So I've decided to make a move." My father and I waited. "I'm going to move back home with the two of you."

My father looked like someone had hit him on the head with a mallet. "You're *staying* here? Here? That's why you quit your job?"

"You said my room was still available."

"Holy smoke," my father said.

"Jerry was surprised, too. He said he didn't know I had a sister." Bee shook her hair away from her eyes. "I'll have to commute back and forth for a little while, to finish some things. But I should be able to do some of the work by phone."

"Holy smoke," my father repeated.

Bee avoided my face; she looked tired but satisfied. She had probably sat up with pencil and paper for several nights, checking the risks, gauging my prospects, weighing conscience against expediency. This is what she'd come up with.

"Don't do this on my account," I said.

"Why not?"

"Because I won't have you quitting your job because of me. If you want to quit on your own behalf, go ahead."

"Fine," Bee said. "I did it for me. I notice you quit your job, though."

"That's different. And I haven't *moved* here. I'm staying for a little while."

"Ditto," Bee said. "Me, too."

My father stood up. "I'm going out to collect the trash can lids," he said. "Maybe I'll clang them together out in the yard."

Bee ignored him, focusing resolutely on me. "This could be good for all of us," she said. "It's been a long while."

To get out of the house now and then and to pay my father some money for rent, I had accepted a part-time job in Atlantic City. Two evenings a week I taught English as a Second Language, substituting for a teacher who had to leave suddenly because of illness, mid-course. Mr. Denzer, downstairs, heard about the job and recommended me. Although I didn't have an ESL degree, I was hired temporarily until they could track down someone else.

The class was held in a run-down Catholic college; a crucifix dangled by my desk. The textbook arrived dog-eared and moldy the afternoon before my first class. Printed decades ago, it consisted mainly of strange idioms and expressions:

Gladys certainly <u>drives a hard bargain</u>.

You look tired, Bill. I'll bet you're <u>burning the candle at both ends</u>.

Don't let Mary find out about the meeting. She always <u>upsets the apple cart</u>.

Howard doesn't like to <u>talk shop</u>. He wants to get the ball rolling <u>right away</u>.

The students, an earnest, humorless bunch, many of whom hoped to find work—or better jobs—in the casinos, labored on essays, pencils in fists. They left at home children, spouses, parents, debts, and televisions to sit cramped in one-piece desk-and-chair sets riddled with obscene drawings and misspelled words. Their average age was probably thirty-five.

I discovered quickly that the course was more than it seemed. The students wrote about themselves, usually focusing on problems they had at home.

Guillermo, from Peru, stood by his desk when he read—old habits die hard. "I was born in a happy family. We are in stitches most of our days. We beat our brains out to keep happy. But I lead a dog's life. We came to this country, out of a clear blue sky, and this should be our reward."

Generally I was at a loss for what to say. Idioms are infectious. "In plain English," I told him. "Don't rack your brain. Let the words flow."

"Like a river," he said, smiling as if I'd praised him. He smoothed his short black hair and sat down.

Following the seating chart—the eleven students sat in a half circle, facing me—I called on two people who read aloud about failing marriages. One man confessed to beating a dog: in a monotone he told a vivid and awful tale of raising a stick over and over, the cowering dog tied by a short leash to a heavy chair. I had to sit down.

"You are distasted," said a woman immersed in a floating yellow veil.

"No, it's all right," I said. "We'll go on."

The class looked disappointed.

"Your former teacher," I said, "Mr. Shendorf. Did he collect your essays and correct them at home?"

A look of alarm went around the half circle.

"We discuss," Guillermo said. "We talk to each other around what we hear."

"I think I would rather collect the essays and work on your grammar."

Guillermo shook his head. Several people folded their essays and tucked them away.

I stood up and smiled. I was brusque. "Every teacher does things differently," I said. I had them revise their essays, helping them individually at their desks. When class was over, no one got up to go.

"Mr. Shendorf always ends our class with a lesson. He advices us each time."

"That's very interesting," I said. "You mean 'advise.' "

"Where are you from?" asked a man named Sifor.

I politely explained that I was not Mr. Shendorf. "See you Thursday," I said. Faces fell.

"When you come and know us again, you will see which way the wind blows," said an old man.

I walked out the door.

The heat didn't go away. During most of August the temperature never went below eighty, even at night. The beaches were overrun with miserable inlanders who had escaped even worse in search of a breeze. Bee spent the weeks going to and fro, as she had said. She brought her computer and some file drawers and set up shop in her old room, technically a guest bedroom but one that had always retained vestiges of Bee.

The walls were a light monastic gray, the floorboards painted white. The shelves above the dresser held a globe; a series of maps, rolled up; odds and ends of encyclopedias (religion from *A* to *M*, the *World Book L* to *R*); and volumes of engineering, science, and philosophy. Bee had collected them from garage sales when she was in junior high. The doorless closet was empty except for a vacuum cleaner and a row of Bee's identical button-down shirts. At the foot of the bed were three pairs of white sneakers and no other shoes.

"That's kind of curious, isn't it," Ellie said, "two grown sisters moving back in with their dad."

We were in the attic, where I was sorting through hundreds of boxes, drawers, cabinets, trunks, garment bags, and duffels full of my parents' and grandparents' things. Because I wasn't yet sure what I was looking for, I'd started out haphazardly, opening a box, riffling through it, and then going on to the next, but when I realized that all the boxes were getting mixed up in my wake, I had to slow the process down. I developed a system, lining the trunks and smaller items up roughly in rows, then snaking back and forth among them—right to left, and then left to right. "Boustrophedon-fashion," Bee said.

Ellie had acquired the habit of stopping by, flopping on my bed and dozing or dreaming the afternoons away.

"I guess you could use the word 'curious,' " I said.

"I wish I had a brother or sister." Ellie rolled over. The box spring creaked and whined, even though she probably weighed less than eighty pounds. "Being an only child stunts your personality. I'll be self-centered when I'm older. I won't know how to interact with my peers.''

"Do you have that trouble now?" I took the black felt-tip marker from my pocket and drew a small x on the boxes I'd opened, sifted through, and closed.

"No. But I might grow into that kind of situation later on." She pulled a bottle of nail polish from the pocket of her cutoff jeans, which must have been a size 0. "Does Beatrice—does your sister—mind that you're up here?"

"Why should she?" I pushed aside a stack of folding chairs and a lamp and found a small manila envelope on the floor. "Actually, we argued about it, but it isn't any of her business. I'm just finding out what's here." The attic was starting to look very orderly. The neat rows that I'd created, with all the boxes evenly spaced, gave the impression of a graveyard, the tombstones old and misshapen, the engravings gone. I opened the little envelope and found three pairs of rhinestone earrings, a copper bracelet, and a pendant in the shape of a hen.

"Oooh, let's see." Ellie stood up and recapped the bottle of purple polish. Her toenails were wet, so she heel-walked to my side to examine the jewelry in my palm. "Screw-ons." She was disappointed. She picked up the pendant, knelt, and attached it to the collar of my shirt. She smelled of flavored chewing gum, suntan oil, and the drying purple polish. "You'll be glad to have her here with you, I guess."

"Sure, for a while. But Bee gets very judgmental. According to her, I do everything wrong. And she'll go crazy without her job and her own apartment. She's incredibly independent.''

"Aren't you?" Ellie plucked an earring from my palm. "Hold still." She gently turned the tiny screw and fastened the clump of rhinestones to my ear. "These are pretty. Did I tell you my new name for the baby? Sherwood. Call him Woody."

"Forget it," I said. Ellie was determined to find a name. She said that if I found the right name, I would suddenly bond with the baby; I would progress beyond abstraction and picture "a real-life face."

"I'm not ready for faces yet," I said. I put Ellie in charge of naming, temporarily, in my stead. "A Sherwood would be fighting in the playground at the age of three. Anyway, yes, I'm independent, in a different way. But Bee thinks I'm an idiot. She thinks I shouldn't have left my job."

"One more." Ellie moved around to my other ear. I felt hypnotized, weighed down. I could hear her shallow, nasal breathing and feel the cool tips of her fingers on my neck. "Do you think she has a point? You're a good teacher. How about Simon? I knew a great guy named Simon. Don't move, I'll fix your hair."

I closed my eyes. "Bee's the one making a mistake. Or more of a mistake than I am."

"Do you mean because her job is better? Is that what your dad thinks, too?" Ellie was gently brushing my hair. "Or what about that guy downstairs? What is he, your cousin?"

"Who, Mr. Denzer? No, he's a renter. But I've known him for a long time."

"He's got his eye on you," Ellie said, licking her fingers and pushing hairpins into an odd-shaped twist at the nape of my neck. "When he came up here last week I could feel it. I'm very perceptive about those things."

In Ellie's presence Bill Denzer had knocked on the attic steps to ask for a can of paint to touch up his front door. Ellie had raised her eyebrows at him and launched into an explanation about how she was helping me excavate my mother's past. She'd used the word "evacuate" by accident, but neither Bill Denzer nor I corrected her. "I think it's very romantic," Ellie said. She handed me a pocket mirror. "This is better than a ratty ponytail. You look elegant as hell. Don't you have a nicer shirt?"

"Bill Denzer doesn't have his eye on me," I said, holding the mirror. Ellie's efforts mainly pointed out the lack of my own. I looked like an aging, overweight starlet on a bad day.

Ellie sneezed. "Hey, at least he's not your cousin. Things could be worse. That's probably incest. Did you tell him about the baby?"

I could feel myself blush. I hadn't told him, but he knew. One afternoon on the deck he took both my hands in his and said, "Congratulations. I'm with you. How do you feel?"

Ellie chattered on. "I like the name Penelope for a girl. Or you know what you could do? You could use the father's last name as a first name, like a family name. Say the father's name is Walker." She propped my collar up around my neck. "Jim Walker. You name the baby Walker Haus."

I took the last hairpin from her hand. "That sounds like a motel," I said, "not a person. Anyway, the father's name isn't Jim Walker."

"What is it?" Ellie asked.

"None of your business."

"Don't get mad." She left my shirt and my hair alone and started fluffing her own hair up to cover her ears, which sometimes poked through the thin blond curtain on either side. "It's just natural curiosity, that's all. I'm still learning about the world."

"You know plenty about the world." I stood up. "Bee's waiting for me downtown. She took a bus from the airport."

"Okay, I can take a hint." Ellie didn't move to go. "What if the baby's born and it looks exactly like the father? What'll you do?" She seemed to be asking herself instead of me. She looked in the mirror. "I mean, you'll think of him all the time. Was he good-looking? Really handsome?"

"No," I said. "I don't know. I don't think he was."

Ellie stood up and walked to the stairs, trailing her finger in the dust along the dresser. "You know, your sister doesn't like me." The attic glimmered with dust because of the boxes I'd moved around; motes of it traveled through the light coming from the two triangular windows and the door. Dust made the air look solid so that the attic seemed more substantial, more alive, than the other rooms in my father's house.

"Don't let it bother you," I said. "That's just her manner." I handed Ellie her plastic bag of cigarettes. "Bee doesn't seem to like me, either, but I guess she does."

"Closeness," Ellie said. "That's great to see in a family." She left with the copper bracelet in her hand.

I had forgotten, on the way to pick up Bee, about the rhinestones and the way Ellie had fixed my hair.

"Lovely," Bee said, loading a clean white duffel into the car. I was parked in the shade of a six-foot sapling; sweat was pooling behind my knees.

"Is that all you've got?" I pulled off the earrings and unfastened the pin.

"That's it for now." She climbed in front. "Most of what I'll need for the next six months is already here."

We let the mention of "six months" sit without comment between us, like a single chocolate donut in a box.

"So, what have you been doing with yourself?" Bee asked.

"The usual. This and that. Eating and resting and reading and teaching. Talking to Dad." I started the car, even though it was already running; the engine whinnied like a horse.

"Left," Bee said. "You want to turn left at the corner there. Are you still spending your spare time up in the attic?"

"I drove myself here, Bee. I can get home." Quickly I flipped the blinker on. "Dad's been up in the attic, too. I caught him coming downstairs with a bag of stuff."

"He keeps his liquor up there," Bee said. "The light's green."

I turned onto Ellen Street. All the streets in Sea Haven were named for women; all the avenues were men. When I was young I used to imagine that every intersection was a marriage; but that there were only five men to some seventy women didn't seem fair.

"I think maybe he's getting rid of things. Carting them out in the dead of night even while I'm home. Do you think it's strange that we have almost no pictures of our own mother? Nothing from when she was a kid, no old schoolbooks, no letters? I wonder if Uncle Harold has anything." Uncle Harold was our mother's only brother; he worked for the post office in California but lacked the wherewithal to send a card.

"You want souvenirs?" Bee was pointing RIGHT TURN with her finger. "Mom never liked pictures of herself. She probably threw them all away."

"She should have given them to us," I said. "She should have considered us."

Bee stared out the window. She always changed the subject when our mother came up. "I don't know why you want to muck around in that dust. It's too hot up there for you."

"It's hot everywhere," I said. "This summer is breaking records. You know, Ellie and I found some bras up there in a dresser, made of something like canvas. It seems there are buxom women in our past."

Bee cleaned her glasses on her shirt. "Some things aren't inherited, I guess. Why is that girl—Ellie—hanging around?"

"I like Ellie," I said. "She's refreshing."

"She's precocious," Bee said. "She needs friends her own age. So do you. Friends and opportunities.

You know there are a lot of schools in South Jersey that—''

"Leave it, Bee," I said. "I can work out my problems by myself."

"At least you admit they're problems," Bee said. "We're making progress."

The sky was perfectly still, as hot and flat as a griddle.

"Are you still feeling well?" she asked. "What does that doctor say?"

"He says I'm large." We passed a row of ice-cream trucks doing brisk business at the side of the road. "I'm starting to feel like a walking vessel."

"Is he able to give you any useful information?" This was a dig at my refusal to sign up for a childbirth education class. Bee thought I should go to a clinic one night a week, pillow in hand, to pant on a floor with a bunch of other pregnant women. But I wasn't like other pregnant women, and I didn't want to engage in corny hand-holding sessions and fill out forms about "my feelings" and "my fears." I told Bee that classes in childbirth were pointless, like classes in car repair: it was better to simply trust your local expert and pay the bill when it arrived. "You're the car, Jane," she'd said.

Now I told her that I knew what I had to know. "In the old days," I said, "women had no idea what to expect. They didn't have to hear all the gory details; they sat around embroidering linen and commending themselves to God."

"I don't suppose you bought any linen." Bee rolled her window up; heat didn't faze her—she probably hadn't noticed the asphalt turning back into tar at the edge of the road. "It's hard not to worry about you," she said.

"No it isn't. There are lots of other things to worry about." I passed Ellie's parents' house, the brand-new Yogurt Hut, and the Sub Station, then pulled up in front of my father's house. "Worry about the economy. Worry about the rain forests disappearing. Worry about murderers riding in buses all over the country looking for innocent people to kill. By comparison, I'm doing fine."

"In comparison to a murderer and a dying rain forest," Bee said.

I stopped the car. Beneath the skin of my stomach I felt a swimming motion, like a snake turning a corner. "Hey," I said. Then it was gone.

"The baby?" Both of us looked at the bulge above my seat belt. But neither one of us, in the steady, choking heat of the metal car, reached out to touch my swelling stomach with our hands.

In my ESL class we continued with idioms.

" 'Around the corner we met some ladies of an evening,' " Geraldo read. " 'They suggest to us that we fornicate and make congress. My friend Hector, even because he enjoy girls with these breasts, say to these two—' "

"Gerald," I said. "Geraldo. What is your purpose in this essay?"

Geraldo was thin and shy, probably eighteen. Unbelievably, he delivered his information with a straight face; he was sincere. "To communicate and persuade," he said, firmly.

"Well, most of the words that you're using don't communicate very well. 'Congress,' for example. I think that went out in the 1940s. People don't use it anymore. It would be more appropriate simply to say, 'We met two prostitutes who propositioned us.' "

Several students wrote the sentence in their notebooks. Arletta, a girl of fifteen or sixteen, would probably show the notebook to her mother.

"Who's next?" I asked. "Someone else please read an essay."

Sebastian, the old man, stood up. He smoothed the wrinkles from his shirt with the flat of his hand; from the neck down he looked like a skeleton wearing clothes. " 'The car,' " he read. " 'One day a girl saw a car. She wants to drive in that. Her father says no, it is not possible. The girl dies after. The father always forever wants to burn that car away. He feels terrible then.' " He continued to stand by his desk.

Sifor spoke up. "That is the same story he always reads. Every time."

"Thank you," I said. "You can sit down."

After class, I buttonholed Guillermo. "What is this business?" I asked. "People aren't coming to learn the language. What are they doing? Sifor speaks perfect English; why is he here?"

"We are used to each other, maybe," he said with a shrug. "We are here together a long while."

"How long a while?"

"Some of us, one year. Some of us more."

"But this is supposed to be a ten-week class."

Guillermo smiled. "I am been here now three times."

"With the same teacher? What's he running, anyway?"

"I am getting much better," Guillermo said. "I am learn so much."

In a moldy pillowcase in the back of an ancient china closet, I found a baby book that my mother had started for Bee. It wasn't in my mother's taste and was probably a gift: fat, cheruby infants dropped through holes in the clouds on the cover; each wore a diaper and a perfect puckered smile. I opened it. Inside, there were equally kitschy drawings of naked children holding flowers and teddy bears, with fill-in-the-blank spaces for first tooth, first word, first step. My mother, in backward-slanting handwriting, had methodically filled in the first few entries. Color of hair: <u>black</u>. (It must have fallen out later.) Color of eyes: <u>blue. Six pounds, four ounces. Beatrice Elizabeth</u>. Disposition: My mother had left a question mark. She probably had no standard of reference to go by.

Under the headings ("Mother's Notes," "Baby's Habits") that required more than a short answer, my mother's responses seemed sketchy. Her tone was scholarly more than happy. She noted that Bee kept her eyes wide open when she nursed and that her ears moved in and out, away from her head, with the effort of obtaining food. In another place, she wrote that the baby seemed <u>earnest.</u> I could picture Bee as a newborn, wide-eyed and diligent at the breast as if trying to say, "Look how hard I'm working. Look what a good job I'm doing.'' But my mother's notes lacked a sense of humor. The last entry read <u>serious</u>, <u>watchful</u>, <u>young</u>. *Young*? Bee was three months old. There was a lock of hair in a plastic bag, like an artifact under glass in a museum.

I brought the book downstairs to show to Bee. She was reorganizing the kitchen, throwing out broken eggbeaters, rusted peelers, and cracked coffee mugs and wiping down the shelves with a foul-smelling solution and a sponge. It was exhausting, having her home. She seemed unable to relax and wanted to regulate our activities, like a director of a nursing home. Suddenly my father and I, who had been peaceably isolated in our separate regions of the house, had to eat at fixed hours, show up for group walks on clear nights after dinner, and sign our names to a piece of paper taped to the refrigerator door, indicating when we were willing to shop, cook, clean, do laundry, and cut the lawn.

"Jesus," my father mumbled whenever he opened the refrigerator and found health-food peanut butter, brown salt-free bread, and a jar of thriving alfalfa seeds, "the world could end tomorrow and we'd have eaten a last meal of this stuff. Where are the hot dogs, anyway?"

I called Bee down from the step stool. "Look." I opened the baby book on the counter. She took off her rubber gloves, wiped her hands, and turned the pages like an archivist, barely touching the corners. She flipped through a large blank section to the back. "I remember seeing this once," she said. "I'd forgotten."

"She never finished it," I said. "It stops at about nine months. Why would she stop?"

Bee seemed reluctant to close the book. "She probably kept the photo albums instead." On the top shelf in my father's study, undusted, were three thick albums showing the two of us growing up. But there were no words, no written records.

"Do you know if she kept a baby book for me?"

"I never saw one." Bee tied up a bag of garbage and set it down by the back door. "I can tell you most of it, though. You weighed seven pounds. Your hair was brown, eyes blue. Nothing in a baby book is going to change what you are now."

I sat down on the stool. A cluster of veins bloomed like a rose in my left calf. "Bee, have you considered a job as a counselor? I think you'd be really good at relating to people. Have you ever met any people by the way?"

"Off," she said, waving me away from the stool. "There are healthier things you could be doing, instead of fossicking in the attic."

"Like washing cabinets," I said. "I want to know why she didn't record anything about me."

Bee climbed up the wooden steps and snapped on her gloves. They were hideously pink and much too large. "I doubt there was anything personal in it," she said. "She would have treated any kid that came along the same way."

"I was the kid, for God's sake. Has it ever occurred to you that our own mother didn't want children?"

"Not everyone likes children." Bee wrung out her sponge. "You'll find that out. Anyway, we're here whether she wanted us or not. Discussing it doesn't change anything.''

I walked to the other side of the kitchen and looked out the porch windows at the beach. Lately I had the sensation that I was waddling, that part of me entered a room before the rest of me caught up. Although the heat was worse than ever, the beach wasn't full. Most of the day-trippers were staying home: there were scares about infected needles washing up beneath the pier. (''We should have thought of that as a strategy years ago,'' my father said.) ''Bee,'' I asked, ''do you know if Mom was sick—I mean, diagnosed—before we were born?''

I heard her stop scrubbing behind me. ''I don't know.''

''Maybe it wasn't good for her to be pregnant,'' I said. ''She could have resented us for that. You're going to peel all the paint off of those cabinets. Then I guess you'll be able to repaint them.''

''They could use it,'' Bee said.

I turned back to the beach, watching the progress of two girls in white bikinis toward the lifeguard stand emblazoned with the sign NO TALKING TO GUARDS. At unpredictable moments I missed my mother. It was like a craving for some kind of food that didn't exist, a fervent, ineffectual desire. The girls on the beach were now perched on the lip of the lifeguards' boat. God forbid anyone should choose this moment to become a victim of the undertow. ''Bee, what do you think—and this is my last question—if she'd kept another book, what would she have written about me?''

Bee waited until I turned around. "Wondering what she thought of you—of us, I mean—doesn't make sense. Mom always kept her feelings to herself." She paused, but I was determined not to speak. I would sit with the taste of lead in my mouth until she told me what I wanted to know. "Okay, all right. I suppose she would have written something similar." It was quiet in the kitchen. "But of course it would have been about you." She dipped her sponge into the pail. "She might have written something about the way you used to wake up. You always made a snorting noise, like a baby pig. I remember we used to laugh whenever you did it." Bee started scrubbing again.

"Did she seem—you know—affectionate?" I asked.

"I thought you already asked your last question. I was four years old at the time, Jane. Nearly five. I remember standing next to the rocking chair waiting for you to get rocked to sleep. I remember Dad telling me not to be jealous."

"Dad was probably jealous," I said. "I think he wanted more of her attention than he got. Was he as strange back then as he was later on? I always wonder when he turned into such a weirdo."

For the first time Bee looked angry as well as impatient. A perfect, delicate furrow appeared on her brow. "Why do you seem to think that in psychologizing yourself you have to dig up dirt on someone else? Dad did the best that he could. He wasn't handed any good luck; he trudged along."

"Good luck like a wife who wouldn't get sick and

die on him? That's what you mean? As if it were Mom's fault when she wasn't here?''

Bee whipped around. "She *was* here most of the time. Who told you she left?''

I stared at my sister and she blushed. "What do you mean, 'left'? Are we talking about the same thing here, Bee?''

Bee went back to the cabinets.

"Mom left twice," I said. "She had two major surgeries. The other procedures were chemotherapy day by day. Are you saying that she left another time?''

"I'm not saying anything," Bee said.

I grabbed her leg. An ocean breeze came in behind us. I could smell dead sea animals, decaying barnacles, crabs slowly roasting in shallow tide pools in the sun. "Tell me.''

"Once," Bee said. "Once more. I was really young.''

"Dad says she didn't get sick until that first time, when I was eight.''

"I don't think she did," Bee said.

"Then where did she go?''

"That's the question. I don't know. I asked Dad once. He said I was remembering wrong and that I must have been confused. But I can remember us at dinner, just Dad and me, sitting here at the table, and I was looking at my food and wishing she'd come home.''

"She left him," I said. "Where did she go?''

"I don't know.''

"How long was she gone?''

"I don't know that, either. I remember she looked different when she came back."

"I don't believe it," I said. "Mom left. And you were old enough to remember. She'd had enough of him."

"Don't sound so happy about it." Bee shook her leg to make me let go. "It must still be hard for Dad."

And for you, I thought, to think that your mother left and might not come back. That's probably why Bee turned out the way she did: distant and well protected, spiny and serious and proud.

"I wonder why she came back?" I asked, and as soon as I asked the question, I knew. Bee was probably four years old if she remembered, which meant that my mother was pregnant with me. She came back to Sea Haven to have another baby and never managed to get away again. I felt things falling softly into place: I was reliving, without knowing it, a piece of my mother's life; without seeing them I was following in her steps. "She came back for *me*," I said. "It's just like me."

Bee's face was a stone. *For me*, I wanted to repeat, but that was the same as declaring, She left you behind; she didn't care. Instead, I said, "Sorry—I don't mean anything by it." But I must have looked elated because Bee didn't want to discuss it anymore. She said that our father was going to eat at Murphy's, so the two of us would eat at home alone.

"He's thinking of selling, you know," she said, mainly to try to puncture my mood. It wouldn't work.

"Dad won't sell," I said. "I'll help with dinner."

"You really don't understand what's happening

here," Bee said. "Dad doesn't see all this like you do." When I went back later to get the baby book, it was gone.

The ESL class, I thought, would improve. I made a speech about leaving personal problems at home and concentrating instead on natural expression and correct, grammatical speech. I assigned more neutral topics. "All of us," I said, "have things at home that worry us or make us angry. But let's talk and write about other subjects in class. "Describe a tree," I said. Geraldo wrote about sugarcane.

"Describe an animal." Ulrika read a few paragraphs about sheep. Someone at the edge of the room began to baa.

"Sifor," I said, "please read your essay." There was a tension in the air, a free-floating surliness.

"I didn't write one," Sifor said. "I have no interest in describing trees. I am forbidden to express myself as I like, in a free country."

"This is a class," I explained. "Not a gossip column. You are here to learn better speech."

"I am here to communicate," he said.

I went on to some drills, repeat-after-mes. Sifor and Sebastian were talking openly, not whispering. Some of the other students joined in. Arletta asked if I knew when Mr. Shendorf was coming back.

There was a light rain falling. I looked out the window, down at my car at the end of the block. There is no way to teach someone, I thought, who doesn't like or respect you enough to learn. "Do what you can," my mother had often said when I was having trouble;

but did she mean that I should do what came to me naturally, or was she tactfully remarking on my lack of talent?

I turned around. Maybe it was the expression on my face; suddenly everyone was attentive. "You want to know when Mr. Shendorf is coming back? I don't know. I think Mr. Shendorf is a charlatan. Look that up: *c-h-a-r*." A few people leafed through their dictionaries. I continued. "I have reported him to the board of higher education. This class is a mess. You may think you are being helped here; you are not. Mr. Shendorf is pulling the wool over your eyes. You are deceived. You are a bunch of sitting ducks. Would anyone like to comment on these ideas?"

It took a while, but their hands went up. I didn't call on anyone; I let them talk.

Their grammar was lousy; sometimes I didn't understand what a student said. I didn't correct them, though. They were arguing with each other, they were expressing their ideas, they were getting something said. When I left I could hear their voices, like a badly tuned group of musicians, rising and falling against each other, getting fainter as I continued down the hall.

My ultrasound exam was scheduled for the next day. Dr. Subramanian said another doctor would "attend" me at the hospital; Dr. Subramanian's office didn't have its own machine.

I went alone because Bee was busy, probably lobbying my father to raise Mr. Denzer's rent. Since Bee had moved in, my father's friends had stopped coming by, and Mr. Denzer, who Ellie claimed had the hots for me, didn't knock on the screen anymore. Only Ellie continued to drop by, usually without warning; I'd find her sitting on the couch with the baby name book in her hands, scribbling possible names on slips of paper and tucking them into a drawstring bag.

In the waiting room, everyone else had brought a husband or a friend, as if they were going to catch a show, popcorn and all. I drank the required three enormous glasses of water and painfully crossed my legs for forty minutes, reading ancient magazines about movie stars before being led by a nurse to a tiny room. Another fifteen minutes went by before the doctor came in. He was all business, saying hello while reading my chart, then washing his hands and whistling to avoid conversation.

In the odd way of examinations, I lay on the table, lifted my shirt and unsnapped my pants, and allowed a stranger to squirt freezing vaseline from a tube across my stomach, then smear it around.

"This is the best part," he said, as if making a joke, but he didn't smile. He seemed like the type who had forgotten how.

I had a backache and shifted around. He told me to hold still, then muttered to himself and unwound some cords. "Your first?"

"And only." I smiled a tight grin.

He looked at my finger for a wedding ring. "This is the transducer. I slide this across your abdomen and turn on our screen—"

I didn't like this man at all. I stared at the wart on his forehead to make him feel bad and to help me forget the oceans of water my bladder contained.

"Here we are." He moved the transducer, the size and shape of a man's electric razor, below my navel in an arc. "Look at the screen."

I turned and looked. A bunch of slow-moving liquid static, and then there it was. A soft gray head the size of a penny, with eyes and mouth; impossible fingers; legs moving jerkily up and down. I could see it turning its head to face the screen, as if to see me, as if to take this opportunity to speak, not understanding that I couldn't hear. It opened its small gray mouth, then turned again. I could see it swallowing, see its heart, delicate firefly, pump away. I could see flesh and skeleton both, lungs and vertebrae and toes.

"Why is it swallowing?" I asked. "It doesn't have anything to eat."

"Amniotic fluid. Passing it through," the doctor said. "Not much else to do in there. There's no TV."

He moved the transducer to another angle, to see the hemispheres of the brain. When he returned to the face again, the tiny creature put a hand up, as if to block our view, as if we were shining a light in its eyes, and turned away.

"They probably don't like this much," he said. "There's a lot of vibration and some noise. I can't tell you for certain about the sex because the umbilical cord is obstructing. But everything looks pretty good to me. Do you want a picture?"

"Picture?" I asked, imagining a photo of myself with my pants undone.

He didn't hear me. The machine clicked twice. "Here you go." He handed me a picture of the fetus raising its hand. The screen was off, the image gone.

I wanted to ask him to turn it on again. The picture wasn't enough. I felt we had been cut off; there was something it wanted to say to me, and when it was born, it would have lost the capacity for speech. It would babble senselessly, nostalgically, for years. I would have to teach it, word by word, naming everything: This is a tree, this a house; we call this an ocean, a clock, a lamp, a graveyard, a dog; a starving person, a newspaper full of facts, some of them true; this is envy, this is sadness, this is fear. This is your mother before you'll lose her: bloated, childless, and young. I would have to wait for this future child to recover what it knew. We could wait our whole lives and never remember what this tiny, soft, gray being had wanted to say.

"You can get up," the doctor said and walked out of the room. When the nurse found me, I was still undressed, lying on the table sobbing, watching the screen.

6

~~

Excursions into Philosophy

"Let us presume that Margaret Truman is an alligator," Bee writes. "Human beings are essentially immaterial; therefore being a human person is not an essential property of human persons."

"Come on out of there, you coward," my father says, standing outside my bedroom door. "We're going to talk."

"Persons may change," Bee writes, "yet remain the same across possible worlds." I have been studying her essay for about an hour. It's hard to read because of all the mathematical symbols; there are even tiny alligators that my sister must have drawn by hand amidst the type. At the foot of the last page is a neat A+. Then, in Bee's miniature script, "Don't show this to Dad."

I *will* myself to understand at least a page, a paragraph. Bee is carrying twenty-two credits in her second semester at Berkeley, getting As in physics, calculus, economics, Latin, and philosophy, an upper-level course called "Modern Thought II." When my father found out about the philosophy, he was furious. "Hocus-pocus!" Now Bee fills her letters to my parents with news of her progress in science, and letters to me with ideas and concepts I can't understand.

When she was admitted, with open arms, to almost every good school in the country, my mother encouraged her to go to Berkeley, as if it weren't enough that she'd be leaving home. My father and I thought she should study somewhere on the East Coast. "What about Princeton?" my father asked. My mother called it a boys' club. "How about Harvard?" he snarled. "I guess that's just a football school?"

I didn't quite believe that she would go. The week before we took her to the airport I kept alive a private hope that, in spite of her 4.0 and her teachers' praise, in spite of the letters from Massachusetts, Texas, and Illinois that promised her money if she would come, Bee would look carefully at our home situation and whip off a quick entry letter to Atlantic City Technical College. Instead she nearly floated through the airport, even though she had never entered an airplane in her life, and from the opposite edge of the country wrote home during her second week, "How do we know that this letter exists? We perceive a version of the letter, not the thing."

"You can't stay in there forever." My father sneezes in the hall. "This is your opportunity to shine." He wants me to join the golf team. He wants me to *be* the golf team, since our school doesn't have one yet. He has spent the last three days arguing with the principal and the PTA, but I'm not sure that I want to play golf on a team. None of my friends know how to golf, and I don't want to be associated with a sport that only people my parents' age and I like to play.

Again I review the first and second pages of Bee's paper and still don't know what my sister knows. For these ideas, Bee refused to come home at Christmas, staying in a special dorm for students with families overseas. She is studying on a scholarship that pays four years of tuition. My parents pay for room and board, leaving Bee to earn the rest: books and airplane fares and other fees. She has bridged this gap by having no social life, taking too many courses, and not coming home. She intends to finish in three years.

"Why are you hiding under a bushel?" my father says. "I guarantee you, by year's end you get your picture in the paper—more than once." What he means is that I will never go to college like my sister unless someone notices how well I can swing a club. He means that I golf well for a dunce.

"I'll tell you what I'll do. I'll wait here for one more minute. If you still don't open the door, I'll go away and leave you to think it through on your own." I know that trick, the footsteps pounding down the hall and tiptoeing back. I look at the essay one more time, then throw it, with its envelope, into the trash. I am sixty seconds away from a low IQ; when I walk through the door I'll put on dumbness like a shroud.

"Who's going to coach us?" I ask, with the door still closed. "It can't be you."

"What do I have, a smell? I won't set foot on the silly course."

I lean my head against the door. "I don't get along

with Mrs. Stegner. She hates me; I had her last year for gym.''

''What's that mummy got to do with it? I got you a real-live coach. That new guy, William Dancer.''

''Mr. Denzer? Who teaches Health?''

My father opens the door with a nail file. ''That's the one.''

Mr. Denzer is the brand-new gym teacher at school. Only twenty-six years old, he replaces Mr. Mattison, who retired. Because Sea Haven High is small, he has to coach football, boys' and girls' basketball, and baseball in the spring. Mrs. Stegner, a woman with colorless hair who has the largest collection of athletic kilts in North America, coaches girls' volleyball, swimming, and boys' and girls' tennis. Both Mrs. Stegner and Mr. Denzer also teach Health, or what used to be called Grooming and Hygiene.

I am one of the lucky fifty percent of the ninth grade who drew Mr. Denzer's name for Health. Clearly he doesn't like to teach it; he stumbles through the book bewildered, scratching his head at the pictures of dating couples, the anatomy of acne, recommendations for washing one's hair. Around Halloween he pitches the book entirely, deciding to wing it and giving disconnected lectures about ninth grade as a ''time of confusion'' when people ''want to do things they shouldn't.'' We sense his desire to say more. Often he asks us about our feelings; no one risks a word. The boys draw breasts and phallic symbols on their notebooks, and the girls imagine themselves in front of a fire with Mr. D., as he is called, wanting to do what he hints at but never tells.

The boys say Mr. Denzer is a fairy. They say even worse, jokes about not dropping soap in the locker room. My boyfriend, Bert, says Mr. Denzer actually cried when Jerry Caldicott hit him in the stomach—accidentally—with a rubber ball.

Most of the girls don't buy it. Mr. Denzer has light brown hair that curls and turns below his ears. He wears ill-fitting contact lenses that make him look dream-bound and sentimental. One of the girls in the twelfth grade says she heard Mr. Denzer talking after school to the science teacher, Mr. Carlisle. "I like them young," he said, winking—or maybe blinking—when she walked by. No one believes this story but we repeat it anyway. We make ugly comments about the younger female teachers' supposed attempts to lure him home.

Bert, who has taken an interest in me for no reason I can understand, says he doesn't trust me to spend the wet spring afternoons with Mr. Denzer, "all alone." "I'll join the team to keep an eye on you," he says, jerking his head to the right so that his hair flops neatly into place above his eyes. Bert is a dope at times but I am enormously lucky to have him: he's two years older than I am, a junior with light green eyes and all the right friends. I know that I'm not his typical choice; I'm not as good-looking as I should be for the role and therefore pardon him any lapses of his own.

"You're really hopeless," Bert says, when we play basketball in his driveway after school. He says this with affection, arm on my hip, a sweet-tasting sheen of sweat around his mouth. His hand is so often at my waist, I have brush burns there. We are always touching each other, hand on hand, knee on knee, toe on toe. Later, when the sun drops behind his garage, we'll kiss in the steam of his mother's kitchen while she cooks dinner at the stove. I feel prickly and guilty doing this, even though his mother, who wears an immaculate white apron all day long, seems to think it's fine. She sings Harry Belafonte songs while Bert breathes lightly in my ear. In my house, on the rare occasions when Bert has visited me there, I stand on the opposite side of the room as if he were my attacker. I refer to him in front of my parents as ''a guy from school.''

Sometimes I think Bert likes me because he's a coward and I am not. ''You're a riot,'' he says, nervous, when I say something rude about the teachers or the principal. His astonishment and admiration make me brave. When the teachers go on and on about my sister—How do I feel, having a sibling offered scholarships at the toughest schools in the country? Are my parents proud?—I get sarcastic for his sake. ''Ask them yourself,'' I say to the principal, which gets me an hour's worth of detention. I become a smart-ass and develop a permanent sneer.

Mrs. Glenn, the geometry teacher, says I'm becoming a ''hard tack.'' I like the phrase and try to live up to it. Mrs. Kline, who teaches French, says I'm *difficile*. I mimic her in the locker room with my friends. We are an odd group of misfits, my friends and I, angry and worried about our hair, which has to look messed up in an extremely specific way. We can't

stand the girls who look prissy, who wear white ribbed
kneesocks and ribbons with the Sea Haven High
School colors in their hair. We wear pants slung low
on our hips, leotards, clogs or platform shoes. We
think this is gypsylike and rough.

Bert admires my friends from a distance. "They're
a riot," he says, holding my hand in the hall. Although
he seems every day to have been starched and ironed,
he is remarkably good-looking. At times I allow myself to imagine us married, in a house built of stone,
miles and miles from any ocean—somewhere like
Kansas or Oklahoma, solid places with trees and dirt
rooted all around, places you can move away to and
never come home.

"Here's what we do," my father says, stirring the soup
that he's concocted: tuna and pepperoni in a chicken
broth. Whenever my mother comes home late he in-
vents a new food: shark and onion sandwiches, baked
potatoes with sardines, spaghetti with olives and cash-
ews. He gets angry if she's not home by five-fifteen.

"This guy Dancer is willing to coach only if we get
ten students and raise some money for the clubs."

I look toward the door to see if the noise I hear is
my mother coming in. "Dad," I say, "kids my age
don't know how to golf. No one's interested. I'm the
only one who plays."

"Horseshit," he says. "Your buddy Bert already
said he would play; you need eight more. The way I
see it"—he drops two hard-boiled eggs into the
broth—"we put an ad in the school paper. Let people
know. Look, I wrote up an ad; I banged it out

this afternoon.'' He shows me a yellow tablet:

Hey! Hey! Hey! Play golf! A ''swinging'' coed sport! (Spring term!) We need ten for a team, boys and girls. Beginners, intermediate, or know-it-all. A great way to make friends. Find out what your parents have been keeping secret all this time. Come one, come all!

If he sends it to the school paper, I will change my name.

''I'm back.'' My mother has come up behind us in her stocking feet; she took off her new black hiking boots by the front door.

My father barely looks up. She hasn't yet paid the price for being late. In the last six months she has accepted and quit two jobs and adopted a series of interests: first yoga and meditation, then modern dance, and now daytime classes in ''life drawing'' and ''drawing nature.'' Ever since Bee left, she's been picking up and discarding hobbies, throwing herself temporarily into every one. She keeps the skull of a bear on her dressing table, and in its drawers some pencil sketches of a naked man.

My father folds up the yellow paper and hands it to me as if to prove that we have a secret. ''We were getting ready to eat without you.'' He bustles off to the cupboard for the plates.

''I thought we might go out to eat,'' says my mother, sitting down in a kitchen chair. She rests her stockinged feet on the dog's back. ''Hello, Spunk, I'm home. You can say hello to me now.''

My father points out that it's six-fifteen. "Dinners out should be planned ahead of time," he says.

"Oh, for God's sake, Gregory." She shuts her eyes and lets her peach-colored hair fall forward. My father and I set the table, working around her as if she were made of wood. With Bee away, the three of us tend to run out of conversation; she had a way of appearing in the kitchen with brand-new topics: news of disaster in Belize or warnings about the effects of offshore drilling on the humpback whale.

"Soup's on," my father says. He puts three mismatched bowls on the kitchen table and fills them with soup. The tuna floats in chunks in the chicken broth with pieces of celery, sliced the long way, leftover French fries, semifrozen peas, and pepperoni. The celery barely fits in the bowls.

"I left some pea soup in the freezer," my mother says, without lifting her spoon. "You could have heated that."

"Jane and I don't have a treasure map of everything in the freezer." My father drinks his soup down with a glass of milk, the newspaper balanced on his knees.

I imagine myself calmly standing, opening the window, and throwing my soup on the lawn. I think of other people's families, of Bert's aproned mother making pans of lasagna and strawberry pies, his father laughing out loud at a TV show.

"Jane," my mother says. She's vivid and tired, her narrow face shining in the kitchen's glare. "Why don't you bring us a cup of tea? My feet hurt."

I boil the water and bring two tea bags, as well as some peanut butter and crackers, to the table. Neither of us will touch the soup; my father, who once won a bet by finishing an entire bowl of chocolate ice cream with ketchup on it, has taken his newspaper into the other room.

My mother bites experimentally into a cracker. Lately she can make the most ordinary acts seem foreign and strange. It's as if she recently came here from another country and is patiently entertaining our alien ways. "I'm thinking of getting another job," she says.

"What kind?"

"Something different." She shrugs, her shoulders two small round pegs moving up and down. The last two jobs she had involved light typing, answering phones. "Something physical would feel good. Something outdoors."

Even at fourteen, I could point out to her that she has limited strength and tenuous skills. "Huh," I say.

She dips her tea bag up and down until the water is black. Her hands are graceful; paint spots freckle her fingers and thumb. "Do you ever think of getting a job, Jane?"

"No. I'm playing golf. And I'm too young to earn real money." I'd like to shock her, to tell her that I intend to flunk out of school and lead a life of crime.

"Do you like golf? Does golf matter to you? Oh, never mind." She waves her hand in the steam. "Maybe that isn't the real question." I wonder if my mother will send me away when the time comes—maybe to some vo-tech school in Alaska. She cocks her head, studying me. She has a habit of thinking about me in the abstract, as if I'm not there. "I can imagine you a lawyer. You're creative and exact." She sighs and brushes the bangs away from my forehead. I tried to bleach them, but they came out stiff and crackled, greenish gold. (''Great,'' Bert said when he saw me, but he looked unnerved.) I was alone in the house when I did it and must have read the directions wrong. I cried in the sink for half an hour, but when my mother came back I pretended that I wanted to look that way.

''Your father's been passed over at work,'' she says, not quietly enough so that I can be sure he can't hear her, in the other room. Her absence of tact astounds me. My father rustles the paper. She sips her tea. ''The store hasn't been doing very well; he thinks they're looking for a younger manager.''

I try to think of another man in my father's office, in that large, square, windowless room full of clothing racks, hangers, file cabinets, and disassembled mannequins. ''Will he be fired?'' I'm whispering, even though she won't.

''I doubt it. But he takes things very personally. I don't know whether you've noticed. Takes them to heart.''

For an instant I picture my father's beating heart, a loud, insistent, hurtful organ cluttered with arteries and veins and booming with indignation like a fist. Then it's only one short step to imagining all three of our hearts suspended in air above us: his; my mother's, shaped like the ones children draw in school, a pink paper valentine with no ventricles at all, rippling gently overhead; and mine, lackadaisical and arrhythmic without reason, sullen, reddish brown, and dull.

''It won't be the end of the world if he loses his job. That's what I told him,'' my mother says, in a tone that makes me want to fall sideways into her arms; instead I take the yellow paper from my pocket and get a pen. I add a final line to my father's notice, "Mr. Denzer will be our coach," and sign my name.

"Plantinga points out that while a statement such as 'Othello was an Eskimo' is false, the statement 'Hamlet wore size 10 shoes' is neither true nor false." Bee sends me a list of books; I find them in the new Sea Haven library downtown. Kant's *Prolegomena to Any Future Metaphysics* is the first.

I can't even understand what's written on the jacket and check out instead a slim volume on the pioneers.

"Bee," I write, "if you don't exist, why are you living in California?" I tell her about the drawings of naked men in my mother's drawer. "Dad got in trouble at work," I tell her. "There isn't enough money left for my education. I'll live at home until they find someone to marry me to." I ask Bee what the parties at school are like and tell her that I wouldn't mind visiting sometime soon. Then I tell her a few things about the pioneers. "Pioneer women," I write, lifting a quote from the book but claiming it's mine, "often made do with scant supplies. Dresses were sewn from feed sacks; children gathered buffalo chips for fuel."

In her response, Bee says nothing about my father's job but tells me it's too early to think of visiting her yet. "Why are you reading about the pioneers? That's a stage you're supposed to have gone through already. Look at my list again. This is the basis of rigorous thought, the key to the mind."

"Yours is still locked," I want to say. I make her

a batch of chocolate walnut brownies and send them
first class with a Wonder Woman comic book on top.
No note enclosed.

Because Mr. Denzer is involved, kids have signed up.
Five boys, including Bert, all of whom already know
how to play, and twenty-three girls. Two of these are
myself and my friend Denise, who chain-smokes and
has never played a sport before. I pay her fifteen dollars to come.

We meet at the top of the practice fields where we
can look down along the wire fence toward the water
tower looming above the pines. Mr. Denzer explains
that these aren't tryouts; he isn't certain yet whether
we will have "cuts" but simply wants to see what we
can do. We spend thirty minutes on our swing, without
the ball, taking turns with the banged-up donated
clubs. Denise and I share a five-iron with a girl in
eleventh grade, a cheerleader who clearly sets her hair
each day. "Nice legs," Denise tells her, the first time
she stands in front of us to swing. To me she says, "I
can't stand seeing someone that cheerful. It hurts my
ears."

Mr. Denzer watches each of us swing. "Very
good," he says to me. The cheerleader stares. Then
each of us gets a chance to hit the ball while the others
observe and make comments from the rear. It's an
erotic sort of moment, a lot of people gathered around
to watch your body sway, while Mr. Denzer mentions
hips and wrists and shoulders, stepping forward now
and then to correct your stance. Denise drops the club
when it's her turn. The cheerleader skitters her ball to

the side. Bert and Jim Palermo hit fairly well, probably just over 100 yards. I am second to last. First I swing, just to get the feel, and two kids laugh because they think I missed the ball. I don't even flinch. I've played in front of my father, performed for his friends, and at the age of ten hit with a group of instructors from the club. I plant my feet and look down at the ball until I see all the little indentations; I can see the tiny hard core and the rubber wrapping, all the layers. This one small, useless thing is what I'm good at, and I try hard not to love it like I do.

"Hot dog," Mr. Denzer says, as the ball clears the fence easily, probably 160 yards. It bounces once on the road and disappears among the pines.

"This isn't long enough for a fairway," I tell him. He smiles when I give him back the club.

Denise and I like to read *Seventeen*, to make fun of the clothes and the columns, which we pretend to think are beneath us. The articles analyze girls like us. They talk about hormones and makeup, the pain of rejection, dating rules. One whole article is devoted to "going too far." We start out laughing and reading selected parts aloud, then become engrossed. I read about girls from broken homes and the way their parents vie for their attention, outdoing each other with gifts and praise and talk. Denise studies tips on "blotting" and runs a tissue lightly across her lips. "Listen to this," she says. " 'I'm a fourteen-year-old with a problem. Whenever I talk to a guy, I get worried about how I look. My teeth are crooked and sometimes I cover my mouth with my hand. I don't notice I'm doing it until people say they can't hear me. What should I do?' "

"Glue her hands in her pants pockets," I say, and Denise shakes her head. "Paper bag candidate." She yawns but finishes reading the page. "Hey, here's a letter from a girl whose mother had—um—cancer," she says, looking up.

"Touching," I answer, and flip the page. I make a note of the cover so that I can read it when Denise is gone.

"Sexuality," Mr. Denzer says, "includes not only sexual relations and intercourse, but the way a person feels about his body, the ease with which he interacts with the opposite sex. It's difficult, at your age, let's say fourteen, to feel completely at home with yourself. Your bodies are changing day by day, gradually becoming more mature."

I stare at the desk in front of me, almost feeling my body ripening like a pear. The tips of my fingers blossom, capillaries in my ears start to overflow, seeds and hidden bulbs in my abdomen swell and reach for the surface of my skin.

Mr. Denzer sits on the corner of his desk, loosening his tie. "I'm sure that some of you have begun to experiment, and part of my job is to tell you there's no hurry. Wait a while. Wait until the time is right. You have your entire lives in front of you."

This speech confuses me at first, because I think the word "experiment" refers somehow to menstruation, which for most of the girls has already begun. Then Denise pokes me with a pen. "Has Bert brought out the old chemistry set?" She cackles.

Bert has not. I begin to wonder if something is wrong with us or with him. Mr. Denzer refers to subterranean passions Bert doesn't feel.

" 'This isn't *long* enough for a *fairway*,' " he mimics over and over. Since we've been playing together every afternoon, he's been grouchy and cool. I try to explain that I've played for years and that there is no better feeling than clicking squarely into the side of that little ball.

Bert doesn't care, but Denise is impressed. "You have to show me how to hit it like that," she says. We smoke Marlboro Lights behind her house just after dark, flashlights propped beside us on the lawn, and practice, practice, practice.

By the end of the second week, all the girls but three have left the team, which consists of eight boys, myself and Denise, and our cheerleader friend. The boys are nice to Denise and Rayna (the cheerleader's name—we call her "Rhina") because we have only eleven, and without ten the team will fold.

Playing with people my own age for the first time, I realize the extent of my skills; I'm much better than the boys. When Mr. Denzer has to be away at a baseball game (with a little help, he's coaching two sports), I act as teacher in his stead, and most of the other kids don't seem to care. There aren't many teams to compete with, since most of the usual high schools don't sponsor golf, but there are enough. We hear about one boy or another, in Vernon or Atlantic City or Long Beach, who is supposed to putt on a dime, but with my long, arcing drives we beat them all. Riding home on the bus, our driver, Fast Eddie, at the wheel, we careen along the bay road, cheering the gulls up from their nests within the marsh. Generally we cheer for me.

The only person who doesn't cheer for me is Bert. He sits in the front of the bus with an open textbook in his lap. "You don't need to study so much," I tell him. "You'll wear out your brain, and it'll shrink to the size of a hamster's."

"Don't be stupid," Bert says.

"That was eccentric," I tell him, "not stupid. Do you want to know what my sister says?"

"No, I don't." He has a look on his face—mouth open, lower jaw slung far to the side—that I've never seen. "I don't want to know what your crazy sister has to say."

"What are you mad about?" I ask.

Bert returns to his algorithms, reading until our bus pulls into the parking lot at school, where my father waits impatiently in the car. "Well?" He wants to analyze every hole, discuss the intricacies of a match that I've forbidden him to see.

"It was okay." I watch Bert get into his mother's powder blue Ford and slam the door. "We won."

"How did *you* do?"

"I dropped it in two on the fifteenth. Where's Mom?"

"The fifteenth? Holy cow." My father puts the car in gear. "I don't try to keep track of your mother. She's probably out roaming a vacant lot, looking for tin cans poised among the weeds. She had her sketchbook in the car."

"She was supposed to come with us," I say.

We drive to our favorite hamburger restaurant near the marina.

"Mom isn't interested in golf," I tell my father. He locks the car and we enter the green tile world of the restaurant, which resembles a giant bathroom with a stainless steel grill off to the side.

"There are worlds of things," he says, slapping his newspaper down on a table before a slow-moving older couple can get there first, "that your mother is interested in. Don't get her started on something new."

"She should be interested in *us*," I say, hating myself. "We never see her."

My father shrugs off his jacket and puts his napkin on his lap, even though we haven't seen a menu.

"I don't think she should get a job. She already had two jobs that didn't work out. I don't see why she can't stay home. Wouldn't you say?"

"I would say"—he signals the waitress—"that everyone steers his own boat around here."

I remind him that, although we live next to the ocean, as a family, together, we have never set foot in a boat.

"Bring me a chocolate milk shake and a double-decker," he says to the waitress. And to me: "No one's stopping you from going out alone."

In a book called *Westward Trail*, I read about pioneer families who live in clearings in the woods. The trees, a towering green, circle the crude log homes like a living fence. Once you step outside the cleared circle, you feel lost: the sun can't shine through the layers of overlapping leaves; the temperature plummets out there; and the shouts from the cabin fade, absorbed by the ground. All day the older children work in the garden or the house while the younger ones are supposed to pull up weeds. The circle always threatens to get smaller and close them in, so the job of the children is to hold the line. Once, when one of the littlest steps on a bed of moss outside the circle of the trees, he is carried away by Indians and disappears. I wonder about the second life this child leads.

Bee seems to be studying similar problems. "Identity," she writes, "is a difficult concept to the extent that we must consider the identity of individuals over time. Intuitively, it seems there must be limits to the degree to which a person can be changed, and be the same."

When I call her late at night on the kitchen phone, she says, "Jane, I forget to sleep sometimes, I'm so excited." She tells me about her professors, who question everything they see. No one in Berkeley, it appears, relies on the evidence of their eyes, ears, fingers, nose, or tongue. "Tell me what *you're* studying."

Mentally I review my classes, simple versions of algebra and English Bee excelled in long ago. "I don't know," I say. "The usual stuff. I'm playing golf."

"Let me send you another reading list. Speak up, I can barely hear you."

It's two in the morning in Sea Haven; my parents are sleeping in their room ten feet away.

"What do you miss about us most?" I ask. "Do you think we're the same people when you're gone?"

"Jane?" she says. "Are you still there?"

Hearing my father roll over in bed, I hang up the phone.

In Mr. Denzer's section of Health, one of the largest units we study is first aid. We learn about tourniquets, splints, and pressure to stop blood flow; we learn the "stop, drop, and roll" rule about burns and know that stroke victims should elevate their feet and keep warm. A Red Cross worker shows us how to resuscitate a dummy and encourages us to sign up for a class "that could save a life." We practice the Heimlich maneuver on one another in study hall. But what we've been waiting for—the capstone of the course—is the emergency childbirth film, a ninth-grade rite of passage and piece of class lore widely discussed in the cafeteria each spring. We have to bring permission slips from our parents to see the film. "Not that thing again," my mother says, signing the slip. "If you decide to skip it, fine with me."

Everyone arrives early. Two of the boys bring vomit bags, selling them for a nickel at the door.

"All right," Mr. Denzer says. "Let's quiet down."

The birth takes place, for some unknown reason, in a fallout shelter, with cans of no-brand food stacked on wooden shelves. There's a table in the center of the room, covered with pillows, a shower curtain, and a white sheet. The only people in the shelter are two women, one of them hugely pregnant in a stiff white gown, the other in a tight-cinched dress. The pregnant woman looks docile and tame, not clearly hurting, as she's led to the table and helped to lie down. A man's voice narrates the film, telling the viewer what to do if she should encounter this emergency herself, perhaps in a bus or a department store. The thin woman, businesslike, looks at her watch to time contractions (the camera focuses on her wrist, on the second hand), and jots them down on a piece of paper at her side. The narrator's voice is serious, in the corny style of the 1950s, but now and then it sounds proud and hearty, almost amused. I start to wonder who the narrator is. Is he responsible for this mess? Where is the woman's husband? Was he radiated in war? The narrator says that it's important to reassure the woman giving birth. We flash to a reassuring smile on the face of the skinny woman, whose hair, even within the confines of the shelter, has been washed and curled, then to the sweaty forehead of the patient, still as bland and unknowing as a pie. Harry MacIntyre, behind me, makes indecent gestures with his hands.

Without warning, after a lengthy viewing of the necessary towels, blankets, dishpans, antiseptics, scissors, and knives, the camera zeroes in on the woman's crotch; I hear a collective shifting of chairs around the room. From this point on, we aren't watching a living woman; we are seeing an inhuman spectacle, a repulsive feat, something none of us, in our deepest moments of shame, could have counted on. The narrow-waisted woman has disappeared. All that's left is a hideous bulging mass of skin, bleeding, purple, hairy, and obscene. I can't tell which way is up and which is down. A jet of blood hits the camera lens. One student gropes for his vomit bag, another lurches for the door. The narrator's voice has stopped, as if what we see can't be adequately described. Mr. Denzer, at the front of the room, cleans his fingernails.

When the film is over, we sit stunned. No one has noticed whether the baby is a boy or girl.

"Ten minutes left to class," Mr. Denzer says. "Are there any questions?"

Not a hand.

He hits the rewind switch on the machine and turns on the light, whistling and untangling the extension cord. We remain frozen in our chairs, like deer caught in high beams late at night. This is what could happen to us: the movie, if successful, should frighten us into celibacy for years.

"That concludes our emergency unit," Mr. Denzer says. "When the bell rings, you can go."

Soon Bert is studying on the way to the matches, as well as on the way home. At the back of the bus, Rayna, her hair parted perfectly on the side as if with a laser, asks what's wrong.

"Nothing," I say.

She smiles, looking sweet. Most days she can't carry her own clubs to the tee.

Denise is practicing her swing, empty-handed, in the aisle.

When we get off the bus for the match against Mount Union, I run up to Bert and grab his arm.

"You don't want me to play well," I tell him. "That's what's wrong."

Bert tosses his hair. He has pencil-thin eyebrows and an Adam's apple like a giant thorn. I don't like Bert much anymore, but that's not the point. The important thing is to keep him, not let him go. I am willing to suffer for his sake, like the pregnant woman in the film. "I don't care if you play well," he says.

"You don't want me to beat *you* anymore."

Bert stops beside me on the grass and studies my face. "You could win without trying. You couldn't lose."

I feel I've been given a chance to prove myself, to win much more than a game. "Watch me," I say.

The smell of Bert's chewing gum, raspberry or strawberry, mingles with the scent of wet grass and exhaust. Bert leans forward and kisses me on the mouth. One of the other boys whistles. Bert plucks the gum from his cheek and throws it away.

"I don't need charity," he says.

Denise gooses me with a putter. "Didn't anyone tell you that kissing weakens your knees?" She puts her arm around my neck and we walk to the tee.

Everything goes fairly well until my father shows up at the match, breaching all of our agreements. I spot him at the edge of the green on the fourth hole, talking to Mr. Capelli, Denise's dad. I turn around to look for Bert but he's heavily involved in a pear-shaped sand trap, shaking his head. Mr. Denzer has already asked me if I'm all right: I hit a thirty-yard drive on the first hole and got an eight on a short par four. "My arm's a little stiff," I said, as Bert walked past us. Mr. Denzer rolled up my sleeve and squeezed my wrist, but I said I was fine.

Now I step up to the tee and stare at the ball. I would like to hit it into the atmosphere, onto a golf course in Virginia or New York. I can feel the perfect revolution of my arms, the turn of my wrists. I stiffen my left elbow and drive the ball off into the weeds. Bert appears suddenly behind me. "Too bad," he says, heading for his clubs.

My father is livid when I reach the green. He hisses at me from the rough. "What are you throwing this for? I've seen you play better with plastic clubs." I rub a spot near my shoulder blade. I take three putts to sink it: par three.

On the sixth hole Mr. Denzer rolls up my sleeve and kneads my elbow. "It doesn't look swollen. Is something bothering you?" He quickly glances toward my father, who now stands in a cluster of parents, pointing at me. Mr. Denzer drops my arm.

I reassure him that I can finish the entire course. I look at the best boy golfer on the Mount Union squad, a sad-looking guy with skin like wax and a mouth like a flounder's, damp and pale. I set my ball on the tee. My father has muscled through the tiny crowd and stands just behind me, as close as protocol allows. His shadow nearly touches my right shoe. I look at the ball.

"*Hit* the goddamn thing," my father says, just as I bring the driver down, and almost unintentionally I do, over the creek and the fake wood bridge, past a family of gulls and toward the green.

"About time." I beat the Mount Union boy by one.

When I catch up with Bert near the locker rooms, the rest of the team is gone. "Wait up," I say, and then wish I hadn't when he turns around. "My dad was there, Bert. I didn't know he was going to come."

"Listen, Jane." His face is tense, as if there were

muscles in every inch of it, all of them flexing and unflexing, doing push-ups and sit-ups under his skin. "I don't care how well you play. So you're good at golf: big deal. If you were playing at a decent school, you'd just be average, you'd be middle of the road." He opens his hands as if to show how little I'm worth.

"What does that make you?" I ask. "If I'm just middle of the road."

"Not a hell of a lot." He tucks in his shirt. "That's why I'm quitting. I got a job."

"You can't quit."

"Sure I can. You've still got ten on the team. You can still show off as much as you need to."

I should ask him not to go. I should look swoony and touch his chest. I can sense all the proper things to do but I'm just watching Bert get smaller, as if one of us were leaving, walking away.

"I've been seeing Rayna," he says. "For a week or so."

"Rayna," I repeat, a little too loud.

Bert says that he hopes we'll all stay friends.

I tell him that should be easy. "She's got a really nice pair of legs," I say, and then go.

Denise is sympathetic. "He was a jackass," she says, carefully watching my eyes. But I don't cry. I don't mourn Bert at all. I feel lighter—not happy, but careless and numb. I think about the pioneers. They were thinkers, in their way. They may not have sat around all day wondering whether the trees were really trees or whether the Indians wouldn't be Indians in different clothes, but they had to think to get along. They were smart, whether they did well in school or not. Most of the girls were married by the age of fifteen.

With Bert out of the picture I begin to flirt with the boys on the team. I put my arm around Jerry Caldicott on the bus. Mr. Denzer smiles. I hide Bill Latisher's clubs. Denise cheers me on. Behind the locker room I tell Jim Worth, a boy with acne on his chin, to put his hand underneath my shirt. I am surprised—and so is he—when he obeys. He calls me on the phone that week, and I sense that he's told the other guys. It doesn't matter. None of them will ever golf as well as I do.

Denise lights up in the shade of the water tower after practice and tells me I'm acting strange.

"I'm still winning. Worry about your own game," I tell her. Denise makes me tired.

She stretches the sleeves of her sweatshirt to cover her hands. "I'm not talking about golf. I saw Bert. You know he's working for his dad."

"What a good boy."

Denise takes one more drag off her cigarette, then stumps it out. She's been smoking less, and sometimes she lifts weights at her brother's gym. "Rayna's afraid of you," she says. "She thinks you've got it in for her because of Bert. She wanted to quit the team but Bert told her not to."

"Gee, that was kind of him," I say.

"I helped him talk her out of it," Denise says.

"Oh." I take the pack of cigarettes from her hand. "A little threesome."

"He wasn't right for you." Denise replaces a divot. Her hair has begun to look almost smooth. "Remember when we used to sit around and plan our futures? What kind of jobs we were going to have and when we'd get married, and how many kids we'd have? How many boys and how many girls? We gave them all names.''

''Yeah,'' I say.

''But you know we never named the husbands. We had names for all the kids but not for the men.''

I look at Denise. I've known her since the first or second grade.

''Sometimes I get afraid we won't remember things,'' she says. ''We'll get old and have these ordinary lives and just take our parents' places when they die.''

Somewhere a part of me knows exactly what she means, but the sight of this new Denise—in the growing shade of the water tower she looks less sure of herself and softer, almost pretty—makes me cruel.

''You know what?'' I tap a cigarette from her pack and light it, blowing a crumpled smoke ring toward her hair. ''I've been studying some things, and I've discovered that people are relative.''

''What do you mean?''

''You and Bert. Rayna, too. If I decide you don't exist, you disappear. I can look at you right now and you're not alive. *Poof!* you're gone. I wipe you out.''

''What the hell do you mean by that?''

''Denise?'' I look around in the shadows as if searching. ''Denise?'' I wave my hands like Helen Keller through the air. ''Oh,'' I say to myself, ''I guess she's gone.''

* * *

"Dear Bee," I write.

Forget everything I said in the other letters. Everything's fine. We're very happy here without you. We play cribbage together on Wednesdays. Dad laughs a lot. I understand Hegel completely. Bert is gone; I'm in love with Mr. Denzer, the golf coach. One day, perhaps I will kill myself.

Your sister, Jane.

"I'm only here," Denise says, "to give you a message. Then you can wave your magic wand and make me invisible again." She slumps against my locker. "Mr. D's calling a meeting about morale."

"So?" I'd like to make peace but don't know how.

"You missed the last meeting," she says. "He wants you to come."

"Maybe, if he invites me personally, I will. He could send me a love note and a rose."

Denise doesn't laugh. "I can't tell if nothing bothers you," she says, "or if everything bothers you too much. Which is it? Why can't you ever tell anyone what's wrong?"

I wave her away.

"Will you be there?" She helps me stuff my books in the locker.

I tell her I will.

I skip the meeting, as well as practice the next day, and Health, too. I miss the match against Millerville. I leave a note on Denise's locker: LARYNGITIS, CAN'T PLAY. On my own locker she writes (on the metal, in a felt-tip pen): YOU DON'T NEED VOCAL CORDS FOR

GOLF. The team wins without me for the first time; I see the article in the morning paper on Saturday.

"Mr. Vensler called," my mother says. "He wanted to tell you about the game."

"It isn't a game," I say. "It's a match. I couldn't play because I hurt my arm."

"That was it, then, a match." She holds a paint-color strip against her bedroom wall. She wants to paint the room a deep violet; she's been covering, room by room, the off-white my father chose ten years ago with aquamarine, coral, and all the colors of the sea. No one has told her that a woman who has spent half her life expecting to die should find a better use for her time, but I am beginning to think that I will. I have been saving up a mountain of things to say. "What do you think of this?" she asks.

It will probably look wonderful; in fact I'm eager to see the colors for my own room. "I don't care about that stupid ugly paint," I tell her, surprising both of us. "I like the walls the way they are."

Slowly, carefully, she collects the strips of colors and sits down. "You're unhappy," she says, in a tone that makes me wonder whether she's welcoming me as a partner in misery. "I didn't know."

I want to tell her there's plenty she doesn't know. Worlds of things she can't even guess at. I'd like to wipe that sudden sympathy off her face.

"I quit. I'm not going to play. It doesn't mean anything to me. I won't ever play golf again."

My mother regards me as she might a portrait subject. "What is it you want me to tell you?" she asks.

I scan my imagination. There is no way to phrase

what I want to know. "Bee isn't coming home this summer, is she?" I stand at the table close to my mother, staring her down. "She's staying again. She never comes home. She moves away, and we never see her. We don't visit, and she doesn't come back."

My mother spreads the colors like a fan. She speaks deliberately, slowly. "Beatrice is an adult. I don't tell her when to come or go. She's very busy and it's good for her to study away from home. She's doing well."

"And what are we doing?" I ask.

"If you think I don't miss her, Jane, you're wrong."

Sadness rises in my throat. "I'm wrong about everything."

"No." She shakes her head. The colors in her hand increase in brilliancy, like gems. I imagine living inside them. "Right and wrong may be irrelevant. Do you want to play golf?"

"No," I say. "Not anymore."

"Then give it up. And pick yourself up and start again."

Although I'm not expecting Mr. Denzer, I'm not surprised to see him in the corner of the equipment shed. I'm hanging my golf bag on the wall.

"Hello," he says. He blushes.

"I'm turning my stuff in," I tell him. "I wasn't stealing or anything."

"The season's not over yet." He crosses his arms. "If you leave, we'll be down to nine. Do you think that's fair?"

"Ten was *your* number," I remind him. "You made it up."

"Yes, I did." He nods and looks down at his shoes, and I feel sick at myself, disgusted. "You're a very talented golfer. You should have a private teacher, not a coach."

My father says the same thing. I foresee the summer as a procession of white afternoons, my father trailing me and some other middle-aged badly dressed bald man in the heat.

Mr. Denzer coughs. "I called the extra meetings to ask if everything was all right; I wasn't trying to assign blame. Things get complicated at home sometimes, I know. People run into problems, and I thought we might touch base and talk things through."

It's hard to breathe. I imagine Bert and Rayna getting married. Then I picture Bee and Mr. Denzer marrying, too, Bee wearing a tan wraparound skirt, a blouse, and a veil.

"I probably should have handled it better," he says. "I should have talked to you alone. That is, if you wanted to talk to me," he adds. I imagine my mother getting sick again and dying, my father losing his job, sitting on the sidewalk in front of Linders with his hat in his hand. Later, he would disown me: I'd be thrown out of school; I'd get a seedy job as a waitress and end up pregnant at seventeen, going away to have the baby in a cinder-block shelter on one of those farms.

Tears are emerging from my eyes. Mr. Denzer puts his hands on my shoulders and draws me in. "It's all right," he says, over and over. I'm still inhaling his aftershave when Bert comes through the door.

*   *   *

Without golf, I am able to devote more time to my studies. And to shopping with my mother, who has quit her art class, in the afternoons. The two of us drink iced tea and eat pastry when things get slow. She seems to want to fix me in a time and place and sometimes seems surprised at things I do. I smoke cigarettes in the open, and she doesn't mind. As for me, I am trying to fix her, too; I would like to commit her to memory but she changes, picking up new habits, gaining and losing weight and changing her wardrobe and her rings, cutting her hair and growing it, drawing on her eyebrows where they never came back in. My mother is a state of flux, as indefinable as air. She's like the ideas Bee describes: at first glance obvious and clear, but the more you look at them the more tangled and abstract they will become. We can't trust our five senses where she is concerned.

I spend more time, too, reading pioneer books instead of answering Bee's letters, which have become less frequent anyway. I read about women who follow their husbands over the plains and through the woods, leaving a trail of dead children and pots and pans. They leave behind whitewashed eastern homes, dove gray silk dresses, and are led bashful and wide-eyed deeper into the forest, gaining new personalities as they go. They arrive at the doorsteps of their brand-new homes disconsolate and unbelieving, fingernails testing the rough mud hut, the log cabin, or straw floor. In later chapters the husband disappears in a winter storm, snakes drop down through the roof in the rainy season, wolves and Indians come to the door. The

women are always pregnant or sick and realize that
their children will grow up wild, never knowing the
clothes and manners of the coast. I love these tragedies
and identify with their heroines, though what country
I feel I've been torn from I don't know.

7

September, October

Mr. Denzer was the only one home when I woke up on a Sunday morning in September and felt the mattress sticky with blood. My stomach was as hard and inflexible as a stone. I rolled over onto Ellie's velvet drawstring packet of baby names—I had fallen asleep reading them, pulling out the white slips and whispering the names to myself: Gwendolyn, Willard, Matthew—and covered my mouth from the sudden pain. There was blood on my palms and now on my face and in my hair, all over my legs; the slips of paper, some as tiny as a fingernail, escaped from the purse and stuck to me: Isabella, Charles, Guinevere. I reached over my head for the bedpost, pulled myself up, and vomited onto the floor.

No one came. I could feel the blood leaving me, sluggishly coursing down my legs with every pulse. I braced my left arm on the pillow and rocked myself to standing by the bed, feeling a corkscrew work its way from navel to spine. The tiny, bloodied paper

171

names began to fall from me, leaves from a tree: Daniel, Daniela, Joanna, John. The stairs weren't possible—I could barely lift my legs—so I pulled myself toward the porch by holding onto the bedpost, the rafters, the rusted nails. Something inside of me folded in half: my body was shaking—not trembling but seizing up in enormous jolts. Watching my feet misstep along the splintered boards, my legs gradually turning into stone, I started to count: seven steps left; six more. A tributary of blood had reached my toe. I passed the dresser, knocking my hairbrush and mirror to the ground. The attic doorway floated in dust and light, like a passage to another world; I was pulling a thread of blood along the floor. I could hear the pigeons under the eaves cooing their songs; bits of feathers rose and fell in the humid air. I gripped the doorway, no longer sure whether I was about to step into Dr. Subramanian's modest office or onto the moon.

Mr. Denzer, about to start on a morning run, paused to retie his shoes and looked up, probably to check the weather. I was waving, having realized that I lacked the strength to shout, when he focused his gaze on the house. He started to run. Up the sand and over the deck, up the outer stairs to my father's porch, through the only open window, breaking the screen, and up the wooden steps to my attic room. Past my grandmother's dresser and her bed, past the scattered bloody strips of names and the broken mirror, over the doorsill to the badly painted deck. He was at my side at the very moment I fell down.

*   *   *

I stayed in the hospital for six days. The placenta—slimy eggplant—had begun to detach from the uterine wall. It seemed to have stopped detaching, and I was allowed to rest at home. "In bed," Dr. Subramanian warned me. "Lying down."

Bee and Ellie had moved Bee's computer out of her room and into the hall and moved Bee's clothes into the attic where mine had been. They hustled me into her room, from where I could hear my father's clocks like a steady thunder far away, and installed a dozen yellow roses in a vase on the old pine dresser. I said I wanted to sleep upstairs.

"Absolutely not," Bee said. "The attic steps are too much of an effort. I'll sleep up there."

"You hate the attic."

Ellie, arms folded, stood close to Bee. They looked like bouncers at a bar. "Down here you're closer to the bathroom. And the phone."

I adjusted the drawstring on my sweatpants—there was less and less string to tie a bow with—and lay down. "What happened to school? Are you going to cut the whole semester?"

"Teachers' holiday," Ellie said. "We came down for the weekend to do some stuff around the house."

I wondered if Ellie's parents knew she was spending most of her time around *our* house, with her former teacher, rootless and pregnant. I tried to fluff up my pillow but Ellie hustled to my side and actually lifted my head like a coconut, setting an extra pillow underneath. I didn't want to be fussed with. I wanted to be back in the attic, left alone. "Cut it out, Ellie. Who's your English teacher?"

"Mrs. Leamy." She winced. Ruth Leamy wasn't known for lighthearted tolerance; in fact Ellie already looked pinched and less confident than she had a month ago. "They got a guy named Mr. Wozniak to replace you. He's really cool. My friend Alison calls him the Woz."

"He's good-looking, then, I guess. Does anyone wonder where I am?"

Ellie shrugged. "You were only there a year. Hardly anyone knew you."

"We'll let you sleep." Bee pulled Ellie by the sleeve. Tweedledee and Tweedledum. "There's a bell on the nightstand if you need us."

"Where's Bill Denzer?" I asked. He had visited me several times in the hospital and had been written up, for saving me, in the *Sea Haven Herald.*

"Who, the hero? No one's seen him. He must be shy." Ellie demonstrated the bell. "We've got a tray for your food. I brought my Mom's silver pepper mill from the house."

"I'm glad you found a way to make yourself useful," I said.

She looked at her feet.

I tried to tell her I was kidding, but Bee quickly shunted her out the door.

During the first week back at home I got out of bed only to use the toilet or the shower. I lay in Bee's room with the window open, barely able to hear the soft pulse of the ocean come and go. Often I lay my hands on my growing stomach, feeling the waves and seismic currents. It was like resting a giant palm on top of the sea. Sometimes I struck bargains with the underwater creature curled within: Stay, and I will reward you; come ashore safe, and you won't regret it. But being pregnant still felt odd more than anything else. It was disorienting, peculiar; it was as if I were gradually taking over the body of someone else—a flaccid, pendulous, self-inflating person with swollen limbs—and I regarded this person from a safe distance.

Bee and my father left me alone in the middle room unless I rang the bell, in which case one of them appeared like an instant butler, tapping once and flinging wide the door. They seemed to be having conferences about me. They worried that I was depressed. They worried that I lacked plans. They worried that any plans I might have made would soon fall through because I couldn't get out of bed. They worried that I wasn't worried about myself. But staying in bed all day brought a kind of relief. I didn't have to shop for baby clothes, or for apartments, or for jobs. I could reject checkers, chess, crosswords, radios, VCRs, and puzzles in favor of dreaminess and hours spent doing nothing. I could think about why my mother, pregnant and with a four-year-old quirky gifted child at home, would run away from her family, carrying me unwittingly along.

At the beginning of the second week, Bee caught me climbing the attic steps. She was always hovering close by, ready to tell me how lucky I was that she'd moved back to Sea Haven to watch over me. I felt her cool thin fingers tentacle my leg. "If you need something," she said, "I'd be happy to get it for you."

"That would be wonderful." I paused, wondering

whether it was worth the effort to break free. "Except that I'm not exactly sure yet what I need. I'm just going up to browse."

"I'm afraid you're mistaken," Bee said. "You were about to sit on the couch under the afghan and try some of the corn bread I just made."

"I don't like corn bread."

"Wrong again." Bee coaxed my right leg down. "This is convalescent corn bread. You're going to beg me to make more."

I remembered the movie *Whatever Happened to Baby Jane?* "I just need an hour or so up there," I said. "I left some boxes open, a bunch of stuff lying around—"

"Forget it. When you were in the hospital Dad went up and reboxed everything and pushed it all toward the eaves. It's all tidy now, up there. I thought he'd have a hernia."

"Was he mad that I rearranged things? What did he say?"

"The usual grumbling. Nothing new."

"Did you help him?"

"He wouldn't let me," Bee said. "He nearly bit my head off when I went up one day to offer."

I took a step down. "What do the two of you do all day? Dad's not working on his lamps anymore, and you don't seem to be using the computer."

"We're taking care of the invalid," Bee said. She handed me a piece of corn bread that resembled pumice stone. "We keep busy. I've been helping Dad reorganize his money. You wouldn't believe what his files look like—they're a mess."

"Dad doesn't have much money," I said.

Bee shrugged. "He's got real estate."

I said, "This house isn't real estate. This house is where he lives. It's where you and I live, too, for the time being."

"Crucial words," Bee said. " 'Time being.' You should know that I put an ad in the paper about your car."

"What about it?"

"You'll want to sell it." Bee pushed her glasses up on her nose. "There's no way you can put a baby in that thing. You'll have to buy something safer, something new."

"You're selling my car?"

"Come over here," Bee said. "Come take a look." She led me to the window overlooking a row of cars parked in front of the house: Bill Denzer's, a tidy blue hatchback, waxed and clean; my father's, a sturdy second-hand Oldsmobile with a Berkeley sticker on the back; Bee's, designed for 130 miles per hour on the autobahn; and mine, a long discolored rustmobile with the tailpipe sticking out a foot in back. "You'll thank me," she said.

A miniature arm or leg smoothed the inside of my body. I dropped the corn bread I was holding, and it shattered on the floor.

Bee picked the crumbs up in a napkin. "Don't worry about it," she said. "I can handle everything from now on."

Bill Denzer began to visit in the afternoons. He brought tulips and handmade writing paper, fresh bluefish caught from the pier. He rigged up a pull chain for the overhead lamp, strung along the ceiling so I could reach it lying in bed; and he checked out books for me from the Sea Haven High School collection, smoothing the brittle plastic covers with his thumb. At first he brought only what I requested: Jane Austen, George Eliot, Tolstoy, the Brontë sisters, and Balzac. These were books I already knew and loved, but I found that now I lacked the concentration to reread them. With the noise of Bee and my father in the kitchen and the liquid, bumping movements of the fetus testing its home, I grew impatient with the creeping pace of the dialogue, the raised eyebrow in the parlor, the inevitable flush on the heroine's cheek. Bill Denzer found the books beneath my bed, dusty and shut. He began to bring me choices of his own.

"I used to love this book," he said, bringing me the memoirs of Carl Yastrzemski. I read a few chapters and put it down. He brought a book about Bear Bryant. A book about square dancers that was much worse than the others, but I read it through. He brought *Alive!* about the plane crash in the Andes, some of the survivors being forced to eat the dead. I read about logging in the Northwest, I read a book about the history of home economics, I read a turgid portrait of Mary Lincoln.

"Selection's limited this time," he would say, standing like a tree trunk in the doorway, framed by the cool gray ocean walls. Sometimes, nostalgic, he brought me yellow Popsicles from the store. When he sat in the wicker chair beside my bed, he moved it several feet away, scraping the dresser or the edge of the windowsill. It was Bill Denzer who delivered the note from my class: it had disbanded. Guillermo wrote, "We have taught you very much." Arletta added, "Well wishes for your illicit child."

I wouldn't have said that Bill and I were close, but there was something comforting about having him around. Maybe because he had saved me, I felt safe when he was near. Maybe I liked him because he was a good listener. Certainly he didn't talk much. When he did talk he usually spoke in platitudes that I found refreshing: "You never know until you try"; "you're only as strong as your weakest link." Maybe I wanted him with me because when he sat beside my bed I could imagine myself again at fourteen, blushing when he turned his liquid brown-eyed gaze at me.

Bill was sincere, which made him easy to make fun of. He didn't understand cynicism or irony, and he lived his life giving pep talks to himself. When he talked about his students, it was always with such candor that I knew they must have both liked him and poked fun at him at every opportunity they got. He knew the names of his students' parents and where they worked, knew who had gotten sick or been laid off, and knew, without embarrassment or glee, the tangled emotional and romantic lives of the twelve- and thirteen-year-olds who would scorn him the following year. He was empathetic, to a fault, and didn't think evil of anyone. If the world were made up of Mr. Denzers, history wouldn't fill a single page.

Maybe that's why, on a day when we sat looking out at the rain against the Benedettis' house next door, I felt comfortable enough to ask him if he would do me a favor.

He looked pleased. Bee and my father had both gone out, leaving him to baby-sit in their stead.

"It's not the sort of favor you may feel comfortable with," I said. "It's in the attic. I'm not supposed to go up the stairs."

"No, of course not," he said.

I hesitated. "I'm sure I can trust you," I said. "But I'm not sure that trust is the only issue."

He waited. He was a sphinx.

So I decided that I had to put it to him straight. I had been looking for something up there; in fact it was slowly dawning on me that I had come home to find it, and though I wasn't sure what it was, I needed to go through every box and nook and cranny until I held it in my hands. "Maybe this doesn't make any sense," I said. "Does it?"

"I guess you can't know that yet." He paused. "Wouldn't your sister like to help you?" He was asking whether Bee approved, whether she knew. The attic was her bedroom now.

"I don't think she'd be very thorough." I looked at him, steady: *Do this for me*. "She'd try to decide what I should look at."

"And you'd rather *I* made that decision?" He stood up, about to refuse me, I thought: he had too much self-respect to root around in someone else's things.

"I'd rather you help me find what I'm looking for."

He smiled. "What if you find something you don't expect?" In spite of his squarish shape and thinning hair, Bill Denzer still possessed a certain charm.

"That won't be your problem," I said. "Mainly I'm

asking you to bring me some things that I can't reach."

"And not tell anyone what I'm doing."

I sat up against the pillows. "You can tell anyone you want except my father and Bee. They're usually out in the afternoons."

"I've noticed that." The house was quiet. Bill cocked his head, pretending to be listening for a key in the lock, a slammed car door. "I think if your mother or father didn't want you to see something, they would have destroyed it."

"How do you know what my parents would do?"

"Conjecture. I've read a lot of mystery books. But then, I never met your mother. What do you want me to bring down for you right now?"

We very quickly developed a system: Bill checked in after his last class at one-fifteen—by rescuing me, he had earned himself a key—and if all was clear, he headed up to the attic where I could follow his footsteps from the creaking of the floorboards up above. I even drew him a map, but my father must have rearranged things completely: sometimes Bill was over by the windows, sometimes in the area where Bee slept, pushing heavy objects across the floor. Soon he didn't want my help or my suggestions, developing instead his own method of organization. Usually he brought down one box at a time, opened up: paperback books, W-2 forms from the 1940s, Bee's high school compositions, photographs. Then I'd tell him what to leave and what to return. Often he waited while I riffled through the contents of a box: it reminded me of being waited on by a salesman in a shoe store, always disappearing behind the curtain for another pair.

We didn't talk about what we were doing or, for that matter, about my "collapse": the fact that I might have bled to death on the attic porch if he hadn't seen me. When I brought the subject up, he would absently rearrange the hairbrushes on my dresser or straighten the yellowing window shades.

"Why didn't you ride to the hospital with me?" I asked, one day when he had brought me a musty cardboard container labeled MISCELLANEOUS. I remembered little of the ambulance ride, but I could still clearly see Bill standing on the sidewalk as the medics loaded my stretcher in. "He coming with you?" one of them had asked. The medics looked like off-duty surfers—yellow eyebrows and flowing hair.

"I needed to call your father and Beatrice." Bill looked dusty and warm. He had spent thirty minutes in the attic and come down with only a shoebox full of blank postcards and broken pens. But I didn't want to complain.

"You could have called them from the hospital." I opened a yearbook of my father's that Bill had found on a previous reconnaissance. No one had signed the inside cover, and in his picture my father looked lonely, skinny, stubborn, and forlorn. "One serious fellow," the caption said. I shut the book.

"Not what you wanted, I guess," Bill said, as if blaming himself for not bringing the elusive *something* I was looking for.

I kicked my feet out of the blankets. My stomach was as round as a basketball. "I'm not even sure why I'm doing this," I said. "I spend my time thinking about things that shouldn't matter at this stage.''

Mr. Denzer stepped toward the bed.

''No, I'm all right. I shouldn't ask you to do my dirty work.'' I flipped through some of the postcards and replaced the lid on the box. ''Next time you'll just visit, if you want, and we'll sit and talk. No more family history. I'll be a well-behaved pregnant person; we'll drink decaffeinated tea.''

Mr. Denzer reached into the pocket of his shirt. He held out five small faded envelopes, each addressed to Miss Caroline Biddle, each with 1942 postmarks. I had no idea where he found them and didn't care.

''Thank you,'' I said. ''Very much.''

He leaned over the bed, straightened my blankets, then quietly started for the door.

''Bill?'' I didn't usually call him Bill. I tried not to call him anything. He turned around. ''You're too good to stick with a job in Sea Haven. Don't you ever get tired of teaching? Doing the same thing every year?''

''No.'' He put his hands in his pockets and rocked back on his heels. ''It's not the same. The students are different every time.''

''They're not like me anymore?'' I laughed.

Bill flipped the switch. It was five o'clock and day was seeping from the room. ''They were never like you,'' he said. ''Not even then.''

Dear Caroline,
   You know without my telling you that I miss you. Here on the base there is no room for privacy, so I am always thinking of you in a

crowded place. Do you still wear your yellow dress? I know it's too much to ask if I ask you not to wear it anymore. You can wear the shoes.

Dear Caroline,
  The sun rose today at 6:21. I was already up, wondering what you were doing. Sleeping, I think. Anyone who sleeps as much as you do must be happy. How can you dislike Joan Crawford? She is the best thing that has ever happened to me, other than you.

Dear Caroline,
  You are a terrible correspondent. My own brother writes longer letters. I want to marry you and buy a tank of fish. A tank of fish and a dog. Having a dog will make you feel better. I think about these things instead of studying. Why don't you write? I think about sitting next to you, watching the fish swim around and around. Is this crazy? I don't know.

"What do you mean, you're reading his letters?"

Bee was driving me to my appointment with Dr. Subramanian. Once a week I was allowed to inch my way downstairs with my sister's help, climb into the car with the seat reclined, and ride to the doctor's office. I looked forward to these outings as if they were trips to distant regions of the world. Because I wasn't allowed to drive, I let Bee sell my car. I also let her give me what both of us knew to be more money than anyone in his or her right mind would have paid for it. Bee claimed that she had fixed a thing or two. "Letters are private," she said. "Where'd you get them?" She reached over to check my seat belt. I slapped her hand.

"I found them," I said. "In the back of a closet—never mind where. Whoever put them away probably forgot about them by now."

Bee signaled a turn. She seemed distracted. "Why don't you ask that unnamed person if it's all right for you to read them?"

Dear Caroline,
   Here is a riddle. What has two eyes, a nose, a
mouth, two ears, a chest, two arms, a waist, hips,
a set of privates, two legs, and a foot fungus?
Please answer. Correct responses win a prize.

"I'm not reading all of them," I said. "It's just a few. They aren't dated, so it's hard to tell the context. I'll put them back as soon as I'm done."

"Done what?"

We drove past the boardwalk and past Linders—now renamed STEDMAN'S in huge red letters, but still the same store—and turned left to Dr. Subramanian's tiny office. We were at least fifteen minutes early because Bee was always anxious about getting to places on time. What she thought would happen during the twenty-three block voyage to his office, I didn't know.

"Admit that you're curious," I said. I had pored over and over the letters. It was hard to imagine my parents so demonstrably, so playfully, in love. Were they still in love in the years before my mother died?

Bee opened the ashtray, looking for dimes for the parking meter. "Curious, yes. Nosey, no." She looked grim and ready, as if we both had appointments with death. Bee had always hated doctor visits, even before our mother died. When we were small, she used to get so nervous in the waiting room that her pulse would soar, her skin would pale, and old Dr. Crown, taking one look at her next to her placid, well-fed sister, would order blood drawn to check for anemia.

"I wonder if they regretted being so unemotional with us," I said.

"I wonder if you'll ever learn to control your impulses," Bee said.

We walked under the hanging placard that said RAJIV SUBRAMANIAN, M.D., and took the clanking, musty freight elevator upstairs. We sat in sticky red vinyl seats for several minutes, Bee flipping through the pages of a *Reader's Digest;* then the nurse led us back to the examining room, where Dr. Subramanian was already gazing at my chart. He was the only doctor I had ever known who preceded his patients into the room, which is probably one of the reasons that I liked him. I always wondered if I should knock when I went in.

"This is my sister, Beatrice," I said; he stood up.

Bee shook his hand but didn't speak.

Dr. Subramanian took my blood pressure, squeezed my ankles and wrists, asked me several simple questions, and measured my stomach with a tape, briefly pressing a stethoscope to my navel. He wrote his findings on the chart.

"That's it?" Bee whispered.

"What do you expect him to do?" I said. "Sharpen some knives?"

Dr. Subramanian pretended he didn't hear.

"Tell him you aren't sleeping well," she said.

I tapped Dr. Subramanian on the shoulder. "My sister says I'm not sleeping well."

"How is she sleeping?" he asked. Both of us smiled.

Bee came and stood between us: me on the table, struggling to get up, and Dr. Subramanian at his desk. "I have something to say," she said. I rolled my eyes to show Dr. Subramanian that I disassociated myself, in advance, from whatever bulletin my sister was about to share.

"Jane's mother," she said, "I mean our mother, Jane's and mine, had a baby that died."

Dr. Subramanian shot a glance at me.

"I just found out," Bee said. "It was full-term. I thought it might be important because of the bleeding." She turned to me, her expression flat, her arms folded, defensive, across her chest. "I made Dad tell me. He was so nervous when you were in the hospital, he couldn't sleep."

"A stillborn?" I asked.

Bee nodded. "Between the two of us. Fifteen months after I was born. Three years before you."

Dr. Subramanian quickly said that a maternal stillborn didn't place me at higher risk, that stillbirth was a fluke still misunderstood, and that there was no additional reason to be worried where my own child was concerned. He was scribbling on my chart the entire time.

"Apparently the child looked perfectly normal. They didn't know why it happened," Bee said. "And there's one other thing."

Dr. Subramanian and I both looked up. Bee was always pale but now she looked white, chalky; her glasses made her eyes look magnified. "I want to know if my sister needs a coach."

Dr. Subramanian smiled broadly. "It's very useful for a new mother to have support. During the labor, before it, and beyond."

I shook my head, trying to assimilate Bee's news. A child between us. A missing link. "This woman— my sister—faints," I said to Dr. Subramanian. "I got my ears pierced when I was ten, and she dropped like a rag doll to the ground."

"Fortunately, then," he said, "piercing ears and giving birth are quite distinct."

Bee helped me up. "So a coach for Jane would be a good idea."

"Of course. But childbirth isn't painless in either case."

"I'm it, then," Bee said, without waiting to see if I agreed or would tell her to inflict her busy self on someone else. What I pictured, when I thought of giving birth, was a thorough dose of anesthesia in some nice hotel, Dr. Subramanian with a needle in his hand and a nurse holding a stack of heated towels.

Bee held the door on the way out. She was talkative and happy; she liked Dr. Subramanian after all. "I know you'll say that they should have told us," she said. "But what would that have accomplished? I was too young to notice Mom was pregnant—I was one.

And later on, they must have been afraid to tell us. You know, with children's nightmares and fears and all of that.''

Bee never had nightmares; I always did.

"Then they probably forgot about it.''

Forgot about a dead baby? I turned to Bee, expecting to see antennae, yellow eyes, a reptile's skin. But she was already laughing, onto something else. "I remember when you were born I had to stay with Mrs. Stiles, it seemed like forever. When Dad finally came to get me, I remember I asked him how you came out of Mom's body." Bee smiled. "He said through her nose. I thought she got pregnant smelling flowers.''

"He said I was born through her nose?''

Bee pulled a massive key ring from her pants pocket and opened the passenger side of the car. "Mom and Dad both did what they could for us," she said. "Now let's agree to leave the two of them alone.''

"Dear Mommy and Daddy.''

Mr. Denzer had found the letter in a second small cardboard box, along with a few golf trophies that I'd won my senior year. I had told him to be careful: I didn't want my father suspecting that anyone was shifting things around again upstairs; and I didn't want Bee finding footprints in the dust. "Don't worry." He waved my cautions away. "I open the boxes from the bottom. I turn them over, take out the staples, and then tape them shut when I'm done. I know where everything is." He did have a way of finding exactly what I wanted. In fact he seemed to take as much pleasure in the search as I did, immersing himself in my family as if it were his own. This new letter was written on construction paper in pencil, with holes in the paper where the periods should have been.

How are you? We rode horses today. I don't like the horse with yellow teeth. My friend Yolanda is from Pnensilvanya! Now is rest time when we write letters. I don't think the peeple here like me. I don't like them.

From, Jane

I didn't show any letters to Bee because I didn't want her asking questions about how I got them. I would have liked to make an exception, though, for *her* letter from camp, long and without misspellings, and full of classifications of bushes, roots, and trees. It ended: "Jane is not very happy here. I don't believe she cooperates well. You will enjoy, however, the quaintly colored pot holders she has made."

I read the letter aloud to Bill, who didn't understand why I found it funny. At the end, though, he laughed to be polite. "Those are real documents," he said. "Your sister must have been very mature for her age."

"Too mature," I said. "She still acts decades older than she is. You know she sold my car? I'll be dragging a baby around on the Sea Haven bus."

"So you're planning to stay?" Bill quickly looked up.

"No, I'd say 'planning' is the wrong word. But it feels comfortable to be here. I like being in the house, even if I'm not doing anything."

"The Haus house," Bill said. "It suits you."

"Thanks. Were there any letters from anyone else in that same box? Do you want to bring the whole thing down?"

"No. The rest wasn't very interesting. These were the best things in it."

I wasn't sure I wanted Bill deciding for me what was interesting, but I didn't have much choice. He was very good-natured about it all. Although he scouted out letters for me, I had the impression that in ordinary times he wouldn't have read someone else's mail if it fell open into his lap from a cloudless sky.

We sat in silence for a while, listening to the burble of gray-and-blue pigeons in the eaves. For once he hadn't moved his chair away from my bed, and he had brought me a collection of love sonnets from Walter Lowenfels, a poet, to his wife. I picked up the book, scanned the jacket, and then studied Bill Denzer carefully and long.

"You should be drinking something," he said, getting up. "Two-thirds of all Americans are dehydrated." He poured a glass of water from the pitcher on the dresser top.

I noticed a beauty mark on his thumb, I noticed his clean square fingers, I saw the soft brown hair that began on his wrist and disappeared into his sleeve. "Where did you get a statistic like that?" I asked him to bring me a pair of socks from the top left drawer.

"I read magazines." He smiled. "I get around."

I heard the scrape of soft wood as the drawers were moved. "Bill."

"Here they are." He held up one white cotton sock.

"It would be easier if you rolled these together in pairs."

I looked at his broad forehead, his clear brown eyes. "I've never heard you mention your parents. Are they still around?"

"I was adopted." He put both his thumbs inside a sock to stretch it out and nodded toward my foot. "My adoptive father lives in a nursing home."

"Adopted?" I pointed my toes, picturing a baby version of Bill, a tiny baseball cap and glove in his bassinet, as he was handed from a faceless mother to an older, well-meaning couple in a ranch-style home. "Maybe your mother was in a situation like mine. It was harder then," I said. "But she could have been me."

"You're keeping your baby." He paused for a minute, then pulled the sock up over my ankle and began on the other foot. I leaned back against the pillows and let him work the clean white cotton over the ball of my foot, the instep, and the heel. "You aren't giving yours away."

"Giving it *up*," I said. "I think that's the phrase. Didn't you ever try to find her? Your biological mother, I mean?"

"No, why should I?" He gave the top of the sock a quick yank. "I don't have anything to say to her."

"She could still be alive," I said. "She could live around here."

"I don't hold any grudges." He put my foot down, gently pinching the toes. It felt good. "But I think she should be sorry."

"Sorry for who?"

He looked surprised. "Sorry that she didn't do what you're doing. That she wasn't as strong as my good friend here. As strong as Jane Haus."

Ellie had been sending mail. Bright cheery postcards with smiley faces, then a series of gifts—baby booties and Day-Glo pacifiers, and one day a silver cup and spoon. "I bet she lifted this," I told Bee, who admired the cup.

Bee pointed out that Ellie came from a wealthy family. "Her allowance is probably what you earned teaching school."

I didn't write back very often, though I did send notes asking her not to buy any more presents. "Go to the movies," I wrote. "Spend your income on yourself." In reply she sent a wooden rattle and said she hated the eighth grade. "All the kids are morons this year." She wanted to come back to Sea Haven.

One day she did, unexpectedly, calling from the bus station to say that she'd arrived. It was the middle of the week, a Tuesday. Bee drove down to collect her and brought her tiny red leather overnight bag up the stairs. Ellie leaned over the bed to hug me as though she'd heard I'd been lost at sea. "It's so good to be here," she said. She was wearing orange lipstick; sprigs of straw-colored hair bristled out from a scrawny bun.

I didn't ask any questions right away; Bee had telegraphed warning looks. Instead I listened to Ellie chatter. She flopped down in the wicker chair, crossing her legs and looking approvingly around, as if Bee's twelve-by-twelve-foot room were a vast boudoir.

"You've done wonderful things in here," she said, bringing out a lighter and a cigarette. "And you don't look bad, Ms. Haus. I mean, you're really looking well." She smoked and wagged her foot and opened my dresser drawers; she was unable to sit still. "You know you and your sister are lucky. You're through with school, you can take time off. You could fly to France tomorrow morning. France! I was there but I don't remember it. People are idiots," she said. "Did you know that two weeks of vacation a year is what most people get?" I said I did. "Two weeks!" Ellie put her cigarette out in the window well. "They probably rent some kind of tacky little house down here for one, and then take the other week at Christmas. God, that's gross. I mean, at Christmas if they're Christian. Are you, Ms. Haus?"

"By heredity," I said. "That's all."

"I believe in God," Ellie said. "I just don't think He pays much attention. How do you think your baby's doing? I know you haven't named it—your sister told me." She pulled my jewelry box from the dresser and sifted through its contents on her lap. "I don't think people are virtuous these days. I mean, most of my friends have done it."

"What do you mean by 'done it'?"

Ellie put on a necklace that had belonged to my great-aunt Agnes. "You guys think I'm so naïve."

"Bee and I do?"

She nodded. "Ms. Haus, do you think the man who got you pregnant will ever come back?"

"I don't know. It wasn't as if he left me; I went away."

"That's what kills me," Ellie said. "I don't see why you did it. I think about your—you know, your situation—a lot. You took a risk. During the summer I used to want to ring a bell in your ear and say 'Wake up!' Every kid deserves two parents. Every kid ought to start with both."

"That's occurred to me," I said.

Ellie sat on the mattress at my feet. "I think the time has come for you to make some more plans," she said. "I don't think it would be a bad idea for you to get away when the baby comes. You could live near me. My parents have money. It would be better than hanging around to marry the mailman." She laughed but looked upset.

"You're not making much sense," I said.

Ellie tucked some loose strands of hair around her ears. "When I'm older I'll probably get married and then divorced a couple times. That's how I am. I'm going to wear white at my weddings, though. I think it's terrible when you see the wedding clothes these days—half the time they look slutty. Nobody takes things seriously anymore."

"What are you talking about, Ellie?"

She lay down suddenly on the bed next to me, face in the sheets.

"You shouldn't be here," I said.

Ellie looked up. "Neither should you."

Bee steamed clams for dinner, and Ellie opened a bag of frozen French fries. My father made a tossed salad—that is, he cut a head of unwashed iceberg lettuce into quarters with a butcher knife. Ellie had spent most of the afternoon with Bee while I took a nap: the two of them seemed to think alike. They had walked past Ellie's parents' house, Bee said, but Ellie never looked in that direction or spoke their names.

The clams were rubbery and cool, the French fries stiff. Bee threw most of her dinner in the trash. While Bee and Ellie cleaned the kitchen I lay on the couch on the back porch, listening to Ellie continue to talk. She listed for Bee all the things that we should buy for the baby: we shouldn't skimp on the car seat or the stroller and should make the extra effort to find flame-retardant 100 percent cotton clothes, which wouldn't itch. She discussed the use of pacifiers and walkers and debated the pros and cons of circumcision. Medically, she said, drying the pots and putting them away in the wrong places, there was no reason to circumcise; some people, though, found the result ''much better looking.'' Maybe, she said, Bee would go with her to visit the preemie ward at the hospital the next afternoon.

''Ellie.'' I flagged her down from my place on the couch in the adjoining room until she peered around the doorway smiling, teapot in hand. ''You can come too,'' she said. ''We'll get you a wheelchair. We'll see what other people are naming their kids.''

''I don't want to know,'' I said.

Ellie rolled her eyes at Bee, who laughed into the sink. ''Didn't I tell you she was this way?'' Ellie asked. ''Stubborn. You should have seen her back at school. We called her 'Brick Haus.' ''

''Ellie, I called your parents,'' I said.

She stood perfectly still. I watched the energy and

agitation and all the happiness drain from her face. She turned back into a thirteen-year-old, nervous and blank in the presence of adults. When I'd finally reached her mother, after speaking to half the Lunds in Philadelphia, Deborah Lund had heaved a graceful, feminine sigh. "I don't know where she gets the desire to tramp around that way," she'd said. I imagined her spritzing her hair as she handled the phone.

"They were worried," I said, wondering if it was true. Bee continued washing dishes. Coward, I thought. "Your mother said they'll drive down later tonight to pick you up."

Ellie threw me the soggy dishtowel.

"I appreciate all the effort it took for you to visit." Lying down, I felt slimy and treacherous; I sat up. "I'm glad you came."

"You could have asked me," she said.

I swung my feet onto the floor and said I was sorry I hadn't asked. "But you can't let them worry all day about where you are." If they're capable of worry, I added to myself. Talking to Deborah Lund made me wonder whether parenthood was a sudden process of attachment followed by years in which the parents become more and more lackadaisical until finally, when their children turn seventeen, they're relatively eager to let them go.

"What if they hit me and stuff like that, and you just handed me over again?" Ellie put her hands on her hips. They were barely hips, just little knobs several inches above her thighs.

"Do they hit you?"

"No." Ellie went into the bathroom and shut the door.

Bee pulled the stopper from the sink's drain. "I think you should have asked her, too."

The rest of the evening went slowly, to say the least. My father found an old movie on TV and turned the volume high. Bee and Ellie and I sat on the couch, our six feet propped on the coffee table, Ellie's overnight bag at her side.

"We had a nice walk today," Ellie said, in the middle of the film. No one had said a word for quite a while. "Your sister and I ran into your old teacher."

"You mean Bill? From downstairs?"

Ellie looked straight at the TV. "Yeah. I mean that guy who still has the hots for you," she said.

My father turned up the volume with the remote control.

"He wears his pants too high on his waist," Ellie said. "But you could probably get him to correct little things like that. It's the bigger things I'd worry about. He's very sly. Lots of ripples under the surface."

"You think Mr. Denzer is in love with Jane?" Bee asked.

"Not that again," I said. "Don't be ridiculous."

My father turned up the set.

"Of course he's in love with her," said Ellie. "You should see the way he looks at her when he thinks no one's around." The volume was deafening now; we were shouting to each other above it. "Oogle-eyes. Smiley. Mr. Swoon." My father stared single-mindedly at the set. The actress's hair was a greenish gold.

"He's not in love with me," I said.

"Yes he is."

"We're friendly, Ellie, that's all."

"Friendly like salt and pepper. Friendly like helium and balloons. He'd make me nervous if I were you."

My father stood up, remote control in hand, and walked to the phone. He began to dial.

Bee turned the volume down. "You really think he's in love with Jane?"

"Hello, Bill?" It was always hard to tell when my father was faking; his ordinary expressions seemed to have been learned in a cut-rate acting school. Ellie and Bee and I watched from the couch. "We have a question up here," my father said. "We need to know if you're in love with Jane." All of us waited. "To settle an argument. I'm trying to watch the damn TV." My father listened. It looked like the listening might be real. "All right, thanks. That's all." He hung up the phone and turned up the sound on the movie again. In fifteen minutes it was over, the credits rolling up along the screen.

"What did he say?" Bee asked.

"Who?" My father yawned.

"Presuming he answered your question, what did Mr. Denzer say?"

"He said 'probably,' " said my father. "I'm going to bed."

When the horn honked out front a few minutes later, Ellie stood up to go. Without saying good-bye, she picked up the velvet pouch filled with names—I had left it on the table by the door—and slipped in a tiny piece of paper. When she was gone, I took it out. It was her own name, Eleanor.

Dear Caroline,

In the Amazon there is a bird that has no feet. It lives for only one season and tries never to land, because it's afraid that it might hurt itself descending, or maybe it won't be able to take off again. All its life this bird lives in terror of building a nest, and in terror of not building one. I don't know, or I've forgotten, the bird's name.

At night, if I read or slept in any position for too long, my hands fell asleep, the sensation tingling first at my fingertips, then gradually climbing up my wrists like a numbing vine. I had to sit up or even get out of bed to stretch, flapping my arms and coaxing the blood back through my veins. One night when I couldn't sleep I heard the freezer in the kitchen close.

"Bee?"

Ice cubes ringing in a glass.

Quietly I opened the door and stepped through. The only light on was the bathroom night-light, punctured with stars. A stocky shadow occupied the rocking chair.

"Dad?"

He seemed to turn around and wave me in. The sky was empty; there was no moon. I stood behind him, close enough so that we could hear each other breathing. My stomach nearly grazed the back of his chair. It had been over a week since we'd talked, and

I wondered if he had been waiting here every night, on the off chance that I would come.

"A cloudy night," I said.

He didn't move.

"I'm feeling better. I get up sometimes to use the bathroom, but I think that's pretty average. Actually, I don't know how average it is. I have no idea."

He sipped his drink. Probably Scotch.

"You'd think that being pregnant would feel like company," I said. "But it feels lonely most of the time."

He put his drink back down on the arm of the chair. "That's what your mother used to say."

I sat down. His profile took shape beside me in the dark. "Bee said you didn't tell her. Was the baby— the one that died—a boy or a girl?"

Again he was silent for a while. It was as if he were flipping backwards year by year through a picture album, to the one still photo of a dead child in a blanket, scalp still glistening from the womb. "Girl," he said. "She opened her eyes once. That was all."

"Did you name her?"

"No. Some people thought we should have."

He must work hard, I thought, they both must have worked very hard to remember that single time her eyelids lifted and she saw them looking down. She carried to the grave an infant's memory of her parents' faces, leaving them decades in which to slowly forget her own. I felt almost jealous. They had loved her perfectly, and secretly, and long. She had had more impact on my mother in a moment than I had had in eighteen years.

I rested my hands on my stomach. The fetus seemed to be hiccuping; every few seconds it would shudder as if frightened or cold. "Why didn't you tell us?"

He sipped his drink and stood, walking carefully, maybe drunkenly, to the porch door. "Your mother didn't want it discussed. She insisted." He slid his hand along the wall to find the switch. "Even with me. It was something she never wanted to refer to again." He was finished talking. Like my mother, he would insist that the subject was closed. I could feel water growing over the place in our conversation where the child had been. Now he was groping for the light, and in the second before it happened, I remembered what my father was going to do. He found the switch and flipped it: a pair of floodlights, mounted on the rear of the house just below the attic deck, dazzled the sand. When I was in high school he had been famous for this trick; it was illegal to sleep on the beach in Sea Haven or to walk the dunes after ten o'clock, and my father had discovered too many birth control remnants in the sand. When he illuminated his victims they squirmed and squinted in the light, hands in front of their faces, buttoning and rearranging their wrinkled clothes. They looked like insects about to be trampled on. Soon enough, everyone knew not to get romantic within several hundred yards of my father's house; students drank and partied by the pier.

Tonight the beach was empty, eerily so. Maybe the sand was wet. Maybe Sea Haven's students didn't find each other attractive anymore.

He flicked off the switch. And only when he carried his drink from the room, the ice gently ticking against the glass, did I think clearly about what he had said: She never wanted to refer to it again. But those weren't his words. What he'd said was "it was *something* she never wanted to refer to." As if there were other things missing, other stories he or my mother refused to tell.

On Halloween morning I got up early, found Bee making charts on recycled graph paper in the kitchen, and told her we needed a dozen good masks, three bags of candy, and a lot of orange and yellow streamers. Pumpkins, too.

Bee looked up. An empty pot of coffee sat beside her on the table; she wore the fuzzy expression of a person who hadn't had time to brush teeth or hair. She still wore her pajamas: men's tartan flannel, oversized, with a drawstring.

"When you're done with that," I added. "What are you doing?"

"Don't ask questions if you're not interested in the answers," Bee said.

"Okay, I won't." I paused while a knee or elbow traced a slow, seductive line from somewhere behind my navel to my lungs. It waited there, glimmering, then withdrew. On the next Halloween I could dress it as a rabbit or a dog, and my father and Bee and I would feed it strained vegetables and slivers of Hershey's bars. "I want to do something fun today," I said. "Something as impulsive as I can handle from inside the house. I'm too cooped up."

Bee was using a ruler to connect some points on her graph. I tried not to think of what she was doing as connect-the-dots. "There aren't any kids on this block anymore. Or not enough to justify the effort.'' She didn't look up.

''Just because there are fewer of them, you're going to cut them out of the profits? What's the worst that can happen? We'll end up eating the candy ourselves.'' I bumped into the table accidentally.

The line Bee was drawing wiggled. ''Yesterday,'' she said, without lifting her sharpened pencil from the page, ''Dad's homeowner insurance premiums almost doubled. I doubt you read the story in the paper.''

''I saw it.'' Both of us knew I was lying.

''Good. Then maybe you'll understand why he and I aren't going to spend the day buying paper streamers and funny hats.'' Bee, I thought, was increasingly crabby. Deciding to be my coach had made her start to act like a stodgy husband. It wasn't good for either one of us.

''What do you want me to do? If Dad wants me to worry, I'll worry. I'm only asking for a little help, Bee,'' I said.

She put down her pencil and eraser. ''I *am* helping. Do you want to know how I'm helping? I'm living here, number one. I actually left a job, and even friends, although you may find that hard to believe, down in Atlanta. You say you want help.'' She pushed her glasses up on her nose. ''I don't think you do. I think your friend Ellie has more sense. She told you to get your head out of the attic, and you sent her away. And who do you spend your time with? An aging basketball coach who sneaks around our house like a thief. Where would you be if you didn't have

Dad to fall back on? Where are you going to live if he sells the house?''

"Dad isn't going to sell the house. He doesn't think only about money.''

"Maybe he doesn't need that money," Bee said. "But you do.''

I looked at my sister, cool and narrow as a green bean. "Not that badly.''

Bee gathered her papers together. "Prices are going to fall. The real estate market has peaked.''

"He won't sell.''

"If he *does* sell," she said, "one of the possibilities, of course, would be that you move in with me. You can't live on sublet money forever. I'm looking into apartments right now." She wiped the table with her hand. "I told Dad I wouldn't upset you. I apologize if I shouted.''

"I'm sure it was just your way of being helpful," I said. "All that generosity can make a person a real bitch.''

Bee folded her arms. She looked like a rag doll with her baggy red pajamas, her boyish hair. "I don't think you understand what I'm offering you.''

"I don't think *you* understand what you're offering. I don't need a moral advisor, and I don't need a self-appointed nag. I don't need a coach. All I want is a goddamn pumpkin, and for you to keep your nose where it belongs.''

"Jane," she said carefully, slowly, as if I were lip-reading every word, "you're being an idiot.''

"That's possible," I said.

"I'm disappointed.'' We sat facing each other on

opposite sides of the table. Eraser rubbings littered the
grainy wood.

"I should have told you earlier about not wanting a
coach," I said. "I should have been clearer. I think I need
to do this thing alone. You don't know how it feels."

"No," she said. "I don't."

"I'm sorry, Bee."

"That's all right." She stuffed her papers in an envelope. "I presume too much."

"Thanks anyway," I said. "Happy Halloween."

Ten minutes later I heard her car start up in front
and pull away.

My father didn't show up that afternoon, and neither
did Bee. Instead of foraging in the cabinets for pretzels
or raisins I could give away as treats, I took a nap on
the living room couch. I was sick of my room, tired
of reading, and unsympathetic in advance toward the
half a dozen children who might arrive expecting
candy. I'd turn out the lights and let them vandalize.

When I woke up, Bill Denzer was standing at my
side. He felt so comfortable using his key that he
didn't bother to knock anymore. "I'm setting things
up downstairs." He shook a bag full of chocolate bars.
"Let me help you up so that you can come and look."

"There aren't enough kids here anymore," I said,
ignoring his outstretched arm and wondering how long
he'd been standing there. "It's not worth the time."

Bill looked into the bag, stirring the treats. He was
wearing a yellow sweatsuit, which I hoped was part of
a costume. "I bought a little of everything, but all of
it well wrapped. I don't want the parents thinking poi-

son." He was trying to cheer me up. Unusual or not, he was currently the best friend that I could claim.

"Okay," I said. I hadn't seen him since my father's famous question on the phone. I washed my face while he waited half an inch from the bathroom door, then let him help me to the front porch, to find the yard below covered with plastic pumpkin shells, the kind children use to collect their candy in. "What are you doing?"

Bill handed me a mask. It had yellow yarn for hair, a bulbous nose, and whiskers. It smelled like the inside of an old soup can. "This way, you can give the candy away without asking the kids to come upstairs."

He led me to one of two reclining lawn chairs on the porch, a folded blanket at the foot of each. A child's sand pail on a string hung over the railing, like a bucket from a wishing well. The bag of candy rested at my side.

"What will you do with all the pumpkins?" I asked.

"Wait and see." He ran down the outdoor steps, a butter-colored blur, and reappeared on the grass below with a cluster of packages.

"Bill," I called over the railing. "I've had a really lousy day."

He was busy opening things, kneeling on the lawn. His yellow shirt rode up his back. (Ellie was right; he wore his pants too high.) "These are actually Christmas lights," he called, looking up, pulling skeins of electrical wire from a bag. "But I think they'll do."

"Bee and I had a fight." I wasn't sure if I was talking loud enough for him to hear. I leaned forward, resting my head against the lower railing, looking down. "We don't know how to talk to each other. We torture each other out of habit. She thinks I'm an idiot, which I am."

Bill started arranging the pumpkins about one foot apart, outlining the lawn. "I'll put one bulb into each of these. See, I've made a hole in the bottom piece." He held up a hollow pumpkin, with the price tag dangling from the handle.

I pulled up a blanket. "I'm not going to need any more letters out of the attic," I said, talking more to myself than to Bill. It was dusk. "My father loves this house. He's got to stay."

Bill attached an extension cord to the lights and finished setting up the pumpkins—two large ones on either side of the front walk, near the landing site for the bucket, and another twenty or thirty leading up to the house. He plugged them in. The pumpkins were strange to see, bright and hollow with identical foolish grins. Bill stood in their midst, glowing up at me with the rest. I felt I had to set things straight.

I cupped my hands around my mouth to give, however foolish, an impression of privacy. "Bill," I said, "I want you to know that I didn't tell my father to ask you that question. I don't want to give you the wrong idea." The pumpkins smiled.

Bill put his hands on his hips. "Do you like it?" You could probably see our yard from the pier.

"I think it's wonderful," I called. "I really do. I just want to make sure that you know the question was my father's. On the phone. It wasn't mine."

Bill spied some trick-or-treaters down the block. With a switch in his hand he turned the pumpkins on and off, blinking the lights, and the children began pointing, calling behind them for someone to come. "That's all right." Bill put on his mask and motioned for me to wear mine, too. "Because the answer I gave your father—" He unwrapped a chocolate bar and put it in the bucket, tugging on the string to send something indulgent and uncalled-for up to me. "—that wasn't mine, either. Here they come."

8

The Chapel of Bones

In the dream that comes to me most often, probably two or three times a week, I am forced to undergo an operation. Both my arms are cut off and my tongue is removed. This is sad and unfortunate, but not surprising. Mainly I am embarrassed to be so helpless.

I convey to my roommate, Gloria, that she should warn my family; as of yet they have no idea of my condition. Clearly I can't hold the phone or even dial; speech is beyond me, too. Gloria, businesslike yet sympathetic, finds the number, calls and matter-of-factly explains what has happened. She nods her head, telling them that I've healed, but that I won't be able to explain myself when they come to take me home. I will sit like a great sack of flour in the back of the car, saying nothing. Conversation will certainly flag. It will seem to me worst at this point that I retain my eyes, which allow me to view my parents' confusion and which are expected, by default, to communicate worlds. I will feel ashamed. I'll feel that I've done this to myself or allowed it to be done, and now we'll all have to live with my mistake.

Then the dream shifts. I am back in the hospital, and it is my father who has suffered the operation. He sits in a chair against the wall. They have cut off his arms and cut out his tongue. He rolls his head back and forth against the bamboo-motif paper on the wall, incomprehensibly unhappy. They have cut out my father's tongue and I must watch him roll his head against the wall in just this way, back and forth, speechless. I am as helpless as in the first version of the dream, and equally silent. I wonder if this is some sort of punishment being meted out against us. But that would not make sense. It must be our own fault we are in misery. We have brought this trouble upon ourselves, and our suffering will always be pointless and without reason.

In the dining hall at lunch, I find Gloria sitting at a table with her friends. I know they aren't very glad to see me, but Gloria is my ally, my spokesperson, my best friend. She encourages me to sit down. "What did the shrink say?" she asks, right off the bat. Her friend Angelique, on my right, shakes her head. Most of Gloria's friends, who are black (so is Gloria), think that therapy is an indulgence for white folks, an indication of our guilty consciences and feeble minds.

"We talked for a while," I say, putting ketchup on a hamburger gray as slate. "She said lots of people have vivid dreams when they first live somewhere new."

"Dreams like yours?" Gloria asks. She made the appointment for me with Mrs. Randall, the counselor, after finding me in our dorm room early one morning sitting up in bed awake, slaphappy and rigid as a pole, a half-empty box of NoDoz in my hand.

I shrug.

Gloria wipes her mouth with a napkin—she eats healthy food, salads and unbuttered bread and raw legumes—and tells Angelique that I wake up several nights a week with the same dream, something so weird and scary that she doesn't want to explain it here at lunch.

"It's not always the same dream," I say. "I have other dreams, too, but just not as often."

"That's a sickness," Angelique says. "Your mind is doing things without you. No permission. I remember my dreams once or twice a year, but they aren't about rape and murder and mayhem." She nods at a woman across the table who is reading *101 French Verbs*.

I try to explain that it isn't content that makes the dreams frightening. You can wake up feeling mainly curious and confused by a Technicolor nightmare in which you have slit a person's throat and watched him die. Worse, you can dream about ripening apples, about walking through an orchard and watching sweet red apples fall from their branches to the ground, and awaken screaming, heart beating like a thin-skinned drum.

"Poor Jane," Gloria says, squeezing a lemon in her tea. "Sleep should be a comfort, not a thrill."

Angelique looks disgusted. She is a hardworking

person, studying premed, and logs enormous hours in the library every day. Next year, she and Gloria will probably share a room, and I will have to find someone new. "Somebody's paying good money for you to be here," Angelique says. "If you can't keep your mind on your books, you're wasting time."

I bite into the hamburger, which is studded with round white bits of cartilage or bone. "I'm learning a lot," I tell her. "Not everyone wants or has to study as much as you."

"You need to sleep," Gloria says, "or you won't be studying much at all."

"I can deal with it," I tell her, and Gloria smiles. She reaches across the table and grabs my hand, just holding it, as if trying to pass her energy to me. I wonder what college would have been like without Gloria, if I'd had a sallow, undecided girl from the suburbs to share my room.

"What a mess," Angelique says.

I wouldn't have liked it here half as much.

Here is a dream that isn't so bad. Each of the people in my family lives in the trunk of a different tree—one hollow trunk for each of us: maple, walnut, birch, and pine. In each trunk there is one small hole, one tiny inlet. We can see out, one eye at a time, or shout hello or put an ear to the small round aperture, but only by jumping or standing on our toes. We are nearly invisible to each other, but each of us senses the others' presence close by. We hunker down in the hollow trees, chewing bitter slips of wood, and wait for something to happen. We don't know what.

This one is worse. My great-aunt Frieda, dead long ago, suddenly reappears, still wearing her 1940s clothes, the long pleated skirts and heavy shoes. I go home to consult my parents about this problem, and when my mother opens the door I see that she's my age, with thick bright hair and red lipstick and a complexion I never knew her to possess. She eyes me with no knowledge of who I am. Soon it becomes clear that my mother's fifty-one-year-old self exists somewhere in submission to this younger one. Even clearer is that the younger versions of these people must be killed. We must drown them in the bathtub. It is my job to tie their hands behind them, ignore their pleas for mercy, and hold their faces in the water while they struggle, on and on, to rise and breathe.

Angelique, of course, is partly right. My parents have taken out loans for me to be here, to stare idly from windows, to study Spanish, American History, Victorian Poetry, and bowling, and on weekends to drink beer at a local bar. On the days when I haven't slept well—these are quickly increasing in number—I suspect that I am wasting someone's time. There is the afternoon in English class, for example, when I fall asleep to the sound of my own voice reading "My Last Duchess." And there's the morning in bowling when the instructor points out that with two more gutter balls, I will have a perfect score. In the kindly way of college life, my inattentiveness is viewed as a cause for concern instead of discipline. This in itself is enough reason to want to stay, but if I need further motivation, I review the alternatives to what I am doing: I could be dipping baskets of pale donuts into liquid fat at a small-town diner, living in a boarding-house on my own; or I could be back with my parents again, working at Linders with my father and dating the younger salesmen from the store. I am far, far better off at school.

When I applied, no one expected I'd get in. I shut myself in my room with half a dozen applications, five of them to schools the guidance counselor said might let me in. I threw those five away and set to work on the only school that was deemed "competitive." In the space reserved for accomplishments, awards, distinctions, I listed the prizes I had won in golf. Same for the three-inch white blotch asking for "other honors." Then I concentrated on the essay. It was all or nothing; inventing a place on the church choir wouldn't get me in. "Why do you feel you will benefit from a college degree?" the form asked. I briefly reviewed all the obvious responses: (1) A college education is an invaluable asset both intellectually and economically; (2) a college education will allow the student to discover her strengths and realize her full potential as a human being; and finally—and most nobly—(3) the degree not only fosters personal gain, but enables the graduate to be an asset to society, blah blah blah. I discarded each of these, ignored the question, and wrote a short essay about a nest of baby rabbits, discovered one April morning when the push mower revealed their home in the lawn. I had been in a foul mood that day because I had to cut the grass instead of going to the movies with a friend. As the blades revolved and clattered above the nest, the mother rabbit leaped from the hole and dashed away. We rarely saw rabbits in Sea Haven; these must have been the offspring of some abandoned pet. I quickly remembered the rule about robins: Touch the nest, the mother will not return. But there they were, five of them, nearly hairless, eyes closed, huddled together in a nest of green. I reached in, apologizing silently to God. Two of the bunnies opened their tiny mouths.

I waited patiently until evening, giving the mother a decent chance to reclaim her home, but she didn't come. The rabbits were mine. I put them into a shoe-box filled with grass, fed them lettuce leaves and eye-droppers full of diluted room-temperature milk. One of them lasted seven days. The others stiffened and died very quickly and were buried in single-serving cereal boxes, each covered with a blanket of cotton balls.

I didn't offer a moral in the essay or say there was anything I had learned. The rabbits died; I buried them; that was it. I got a phone call in March from the dean of admissions. She was curious about my essay on the rabbits. Had I meant to put it under the question about formative experiences? (In that space, I had described the sound of the ocean.) No, I had not. Well, she had only wanted to know. It was unusual, that's all. I told her I was an unusual girl. When they let me in off the waiting list, I carried the letter in my pocket like a ticket for a train. Bee—in graduate school in mathematics in Chicago—called to say congratulations. My parents tried not to look surprised. Piling my clothes and trunk and bicycle into the car, and unloading them three and a half hours later when we got to school, they still wore shocked looks on their faces. They met Gloria, toured the bookstore, ate lunch in the dining hall, and then said good-bye, handing me a box of Vanilla Wafers in the parking lot. "It'll be odd," Bee had said, "when they drive away." And in fact it was. They opened the car doors, waved, and stepped inside. In sight of the other students passing by, wheeling stereos and boxes of textbooks along on skateboards, I thought, Thank God we've never been a demonstrative family. They started toward the exit of the parking lot but had to wait for the traffic to clear. I stood on the sidewalk near the car, and all of us smiled. "This is it," my mother said. For some reason, in reply, I shook the box of cookies up and down. "Write to us," she said, as they pulled away. I thought I had stopped shaking the cookies, but every now and then I heard them rattle in their box, as if trying to reassure me, to tell me I had always dreamt of leaving home.

During the first week of school I felt blissful and free. Gloria and I sat up late in our room and talked: both of us *wanted* a lot—we knew we were on the cusp; this was the part of our life that would decide which way we'd go. She mentioned economics and New York. I mentioned travel. Both of us mentioned love, but only briefly, as an aside: we were going to make something of *ourselves*. While we talked, Gloria arranged our room, a cinder-block square. The dressers are built right into the wall, next to the closets, so the only furniture left to situate is two beds and two desks. Gloria tried every combination, finally settling our desks side by side (beneath the built-in bookshelves), with my bed under the window, hers by the door. Almost everyone else on the hall has done the same.

The hall is a microcosm and a haven. Because of the way we've been thrown together, we enter each others' lives with enormous force. Suddenly expected to be adults, to use the word "women" instead of "girls" to describe ourselves, we engage in painfully frank conversations, explaining ourselves to each other, eager to convey entire histories in a day. "Here are the things about me that you'll need to know," we seem to say. "This is the world in which I moved. Here is a list of the people I love. Here are the ones who were cruel to me. These are the reasons I hate my brother/envy my sister/never will speak to my father again." All of us seek and are replacements: we spill out this shorthand emotional history, telegraphing HERE I AM, COME CLOSER, scanning the listeners' faces for confidantes, friends.

On our hall we have one of everything: a resident musician, a genius, a motherly figure, a baby, a village idiot, a prostitute, a drunk, and the mildly insane. Psychologically we comprise a tiny world, with rich and poor, hardworking and lazy, baker, typist, professor, lawyer, priest. Proximity invites confession, and confession is a ticket to intimacy. This is where my dreams are useful. They make me interesting and colorful; I pull them out during conversations like Little Jack Horner's plums. "Oh, I get it, it's something about castration," Vivian says, after I tell her about my "operation" dream. (She pretends she's used to pronouncing words like "castration" aloud.) "No," says Lynne. "The sword is mightier than the tongue."

At first I don't let on that the dream is terrifying as well as nifty. But eventually, when I actually scream out in my sleep and walk the halls at night, people get the idea. They begin to talk less about dreaming when I'm around. More than anything I dread the nightmare's metamorphoses. Even the subtlest alterations are horrific: the misplacement of a chair, the unexpected appearance of another patient, a blood-soaked cloth in my father's hand. To withstand the dream, I need it to be the same. One morning when I wake up around 5 A.M., shaking and tearful from that other place, I decide to get ready for the day. I put on my robe and head for the bathroom, happily hearing that it's occupied, although by a woman named Marjorie whom I don't know well. She leans over the sink in a yellow ribboned nightgown and wooden clogs, splashing water on her face; on the shelf is a small tin bucket neatly arranged with shampoo, soap, toothbrush, hair dryer, brush and comb. While she brushes her teeth, I tell her my latest version of the dream. I spill it all, even the grisliest details. "The worst part," I explain, while Marjorie flosses her teeth an inch from the mirror, "is that when it begins I know I'm dreaming, but I can't stop. It's like watching a movie when you're scared but can't look away." I feel proud of myself, adult, purged of information, thoughtful and true. Now Marjorie will marvel at what I've said, express amazement and sympathy, and share a story of her own.

Marjorie cleans her ears with a Q-tip. Not a crevice has gone unscrubbed. "You're a real weirdo," she says. Later I find out that she's a sophomore. Gloria says she has water on the brain.

*   *   *

Mrs. Randall, the counselor, is a woman in her fifties who has gray hair cut like a helmet and an outsized nose. She smiles in a reassuring way, wiping imaginary specks from her glossy desk. "You know, the college offers seminars," she says, "to help its students adjust to living away from home."

I know the seminars she means. Weekly sessions called "Joining a Group" or "Making Friends." Participants borrow each others' handkerchiefs and talk about acne and abstinence. "I love living away from home," I answer truthfully.

Silence falls. I'm supposed to help Mrs. Randall out. "*Living* away from home, I mean, is great. It's just the dreams."

Mrs. Randall leans back in her chair. She repeats—as she did last week—that dreams are the mind's way of sorting out emotions, perceptions, experience. "We dream more often when we're young or under stress, or when we're undergoing something new." It took me a week or two to understand that I was Mrs. Randall's prize: most of her clients are homesick or thwarted in love or discovering their sexual preference for the first time. I suspect that she'd like to take our sessions further than her master's in social work allows: I picture her swinging a pendant on a chain, dimming the lights, humming a mantra in her leather chair. She asks if my parents know about the dreams or the counseling sessions.

"God, no." I mentioned to Bee in a letter that I was having nightmares and had made an appointment to "talk to someone"; that was all. Bee wrote back—on a sheet of paper riddled with numbers and signs—saying that dreams were a very good thing. She tended now to sound less confident, depressed. "We grew up badly, Jane," she wrote. "We could have guided each other but we didn't know how." Her letters had lost the spark they'd had before.

"How many times," Mrs. Randall asks, "have you had nightmares this past week?"

I shift around in my chair. Mrs. Randall's office is designed to look like a living room, with African violets and armchairs and magazines, but I always find myself looking for the one-way mirror, the observation window hiding a team of scribbling scientists in another room. "Probably three."

"Did you write them down?" Mrs. Randall subscribes to the idea that keeping a journal is half of any cure. But I don't need to record my dreams with paper and pen: they're imprinted—a book of nightmares follows me wherever I go. I shake my head.

"I think it would be useful," she says, curt. "Can you tell me, were these equally, ah, disturbing or severe?"

"It's hard to rank them," I say. "They all wake me up. Don't you ever have dreams?"

Mrs. Randall smiles; then she turns brusque. "What would have to happen for you to feel that these nightmares wouldn't bother you anymore? That they wouldn't make you lose sleep?"

When she asks me this kind of question, I try not to feel like I'm being quizzed, but I hear formulas and games: "If *two* geese lay *seven* pounds of golden eggs every *four* days, how many ingots must they ingest in a year?'' There is a trick to answering correctly, but I just don't know what it is.

"It's a difficult question," Mrs. Randall says, looking demure.

"I guess I would have to be born into a different family," I say. "Is that what you mean?"

Mrs. Randall tells me to schedule another appointment on the way out.

Most of the people on campus who are "having trouble adjusting," as the saying goes, rely on their former lives for comfort and spend long afternoons by the campus post. You can tell by the looks on their faces when they open their mailboxes whether they've gotten news from home. They pull out the brightly colored flyers announcing campus speakers, religious services, dances, rallies, and clubs, then reach in again for the plain white envelope with a stamp. The hands move quickly, and the person shuffles to a private place, bumping into others on the way.

Dear Kim. Dear Son. Dear Grandchild. Here is a picture, a check, a box of oatmeal bars, some news from home.

Aunt Carol is dead. The Wilsons moved. Jimmy took over your bedroom. Nancy Napperstick got married. The gutters on the house are rotting through. We ate meat loaf for dinner; it was burned. Clipped the roses. Buried the guinea pig. Snow fell, probably half an inch an hour. . . .

I walk through the mailroom twice a day, on my way to bowling at 10:15 A.M. and after Spanish or English at 3:05 P.M. I don't get a lot of personal mail.

Bee writes once or twice a month. My mother sporadically sends clippings and news, from minor items about the boardwalk to lengthy feature articles about the construction of a museum in East Orange, eclectic notes I complain about but nevertheless enjoy. She says that her work—another clerical job that calls for virtually no intelligence—is going well, and she ends each letter by saying that education comes in many forms. My father, oddly enough, is the real correspondent. He sends letters twice a week on Linders stationery, sometimes—I can tell from the mistakes—typing them himself on his lunch break on an old machine. More often the secretary, Carol Massey, transcribes them from the Dictaphone instead; they arrive with a lowercase *clm* at the very end.

"That's unusual," Gloria says politely, when I show her Carol's mark. Gloria and I sometimes share our letters, although she gets more than I do. She has her parents, a doting grandma, two pen pals, and three younger brothers who write adoring letters every week. The youngest one's drawings hang on her closet door.

"Yeah, I guess it is."

"I mean, somebody already read it," Gloria points out.

I look at the spread of mail in her hand like a deck of cards. "He used to have his own secretary," I say. "But now he shares one; he's going to get in trouble for this kind of thing. You didn't get any packages?" Gloria's mother owns a bakery.

"Maybe Friday. What does your father say in the letter?"

"I don't know." I've been holding the open letter in my hand for half an hour but don't want to read it. The last letter he sent started off with news of Linders, sales figures and salaries and things, and went on to a story about his uncle Karl, who came from Germany at seventeen, built a shoe business in Secaucus, then lost everything in the stock market crash and killed himself. The story was presented as a lesson, but what the moral was I couldn't tell. Now I look nervously at his letters rather than read them. Sometimes I carry them around and then throw them away. Sometimes I leave them on my desk and tell Gloria to read them for me.

"This one's *fine*," she always says. "Go ahead and read it. It's eccentric, but it's nice."

"I'd rather you summarize it for me." I watch the Frisbees like tiny colored spaceships crossing the quad.

Gloria sighs. "Next thing I know, you'll have me writing back."

Gloria is the best friend I've ever had.

Here's a brand-new version of the dream. My mother stumbles down a brilliant hospital corridor, the sun flooding in behind her so that her face is dark. She runs clumsily in slow motion toward the chair where my father sits. As soon as she arrives I find that, at his side, I hold in my hand a piece of paper, yards long. It gets longer as I look at it, unfurling crazily like a motorized magic scroll. Without reading it, all three of us know what it is: a permission slip for the surgery, which I have signed, my signature a thousand different shapes and sizes, sometimes printed in block letters several inches high, sometimes scrawled backwards in calligraphy. My mother refuses to touch me. I try to explain that I don't remember signing. It couldn't be me! How could I have written my name in so many ways? My hands, as I talk, are tangled inextricably in the paper, which rattles deafeningly around us, drowning out my explanations and my pleas. My mother lifts my father in her arms, his head falling sadly against her breast, as the paper rises up and covers me. I lose sight of them as they travel slowly down the hall.

I turn on the light, gasping. Gloria is gone, spending part or all of the night with her new boyfriend, a junior trumpet player named George. I sit up in bed for the next four hours with the lights on, drinking coffee and eating caramels by the bag.

When Gloria gets back, drowsy and limber, I am riding a sugar high, my bedsheets littered with plastic wrappers and my teeth nearly singing with decay.

"You've got to shake this off," she says, climbing in bed.

I tell her I'm fine. I am grateful to have her here.

"Don't forget about your Spanish literature test," she says, and then falls asleep almost instantaneously, sinking gratefully and confidently into dreams.

Her reminder is a piece of real kindness: until breakfast at eight o'clock, I have something to do.

The test doesn't go very well. Before the professor, Dr. Boom, has finished writing the three questions on the board, I fall asleep. My eyes are ringed with dark circles like a raccoon's. Dr. Boom (his real name is

Professor Montoya, but everyone calls him Dr. Boom because of his expertise in Latin American "boom" literature of the 1960s) is a stocky Argentinian who wears tight black jeans, a leather tie, and a tweed jacket. His classes, like this one, titled "Versions of Reality," are always filled. He taps me on the arm, not unkindly, and points to the board. Question number one reads, "Discuss the concept of *identity* and the use of *masks* in the work of Octavio Paz, relating your ideas to the short fiction of Carlos Fuentes."

Although he knows, because I have told him, that I do only roughly half of the reading for this course and write my papers in under an hour, Dr. Boom reserves a place in his heart for me. During the class discussions, while the other students are scratching their heads, trying to decide whether the characters in the novels are dead or alive or ever existed in the first place, Dr. Boom and I zero in on the fine details. He paces the room, parts the beard hairs on his neck, and says *"curioso"* when intrigued. Now he points to the upper right corner of my blank page. "Your name," he says. "Here." I write it down. "Good," he says, *"buenísimo."* He smiles.

The second time he wakes me up, I see I have written half a paragraph, but which question I'm responding to is unclear. The third and final time he wakes me, I am just entering the nightmare, as if opening a heavy door without wanting to. I'm frightened and grateful for the tap on the back of my head. The rest of the students, I see, have already gone.

"You are sick?" he says, glancing down at my page.

"Tired," I say.

He pauses. "One more chance next week." He picks up my paper and tears it. "Different questions. This is fair?"

"*Gracias*," I say.

The dream visits me once when I think I'm awake, during the day. From then on I'm vigilant, sleeping with the radio by my pillow turned on low and reading only colorless, innocuous material after ten at night. Eve so, one night I feel myself drop, slipping inside the dream like a hand in a glove. I land in the hospital's hallway but don't see anyone there. I look in each private room and in the lounge (by now, even asleep, I know the landscape of the dream; I walk around inside it as if it were a vacant stage), my heart pounding in anticipation and awful dread, but my father must have been discharged. I walk into a hall closet and bury my face in the towels, tired and spent. When I emerge, wearing a gown, there are several doctors in the hall. We chat a while. Then the four of us walk through a set of swinging doors, put on our gloves, cover our hair with green nets and our mouths with masks, and soon we are standing in front of the table on which my father lies supine, terrified, shaking his head, catching sight of the knife in my hand just as the ether goes over his face. This is the only dream I wake from before it is done.

Gloria says I need a better shrink. Angelique says I need electroshock treatment. Mrs. Randall says that persistent, frightening dreams imply emotional issues begging to be resolved. "How many hours did you sleep last night?" She looks stern.

"Last night? I did some catching up on my reading." I don't let my back touch the back of the chair. Sleep is like water that I desperately hold my head above.

"Did you sleep the night before? Jane, you look awful. You aren't happy." She likes to put into words what she thinks I may not notice on my own.

I tell her I'm not going to jump off a cliff. "Except for the lack of sleep, I'm fine. When my roommate's there, it's easier to rest."

"I met your roommate." Mrs. Randall sighs. "She came to tell me that she's concerned. She said you fell asleep in your English class again."

"Oh, that." I'll have to talk to Gloria about tattling.

"If things don't get much better, I'll recommend that you go home. These dreams may be telling you that you feel ambivalent, even guilty, about being here. You've severed the family ties." She actually presents this interpretation as if it were something new.

"I'm not going home. The last thing I need is more leisure time."

"You look exhausted, Jane." Clearly she's wondering whether I'm still in her jurisdiction.

I tell her I have to leave early to take a makeup Spanish lit test.

"You can't possibly pass a test in the shape you're in."

"Yes, I can," I say.

But this time I'm wrong.

*   *   *

"Too much work?" Dr. Boom parts his beard with a finger. We sit in his basement office, on either side of a metal desk. A picture of a woman and two young children hangs in a frame on the wall.

"I haven't been sleeping," I explain.

He suggests that perhaps I should talk to a counselor.

"Good idea." I nod. "I already have."

We continue to sit. Then, taking both of us by surprise, I start to cry. At first I'm not certain this is crying, even though there are tears coming out of my eyes, because it was so unexpected; I haven't prepared for it and don't know when I'll stop. I look at Dr. Boom in true confusion, which he understands as true despair. *"Dios, Dios, Dios, Dios, Dios,"* he says, rummaging through his desk drawers for a tissue. Not finding one, he jogs out the door and down the hall, returning with someone else's box. I blow my nose.

While I finish crying he pretends to search through his files. He puts a pamphlet, "Study in Mexico," in my hands. "Technically, the deadline for applying was yesterday. And I would prefer to see you study on the program in Buenos Aires. But maybe this is better than nowhere?"

I picture a desertlike expanse, far from the sea.

"You won't know the other students," he explains. "They're mainly from the university. Do you think you might like to go?"

It takes only two more sessions with Mrs. Randall to make her agree.

To my parents, I write a brief but optimistic note about my plans, outlining the cost (less than a regular term on campus; I will take a bus to minimize transportation expenses), the number of credits, and the experience. (I know my mother will feel strongly about this last.) I drop it lightly into a box on my way to bowling at ten-fifteen.

From my mother, I receive within the week an article from the *Los Angeles Times* (I don't know where she got it) about female architects—its relevance isn't clear. At the bottom of the page, in her scrawled hand, is the word "Congrats!" From my father, nothing for several days. Then it comes. I have gotten unwary, out of the habit of having Gloria screen my mail. I slit open a phone bill, glance at a flyer about a rally in favor of divestment, then find myself holding a letter.

> *Dear Jane,*
>   *Did I ever tell you about my cousin Ben. He was dead when you were born. You never met. One day Ben threw a brick from the second-story window and hit me with it on my head. I was eight years old. This is why I have the scar on my left temple, which you have never asked me about. I remember all of this because I am losing more of my hair and the scar is showing now. Maybe you didn't know the scar was there.*

He goes on to give sales figures from Linders for the months of September and October. It is now December 3.

> *So you are going to Mexico. This is not what I expected you would do with your time in college,*

*but it is your time after all and who am I to tell
you what to do. We are both too old. As for your
mother, she would encourage her children to
float down the Nile in a rubber ring simply because she lacked the opportunity herself. She's
an odd woman, as you know. I am not sure what
is left for the two of us. Although I have always
loved her, she has not understood me and not
understood that some experiences aren't worth
the while. Enjoy yourself as much as possible, if
that is what you expect me to say. I assume you
will forfeit your entire year of freshman golf.*

I leave my backpack on the floor and walk like a
robot to the dorm, unlocking the door without knocking, despite the yellow Post-it Note that serves as a
code, to find Gloria in bed with George. They're sleeping, George with his face turned toward the wall; they
look peaceful and still. Gloria slowly opens one eye
and sees me holding a piece of white paper and an
envelope torn in half. She pulls the sheet up to her
collarbone. "It doesn't matter what they say to you
now," she says, and George makes a kind of snore.
Seeing my wrecked expression, Gloria reaches sleepily
out of the covers and takes my hand. "Go," she says.
"Adios. You're already gone."

I take a short Christmas vacation in Sea Haven, where
my mother keeps me at a distance because of a cold.
Sneezing and sucking on lemon drops, she drives me
to the bus in Atlantic City, handing me two chicken
salad sandwiches and a stack of ten-dollar bills. "See

everything," she says, taking my hand as if to shake it. "Write when you can."

Unexpectedly I tell her, "Look after Dad."

She grins, pressing her face against mine. I am heavier than she and newly taller, so I end up kissing her temple. She smells wonderful, like a faint, exotic clove. I plan to ask if she will miss me, but the bus driver shouts and she starts to cough, so I never ask. When the bus pulls out, I see her in pieces: first her wide, thin-lipped mouth, then the round caramel eyes people comment on, then the lovely prominent bones that form her jaw, then the delicate nose. It's a complicated face, a difficult face to put together. She waves her tapered hand, her narrow fingers, until I can't see her. Despite her cold, I never warned her to look out for herself.

I ride in the green vinyl seat for two and a half days, washing myself in rusted depot sinks, eating bruised apples, prewrapped pies, and potato chips, and watching the country go by. Miraculously, I sleep well all the way to the Mexican border, although the other passengers look nauseated and worn. I dream only once. In the dream, the end of the world is near. The cities are flooded, there is nothing left to stand on but rotten boardwalks, and we are expecting, at any moment, a tidal wave. It will cover us and be done. Families stand together on the boardwalk, some with binoculars, some shading their eyes with their hands against the sun. My father paces, curious and expectant rather than alarmed; he is almost happy, anticipating the big event. In the water, which laps at the edge of the boardwalk at our feet, is a deep-sea diver in traditional turn-of-the-century costume, complete with an iron helmet with a tiny door. In his gloved hand he holds a list of the people who will survive. I urge my father to speak to him and save us. "Get on the list," I whisper, teeth clenched. But my father doesn't have his heart in rescue. Lazily he walks over to the diver and asks, in the tone one would use when requesting ketchup for a hamburger, "Any room on that list for an old guy and his kid?" The diver scans the list once, then turns away.

I wake feeling sad but refreshed, and sleep again.

At sunrise we reach Monterrey, and after another thirty minutes we are in Saltillo, a town of one- and two-story white buildings and a small central plaza full of graceful palms. I meet my Mexican family casually and with ease: a mother and father who look not much older than I am and three small children, two with tiny gold hoop earrings in their ears.

In the weeks that follow I learn from the maid how to make tortillas. I baby-sit now and then for tiny Arturo, Dorotea, and Claribel, who laugh at my accent and my hiking shoes. I walk brazen and sleeveless in the sun. My Spanish, everyone tells me, has improved. I write postcards to Gloria, wishing her well with Angelique, and tell her stories about Cortés and Tenochtitlán. I describe the violence, the beating hearts torn out at the top of pyramids, the bearded gods who arrived in the form of Spaniards, the treachery of interpreters hungry for gold. I tell her about the man on the side of the highway near Linares, carrying a full-sized cross on his shoulders and wearing Levis and a crown of thorns. I describe the woman washing shirts in a public fountain in the park, the leper collecting coins in an old Coke can. I avoid the other American students and take field trips on the weekends on my own, attending cockfights, bars, and even, accidentally, a funeral in a small abandoned town.

I develop a love of Mexican churches—the cool, bone white interiors, the gaudy saints like mute dolls. The chapels in every town I visit boast something new: a row of women's braids tied with white ribbon and hung as offerings; a Christ carved from vegetables and beginning to rot; a papier-mâché wishing well filled with children's corrective shoes. The omnipresence of belief is overwhelming. I bask in it and marvel at such harmonious agreement on higher things.

During one long weekend away, I wake up in a three-dollar hotel in which I've barricaded the door and slept in a sheet that I carry folded in my backpack. I put on my large unsexed overalls and hiking boots, tuck my money inside my shirt, and go downstairs to a breakfast of fried egg, whipped chocolate, and bread. I feel conspicuous but hardy, invulnerable. I pay seventy cents for the food and ask the young boy behind the counter where I can find the major tourist attraction in the area, the old church. *"Capilla de Huesos"*: I have to say it twice. The boy points the way, and the entire clientele of the restaurant watches me go.

I cross a dirt road, hang a left past a group of men playing horseshoes, a girl in green chasing a rooster through the dust. After turning several more corners, following a low adobe wall, I assume I'm lost, and then abruptly I find myself at the chapel door. The guidebook referred to the "unusual use of human skeletons in this poorly maintained structure'': it was one of the first things added to my list of places to go. I walk in. A few rows of small wooden benches, an altar and a cross, and a raft of candles: that's all.

It is only by standing in the center of the one-room building and allowing my eyes to become accustomed to the dark that I begin to see the bones. The four square walls and arched ceiling of the chapel are porous, uneven, oddly made, full of fissures and unexpected slopes, curves, and knobs. The devotional candles in the rear corner illuminate a simple juncture of two walls, the angle defined by horizontal rows of tibia or perhaps femur, on either side. A line of knee-caps, like an unclasped pearl necklace, is inlaid between the two from ceiling to floor. The effect is graceful, if bizarre. The surface to my left, just beyond the pews, is composed of smaller bones fanning out in a circle like a child's drawing of the sun: radius and ulna, metacarpal—the names come back to me from biology like a poem. I wait for revulsion to find me but the arrangement of the bones is too truly lovely, too careful and thoughtful for squeamishness. The grace and design of the collocation mimic that of a living body: the separate bones nearly but never touching, the beauty that at first doesn't seem like beauty, the juxtaposition of fragile and strong. Inlaid in the wall before the altar is a cross composed of thousands of the smallest digits, the tarsal and carpal bones, the uneven rounded pebbles. And above me, grouted into the concave ceiling, are the skulls. The rounded oval lids of them bulge through as if at that moment being born—the empty eyes must be gazing through the mud at heaven. The bones have taken on the color of adobe: all is earth-colored and quiet. The donors—or were they victims? the guidebook doesn't say—literally form a part of what they loved.

I don't write to anyone about the chapel and how long I stand there, thinking about all the separate lives of the bodies around me, how they feared death and loved each other, how they once walked, ate, sang, called dogs, prophesied the future, and engaged in acts of passion on bedroom floors.

In fact I lose the desire to visit churches and spend the next weekend with my Mexican family, keeping the maid, Marta, company while she scrubs the family's wash on a laundry stone.

It is here, under a cloudless blue sky, while I am dreaming of the things I'll do, that the program director finds me. For some reason he speaks in English— maybe so Marta can't understand. "I am sympathy," he says, and shows me the telegram calling me home.

9

~~

November

"Dad," I said, one afternoon when we were rocking on the back porch. "Your birthday's coming up. What do you say we have a party, do something fun?"

"No reason to," he said, flipping the pages of the paper.

"What do you want for a present?"

"Present?" He yawned. "I need a dozen rolls of toilet paper, a jar of mustard, and a new mailbox. Anything else would just get in the way."

"I'll make a note of that," I said. "Why do you need a new mailbox?"

"Obviously," he said, "because I want to strap it onto my head and dance around the neighborhood." I hadn't seen my father much lately; he'd been spending a lot of time with Murphy, coming home mainly to sleep and read the paper and to leave notes around the house about where I could find him "in case of emergency." He posted the numbers of the police, the fire department, the poison control center, and the weather bureau by the phone.

"Bee tells me that your insurance went up," I said.

My father was studying the paper, reading about hurricanes off the coast of South Carolina.

"You know, you could bring in some extra money pretty easily," I said. "You could fix up the third floor. Add a couple of dormer windows and Sheetrock and paint. With a separate flight of stairs it could be an apartment of its own."

"That's all I need: someone vacuuming over my head as well as under it," he said.

"I guess that would depend on who your tenant was."

He looked up from the paper. "The insurance would be impossible."

"But the mortgage is already paid."

"What would you know about it?" He rattled the paper. "Good tenants are hard to come by. Not many of them would put up with a cad like me."

"It might be worth it to them," I said. "Depending on what their situation was. They might be more than willing. You could look for someone who knows how to appreciate a place like this."

He looked at me over the rim of his reading glasses. "Only a jackass would be willing to move permanently into an old man's attic. I couldn't let that happen, could I?"

I shifted around on the chair's cushion. I was now allowed to spend much of the day sitting up. No climbing stairs unless I was on my way to the doctor, no driving, and no exercise, but I could sit for several hours at a time.

"Dad," I asked, "did you ever think of getting married again?"

He looked out at the ocean, gray and tumbling, less than one hundred yards away. "Who would I marry? You have some unfortunate dwarf friend who needs a companion?"

"I'm being serious. You were fifty-something when she died; you were still young."

"*You* were young," he said. "I wasn't young."

"Did you go out with anyone, after?"

"Who would I go out with? Just because your mother married me doesn't mean someone else would make the same mistake. When we dated, most of her friends thought she was nuts. Generally I agreed with them." He pushed my feet off the coffee table. "That belonged to your grandmother," he said. "Take care of it, and maybe you'll get it when I die."

"I don't want this table. It's ugly."

"That's what I like about you. Sentimental to the core. The Bible was right: 'sharper than a serpent's tooth . . . ' "

"I know, 'the sting of a child.' Are you going to think about the third floor? About my idea?"

"That's not an idea," he said. "It's a disaster."

"Dad, listen—"

"What do you do all day?" he asked. "Dream up ways to drive the aged underground? Tell me this: Why is your sister hunting all over creation in some kind of frenzy for an apartment? I thought she was going to relax and look after you."

"Maybe she's bored."

"Beatrice doesn't get bored. She could invent an occupation with two paper bags and a chicken bone."

"Well, maybe she feels bad."

My father mimicked a look of expectation—eyebrows up, lips pursed together unevenly.

"Okay, we haven't been getting along that well. And she didn't react the same way I did to certain pieces of news that neither of us was ever intended to find out about."

"I'm all aquiver with curiosity," he said.

I waited. He honestly didn't seem curious. "We know that Mom left," I said. "She left even before she got sick that first time. You don't have to tell me what happened, I'll just talk, and when I'm done, you can tell me if I got it right. I figure you and Mom had some kind of problems, and I won't ask you what they were, but she packed up and left. Maybe the stillbirth was too hard, or maybe it was a combination of things. I figure Bee was probably four because she was old enough to remember. She remembers more than you think." I felt tired and newly sympathetic toward my father, who still protected the woman who left him temporarily, then for good.

He didn't nod or shake his head, so I went on. "If Bee was four, Mom was pregnant again—with me. Maybe she didn't know it when she left. Maybe she felt the same kind of disconnectedness that I do, and maybe that's what she meant by 'never enough.' But eventually she came back here like I did, pregnant and trying to figure out what to do. She came back to have her baby by the ocean."

My father peeled a strip of dirt from beneath his thumbnail. "Very enlightening. High drama. A+ for interpretation."

"Is it true?"

"That depends on who you talk to."

"No it doesn't; nobody in this family really talks."

"You think we should move toward physical violence?"

"Maybe." I turned my chair toward his. "Bee doesn't even want to remember things that happened when we were little. All she can think about are interest rates and how much this house is worth on a given day."

He continued checking his broad flat nails like a manicurist. "This house has been on the market for almost a year."

"Not seriously, though. Not priced to sell." I realized that I was talking much too loud.

"Janey, listen." He leaned toward me; our faces seemed closer together than they had ever been. I saw every whisker, every crease. "I'm almost sixty-nine years old. When you get to be my age, there are things you don't want to think about anymore; you put them away and call them finished. You get practical. You play the odds and get things done."

"You were always practical," I said.

"Now I'm old and wrinkled and practical as a prune. I'll be dead in a couple years."

"What if I'm not ready for you to die then?" I'd meant to say something funny, to lessen the tension in the room.

"Then," my father said, slapping my knee with the

Sea Haven Herald, "you'll have to get along in this mean world on your own."

I told myself that I needed Bee less, and it was true. I was more mobile, less dependent. I could cook and wash clothes and get out of bed to answer the door. Bee did the grocery shopping and my father did the cleaning, but they didn't have to hover by my side. Some of my earliest memories involved Bee standing next to me in the bathroom when she was eight and I was four, handing me the toothbrush, the paste, and gently wiping my hands with a warm cloth while our mother read pieces of books that she would never finish in the next room. I had always been Bee's job; I didn't want her to be responsible for me anymore.

And Bee was busy, like her name. She was freelancing and consulting and looking for more work and an apartment, and she had struck up an acquaintanceship with Ellie's mother, Deborah Lund. They met for lunch and talked about activities for Ellie, and probably (Bee didn't say so, but I knew) activities or teaching positions for me. We didn't talk. Bee was solicitous, polite, and distant in a way that made distance between the two of us seem inevitable. I knew she disapproved of the increasing amount of time I spent with Bill, but neither of us brought the subject up.

One afternoon when everyone was out, I called my tenant in Philadelphia and asked him to send my winter clothes. I offered to pay for his trouble in the form of a month's free rent, and almost immediately a cardboard box arrived in the mail. I had asked for a selec-

tion of baggy winter clothes—the only ones likely to
fit from January to March—a number of books, and
the contents of my nightstand's three drawers. I
thought when I slit the tape of the box with a knife, I
might be flooded with visions of my job, of my apartment, of the self-sufficient, normal way I used to live.
I would feel a healthy pang of nostalgia for the time
when I was teaching and not pregnant, when I hadn't
yet sensed the lovely but ominous floating movements
of a person-to-be. I braced myself, cut, and lifted the
flaps: a collection of well-worn corduroy pants and
sweaters, some dog-eared paperbacks, and plastic bags
full of playing cards, correction fluid, hand lotion, cal-
endars, and scraps of paper with obsolete messages.
Junk. I'd always thought that possessions should take
on a certain weight with the passing of time, but my
belongings looked impersonal: they were generic,
eclectic, made in shoddy factories by underpaid per-
sonnel around the world. Taken together, they had a
doomed and wistful look—unappealing. I sifted
through them halfheartedly, stirring them with a yard-
stick on the floor.

It was three-fifteen. Bee was probably touring an
apartment, looking at a tacky two-bedroom place with
oil reproductions of yachts and kittens on the walls
and, if she was lucky, a pair of my father's seashell
lamps. When she moved in, though, unlike her sister,
she would know how to make the apartment hers. She
would hang up the picture of the two of us on the pier,
Bee holding a flounder as long as her arm while I
stared at my shoes. She'd bring the collection of as-
tronomy charts she used to tape above her bed, the

paperweight she'd made of cat's-eye marbles and model airplane glue. She'd cover the kitchen table with her "periodic-tablecloth," and the walls with her nut-and-bolt collection. She would hang kites and rope and mittens, as well as her thirty-one-foot gum wrapper chain, in the hall. Bee, like my father, didn't agonize about where she should belong. She didn't riffle through other people's garbage as a way of trying to make herself feel at home.

I made a pot of almond tea and opened the kitchen window, letting the cold salt air come in. I saved my winter coat, two pairs of pants and my hiking boots, and the box of books. I knotted the rest in a plastic bag and sent it out, watching it land with a satisfying *whunk* on the frozen grass, where Bill Denzer would surely find it and fit it neatly inside the metal can.

I insisted on a party for my father's birthday. Bill helped. He bought hats and blowers and streamers and made a cake and, on the morning of the celebration, carried it hidden in a box upstairs so that, together, we could frost it. He seemed disproportionately happy, and I remembered that the only member of his own family was probably comatose in a nursing home. He brought the cake and the bowl of frosting into my bedroom, closed the door, and handed me a knife and a spatula and a spoon. We heard Bee arguing in the kitchen with my father about plasticware: he wanted to set the table with disposable things and park the trash can beside it. I could hear the heavy can being dragged to and fro.

"Your father must be happy to have the family all

together for his birthday," Bill said. He was filling up a pastry bag with something gooey and blue.

"In body if not in spirit." I globbed the frosting on with the spatula. The top layer of the cake began to disintegrate into crumbs. "Bill, do you think Bee hates me?"

"Why would she hate you?"

"People don't need good reasons. It's just that I accidentally reminded her of how obnoxious she can be. And she doesn't want to listen to my ideas for the third floor."

"Your sister's very logical," he said. "The third floor may not be the best idea. Something else might come along."

"We'll see. I'm making a mess of your cake over here; come and look."

Bill took the spatula from my hand and quickly frosted the top and the sides. "Use a circular motion; that way the cake doesn't tear." He wiped some frosting smudges off the plate with a paper napkin. "I would offer to talk to her for you, but I think she avoids me."

"Bee doesn't avoid you," I lied, wondering who I was defending: Bill or Bee.

Bill flipped the udderlike pastry bag over his wrist. "I think it's important," he said, "that your family likes me."

"Everyone likes you," I said, scratching my stomach where it seemed there was not enough skin. The fetus was thumping away in there, as if shouting advice, trying to put its two cents into the conversation.

"I'd like to correct any false impressions, then," Bill said.

The thumping stopped. "Listen close," it seemed to say. I looked at Bill's back, as white and blank and inexpressive as a closed eye. He held the pastry bag with an expert's hand, drawing a smiling face with enormous features and bushy brows, and a hat with a tassel like a sparkler on the top. It wasn't a cake for an old man, but it did look good.

"I didn't know you could draw," I said.

He squirted a small blob of frosting onto his thumb and held it to my lips. I hesitated; it was sweet. The clocks were ticking gently in the other room. "Well it's time," Bill said, wiping my mouth very softly with a napkin, "that you pay more attention to what I can do."

We ate ham and brown rice, applesauce and peas. We discussed the future of the county golf course and the local scandals in the news. Murphy, who wore a Donald Duck birthday hat throughout the meal, talked about his newest grandchild, a wonder-boy of eleven months who weighed as much as a five-year-old. "You'll be in the thick of it soon enough. You'll find out." Murphy winked. He winked by habit, as if he were flirting with the air. "My youngest, Karen, can tell you. It's a heckuva job, raising kids."

Karen, the snake, had sold Murphy's house from under him. "Will you be seeing Karen at Christmas?" I knew the answer to that one already.

"Oh, no, she goes to her husband's parents'. I might take the trailer for a spin, visit my sister in Wisconsin." Murphy laughed. He buttered a roll; his palm was as broad as a baseball glove.

Everyone knew that Murphy hadn't moved his trailer since he bought it and that he usually spent Christmas day with my father, drinking Scotch and watching religious reruns on TV.

"You can come for dinner here," I said. "We'll make turkey. Right, Bill? Bee?"

Bee was picking at her food, moving individual grains of rice around her plate with the tines of her fork. I wouldn't have been surprised to see her build a tiny log cabin, notching each grain and fitting it to the next.

"Sure," Bill said.

Murphy delved deep into the peas with a gravy spoon. "You know, there's lots of good things about a trailer. It's smaller, that's one. And in the park you've got your hookups and all you need. You've got people close around you all year long."

"Who wants more ham?" my father asked.

"The place where I live," Murphy said, "you've got retired folks, sure, but young couples, too. Little kids. It's a mixed bag."

We finished the ham. We ate the rice. We scraped the last pea from the bowl and even finished the stick of butter. Then we lit the candles, sang, and ate the cake. No one seemed to be having fun.

After giving my father a set of swizzle sticks shaped like golf clubs, Bee said that she had to go. She had an interview in Philadelphia in the morning: I imagined her in a sleeping bag on the floor of Ellie's room.

Bill looked at his watch; he had to catch the end of a PTA meeting at school.

"I don't have anywhere to be," Murphy announced. "I'll stick around. I'll wash dishes. Me and Jane."

Murphy stuck. He washed the dishes, dried them, and settled down with a beer on the old blue couch. Even when my father drove to Caleb Street for milk, Murphy stayed.

"Life's a funny kind of thing." He looked at me sideways, shaking his long, horsey head. His brown-gray hair was cut like a schoolboy's, with bangs: he cut it himself with a kitchen scissors once a month.

"I think I'm going to bed now, Murphy. You can sit here if you want." I stood up.

"Strange things can happen." He winked, looking miserable to the core. "Who'd have thought I'd be sitting on your Dad's couch, keeping you up? I don't know. Not me. I couldn't have seen it."

"Why *are* you keeping me up?"

"It's good news." Murphy sat forward on the couch. "That's how I see it. Pretty good. I congratulated him already." He nodded. "I was first."

"Congratulated who?" The creature inside me rolled over like a wave breaking.

Murphy finished his beer in a swallow. "Hey, it's nice. You haven't seen my trailer, I guess, but this one's even nicer. Sky blue. I knew the lady who died and sold it. Actually, she didn't sell it; she was dead. Her nephew sold it. The lady died cleaning the kitchen—it's real clean."

"What are you talking about?" I sat back down.

"It's right near mine," Murphy said, seeming to

apologize as he spoke. "He'll be close by."

"My father bought a trailer? Is that what you're telling me?" I wiped my hands on my sweatshirt. "Well, if he's thinking of leaving the house to me, I won't take it. I want him to stay right where he is. I've already talked to him about it. We could remodel the attic, and I'll live upstairs. This place is his; he couldn't live anywhere else."

Murphy sat still. Even his winking eye was quiet.

"Is it still his?"

Murphy had known me since I was born. He had caught me when I nearly fell down the back steps at the age of two; he had taught me to swim and kept me from drifting out to sea in a rubber ring. He had bought me flowers on my twelfth birthday and lied with me to my parents when I banged up the car. Murphy was rescue. He was a Coast Guard vessel guiding the foundering craft to shore.

"It was his this morning," he said. "It isn't now."

Bee was gone; she knew. And my father was probably driving one hundred miles for a quart of milk.

"This way's easier," Murphy said. "This way it's all done and there's no fighting. Everything's settled, without an argument. It's done."

I wondered to myself: Would it be so awful if we argued? Isn't that what other families do?

"Wait till you see it," Murphy said. "You'll come and look. Sky blue. I'd say he got the best one."

"I won't come and see it," I said, already feeling my mother and father and all my grandparents vanishing into dust. I could feel the ocean receding, a never-ending ebb tide pulling away.

"No, not right yet. You're too busy. Hey, you've got plenty to prepare for." Murphy looked relieved. "The thing is," he said, "your dad's crazy for you and your sister. And she was right: He had to sell it. There isn't anything he wouldn't do. He got a good deal."

I looked at Murphy, who was nodding to himself. It struck me that people, in their instincts, are like animals gone wrong. Seeing Murphy mechanically nodding, bobbing away, I thought of the species in the *Leary's Bird Book* that my mother had always kept by the windowsill. I remembered reading in it once that different types of birds communicated tenderness, interest, love, with the limited tools they were given: tapping on trees, scratching clawed feet in the dust, submerging each others' heads beneath the pond. All the highly stylized rituals for expressing love. We were worse than hens and pigeons: we had the means, the gifts, but wouldn't use them.

"Tell him to stay away from this house if he doesn't want it," I said to Murphy. "If he needs to leave me a message, he can pin it, with his keys, to the front door."

Within twenty-four hours a SOLD sign appeared in the front yard. Several realtors stopped by with brochures; contractors and architects came; I found footprints in the early morning frost on the whitened lawn. Bill, eternally well adjusted, started looking forward to a condominium downtown. On a weekend trip from New York, our neighbor, Mr. Benedetti, saw the sign and rang the bell. He'd heard that the house had been bought as an investment by a millionaire in Dover, who paid $280,000, mostly cash. He would tear the house down as soon as the paperwork went through.

"It's a hell of a price in this market." Mr. Benedetti scratched his head. "Your dad sold right up at the top. That guy will never get his money back, even if he builds the Taj Mahal."

"I'll be living here until spring," I said. "Murphy told me. He said the new owner will rent me the place until early March."

"That's because builders start work in spring." Mr. Benedetti looked down at my bulging stomach. "The day they get you out of here, it's gone."

My father invited me out to the trailer which, I heard over and over, was not only sky blue but in mint condition from the woman who'd died in its kitchen on her knees, waxing the miniature vinyl floor. Bee had seen it and even spent the night. I pictured her curled on a three-foot sleeping mat, an army blanket for her pillow, the headlamps of motorcycles from the highway lighting her hair. She had flown from Philadelphia to Atlanta to close up her affairs and then moved into a month-by-month rental in Kerry Beach. I hadn't seen her. Since I had only a few weeks of pregnancy left to go, Dr. Subramanian let me take short walks and go carefully, and slowly, up and down stairs. I was free to leave the house, now that I couldn't stay.

I spent my time dozing and reading. Bill often cooked for me and cleaned. He would come upstairs at four or five with some kind of lie about buying too much meat at the grocery store, then lure me into his kitchen, setting me up with a token peeler and some new potatoes in a corner chair.

"You need to look for a place to live," he said. "You won't have time later."

I didn't care. I cultivated a vision of myself beneath an overpass, holding a baby in a ragged blanket. My father could find me, like the match girl, curled up and frozen in the snow.

"If I hadn't gotten pregnant," I said, "he wouldn't have sold."

Bill didn't respond. I noticed there were fewer cans on his cabinet shelves. He was getting rid of things, paring down.

"If he were insane," I said, "I could have him committed, and have the contract declared void."

"I don't think your sister would go along with that," he said.

I said "What sister?" and had to put the peeler down. Bill pretended he didn't notice me watching my own hands trembling; he hummed a Frank Sinatra tune into the stew.

I remembered Bee telling me when I was little and broke a toy that I shouldn't be upset about impermanence—that was her word. "Nothing material lasts forever." But years from now I would bring my child to this spot, look up at the bleached-blond renters holding martinis on the redwood deck, and say, "This is the place that should have lasted. This is where you should have lived."

Picking up the peeler again, I told Bill what I would have done if the house were mine. I would have rebuilt the porches, put skylights in the attic on the south side, added a new flight of stairs, moved out the junk, and made three third-floor rooms.

"You wouldn't have been able to insure it," Bill said. "That's one of the reasons your father sold."

"He sold to make himself miserable. He sold so he and Bee can sit around the little stove in his trailer and talk about how I made them sell the house because I didn't have any money."

"Maybe you'll see some new possibilities come along," Bill said.

"Yeah, maybe suicide," I said. "You know, he came to the door last night, but I wouldn't let him in."

"I know," Bill said. "He came down here."

"What did he say?"

"He said his own daughter had bolted him out of the house. He wanted his red bathrobe and some cooking pots."

"Tell him I cut the bathrobe into pieces and burned it."

"Too late. I snuck in this morning when you were asleep and drove it over to his new place. It isn't as bad as you might think; it has some charm."

"Vinyl does not have charm, Bill," I said. "I thought you'd be on my side. He's going to be crazy in that box in another month."

Bill opened a package of frozen peas. "I *am* on your side. More than you know."

I sulked in front of the potatoes. They were badly peeled, with flecks of skin still clinging to them here and there.

"I have something to show you," he said. "It was going to be a surprise, but come and look. You can tell me how to finish it." He led me out of the kitchen and down the hall in the direction of his spare room, the room where my mother used to do her painting. "What do you think?" On top of neat squares of newspaper, in the middle of the room, was a crib. It had been stripped down to the wood; the smell of paint thinner lingered in the air.

"I wanted an old one with some style, but I made sure it's up to code. I can leave it this shade or stain it. I think it's oak."

"It's beautiful," I said.

"I asked Beatrice not to buy you one, once I found it. And I bought this, too." He unfolded an oblong quilt embroidered with tiny multicolored fish. "It's washable. You'll still need a bumper pad, so the baby won't bang its head against the sides." Bill gently bumped his fist against the bars, testing.

I said, "I guess, if it were left to me, the baby would sleep in a dresser drawer for fifteen years." I ran my fingers over the carved headboard. "Thank you. It's extravagant, really, Bill."

"No, it's not. I feel like I already know this baby. I want to know her even better when she's born."

"Her?" I walked around the crib, admiring the wood.

"Or him. I just imagine the baby being a lot like you."

"It could look very much like someone else."

"No," he said. "It couldn't."

Bill stood on the opposite side of the crib from me, holding the rail. Looking at his hands, I saw that his knuckles were turning white. "I've been talking to Clara Nestor, the principal," he said. "She might need some extra substitute teachers next year. You could work when you wanted to, part-time."

"I haven't thought about it enough, Bill," I said. "I don't think I'll be able to afford to work part-time."

"You will if I help you," he said.

I looked at Bill and knew he could already feel the weight of a six-pound baby in his arms. The crook of his elbow craved a small, sweet head, the palm of his hand already caressed the rounded toes. He was ahead of me, I knew. I still thought of the baby as a little sea horse, faceless, a tiny water buffalo. I asked him where he bought the crib.

"I got a tip on where to find it from Benina. She was keeping an eye out for me."

Benina was a former student, one of two recent Sea Haven girls who'd had children while still in high school. Bill had seen them through, visiting their parents to help break the news, calling doctors, babysitting, and in one case, going to the wedding when the baby was three months old.

"One wayward girl to another," I said. "Tell her thanks. Did she ever give that presentation to your class?"

"No, she got nervous." Bill took my hand and led the way back to the kitchen. "I told her she should do it only if she felt comfortable. She didn't."

I took my hand back, pretending to scratch. "Do you think the PTA would have bothered you about that? A sixteen-year-old single mother as a guest lecturer in a Health class at her own school?"

"No, why should they? Do you think it's a bad idea?"

"No," I said. "Not at all."

He lifted the lid on a pot, and the smell of beef curled up in a spiral toward the lamp. "Then come and make a presentation yourself."

I paused. I owed Bill quite a lot. "You just want to get me into a classroom again."

"That's part of it."

"And what's the other part? What would I say? Do I tell them how to lead their lives so that they don't end up like me?" I rubbed an achy spot in my lower back.

Bill put down the lid and took my hand away and rubbed the achy spot himself; it felt good. "You just said it wasn't a bad idea. You can say whatever you like. I'll introduce you as a former student. You'll sit and talk. It could be as long or as short as you make it."

"What could it accomplish? *Former student screws around, loses job.*"

"I don't see it that way," he said.

I stood up and stretched. "That's how most people see me. And Health is a class in moral issues these days. There's a right and wrong. You don't want me as an example to live up to."

"I can use you as an example of something that happens, good or bad, and let them think."

I told him I'd consider it. He brought two glasses of milk to the table and we sat down. "Only four weeks," he said, looking at my stomach.

"Go ahead." I nodded, and he put his palm on my hip, sliding it around to my navel, which now stuck out like a Frankenstein's knob. Nothing stirred. I poked my stomach on one side. "Maybe he sold the house because he didn't want a single mother on the premises."

"Shh," Bill said.

"And my sister put him up to it. She's possessed."

Bill put his other hand on my stomach, then pressed his ear against me, too. He closed his eyes. Because he lay there for a while, as if asleep, I moved my hands through his hair until the stew was done.

I met Bill at school on the following Wednesday at ten-fifteen. The glossy cinder-block walls were dingier, the floors were retiled in an institutional shade of blue, and the trophy case by the locker rooms was full; four of the older, smaller trophies held my name. Still, I felt as if I were coming back after spending a summer away. The kids dressed differently—better, I thought— the girls didn't wear pastels. A student who looked drunk collided with me. "Stellar," he said, reeling. When the door to Bill's room opened, I knew that this place and time had waited for me; a room and a moment had preserved themselves so I could reenter them, almost fifteen years later, like a dream. The chalkboards seemed to sigh when I walked in.

Through the back windows—the desks, firmly bolted to the floor, faced the front—we used to watch gym classes playing softball or flag football: the girls in short shorts with goose bumps on their legs, the boys in cutoff T-shirts, feinting and shadowboxing from nervousness or adrenaline or cold. Unable to watch them without turning completely around in our bolted chairs, we'd had the impression that enormous physical excitement was occurring just behind our backs, while the delicate puncture of an egg with a wagging sperm was illustrated via overhead projector up front; we sat sandwiched between the technicalities of sexual excitement and its release. Even now, a series of posters along the sides of the room warned about drugs and drinking and other evils of the day. "Come in," Bill said. I had sat in that room when he was my teacher, when I was fourteen and he was twenty-six.

"I've always hated these desks. They don't give the kids enough room. Sit in my chair. I'll introduce you and then go. You won't feel inhibited that way."

"Inhabited?" I asked.

I spotted the seat that I'd usually sat in: halfway back on the right-hand side. I remembered Denise, who now had three stepkids by a second husband, whispering comments about Mr. Denzer's wardrobe and the way he combed his hair. "Camel eyes," she'd said. In fact they still were: large and limpid and dark brown, with long, thick, feminine lashes. Bill went to get me a glass of water while several students shuffled in. They looked at me, amused, as Denise and I would have done. One boy slammed his books on a desk and asked loudly from the back of the room: "Are you a new student?" When I turned to answer, he was talking to a friend.

The bell rang. Bill returned with the water, made a few announcements, and then simply said, "Our speaker for today is Jane Haus." He whispered something to a drowsy-looking female student in the front and walked out the door.

Confronted with a new class at the beginning of every academic year, I used to suffer a crisis of confidence. What on earth could I teach these people? I knew nothing useful myself. They needed to know how to get along in the world, to find jobs, to maintain their cars, to earn and spend the correct amount of money relative to their financial situations, to be generous with others but protect themselves, to cook and type and fall in love successfully, to be well adjusted according to the local norms. Where could the rules of punctuation possibly fit in? Every year I felt more desperate than the year before.

Although I had no idea what to say, I started to talk. I told them that I knew they found lectures dull but that Mr. Denzer had asked me to come. I explained that I used to be his student and that he was my coach when Sea Haven High had sponsored golf. Someone asked me a question about the team, and we discussed it for a while. They were disappointed that I hadn't continued to play. "For too long I thought it was the only thing I could ever be good at," I said. I felt there must be a useful lesson in this example, but I wasn't sure how to extract it, squeeze it out. "The reason I'm here," I said, "is that this is a Health class, which involves sex. You can see by my ring finger"—I held it up—"that I'm not married. You can see by my stomach that I've had sex." Someone laughed. "I'm twenty-eight. I could be making a mistake. I left my job. I'm living in my father's house. Strangers like yourselves probably take pity on me. Are there any questions so far?" No one raised a hand. "I guess I could tell you what it's like to be pregnant."

"What's it like, then?" someone asked.

It was time for a confidence. "I don't feel I'm able to enjoy it," I said. "It feels strange. I feel like I'm harboring an alien in there."

Things went more smoothly after that. There was an exchange of information—the questions were frank. Some were subtle, some moronic. Probably two or three people learned two or three things. The rest were awake. That's school.

Bill took me to lunch. We slid our plastic trays along the silver track. There lay the universal fare: green beans bobbing in liquid, whipped (not mashed) potatoes, slices of pressed meat from another world. Women with burns up and down their arms, wearing shower hats and see-through plastic gloves, stood listless in front of these dishes while students bought Hohos, Yodels, Twinkies, chips, hot dogs, ice cream, and milk. The teachers, of course, selected the "platter," although we pushed it around on our trays and threw great lumps of it away. Over a cube of chocolate cake Bill told me that I looked wonderful. "I knew you'd fit in," he whispered. I asked him if he still showed his students the childbirth film.

He looked confused.

"You know, the one in that weird emergency shelter. Very graphic."

"I hardly remember. Did I show that while you were here?" He bought an extra half-pint of milk to put in my purse.

The second talk was easier. I rattled on about being unemployed and pregnant and feeling unsure of myself. Sometimes it works: reveal your insecurities and break the student/teacher barrier down. The way this strategy backfires is if the students take the opposing role and dispense advice. One person asked if I would hate myself forever for what I had done. Another asked if I'd gotten pregnant "the first time." I wasn't sure how to answer. Did he think I had been a virgin until my late twenties? I said that I hadn't been "careful." A murmur picked up and then quickly died down.

Finally a blond, limp girl in the back of the room, who had been gazing out the window since I arrived, asked without raising her hand, "Do you see your baby's face? I mean, do you feel like you know it now as well as you ever will?" Several students rolled their eyes. This girl was clearly considered a loon.

"Say that again," I said. "What's your name?" She had already gone back to staring out the window. Someone in front interrupted, asking a dull but prurient question. The bell rang. I pointed out the girl to Bill. "Oh," he said, "Michelle. A lost soul." We watched her click her coral fingernails against the lockers on her way to another room.

The third and final class of the day, Bill said, would be the best. The kids were sharp and articulate; they were curious; they were bright. For some reason, before he left, he told them that he lived in my father's house. Then the questions poured in. Did Mr. Denzer take care of my invalid father? Did they share meals? Where was my mother? Was Mr. Denzer the father of my child? I steered them back to pregnancy and birth. They began a litany of horror tales. Someone's cousin's stomach had burst open from an appendectomy scar. Another girl's mother had given birth to twins on a hard tile floor. A boy knew someone who had borne a child with flippers instead of hands. "Kind of like wings," he explained, wiggling his fingers by his shoulder blades. "But he couldn't fly." They wanted to know how much I ate. How much I weighed. Whether my hair had gotten thinner or fallen out. What would go through my mind when I gave birth.

"I don't know," I said to this last. "I'll probably hope it's over soon."

"You'll probably think back to your own mother," someone said. "Because she went through the same thing, but you won't be able to ask her questions."

"What questions would I ask her?" This, of course, was another ploy: Turn your own question back to the class, and try to dream up a possible answer while they stew.

The room went still. No one seemed to want to touch it. "You might ask her if she loved you right away or if it took a while," someone said. I congratulated Bill on his students' minds, and then I drove home.

One item at a time, my father was pilfering the house. At first he took very little with him: his clothes, one rocking chair, the bathroom rug, some books. Then the coffee table vanished, as did the kitchen table and chairs. There were indentations on the rug and faded outlines on the walls from where the furniture had been.

Initially I didn't let him in the house if I was home, so he had to collect his things when I was out shopping or taking a walk along the sand. But soon it became impossible to refuse him. He would appear looking lost and forlorn at the old storm door, like a traveling salesman blown to Sea Haven by mistake. Or he would show up with a razor and a caulk gun to caulk the tub, as if there were any reason to fix a house that would be torn down. We worried about each other. He compulsively checked the refrigerator for spoiled food. He checked the phone. He had written down his number so many times that I kept finding it on slips of paper everywhere—in drawers and cabinets, taped to walls, and glued to the receiver so that it flapped or fell off when I picked up the phone. He checked the weather bureau and gave me reports. At the first sign of any storm I was to get in my car and drive to the Giles Street bridge. "All the other bozos will be driving north," he said. "You'll beat the rush."

"Maybe I'll stick around for the flood instead and name the baby Noah." He didn't laugh. Once he accidentally called me Caroline. I suspected that he hated the trailer but wouldn't admit it. My own father, who had grown up in front of the ocean and seen the hurricanes of '46 and '69, was going to spend his last years in a metal shoebox the color of the sky. I found it hard, in his presence, not to make hostile comments about Bee. I pointed out that she was an egotist with a heart of stone and that she lacked the imagination to match the frequency with which she dictated her ideas. My father said that if I needed her, she would still come.

"When I'm dead," he liked to say, "your sister will still be here. She's your only family."

"Not for long," I said.

"Children don't count," he answered. We sat, as we always had, in the matching rockers on the porch. "Not for at least a dozen years. It takes them a decade or more to turn into people."

"And then they stab you in the back, right, Dad?"

"Not always. Not every day."

"Bee shouldn't have made you sell," I said.

"She didn't make me sell," he said, impatient. "Are you going deaf? Do you think I lack a mind of my own?"

"I think you got persuaded. That happens. I bet Mom even persuaded you now and then. I bet she persuaded you to go to bed with her before you were married."

He actually guffawed.

Impressed with my own candor, I was unwilling to stop. "One of the other things no one told me was that she was pregnant before you got married. Did her parents mind? What did they say when she told them?"

My father rocked quietly for a while. "They wouldn't let her in the front door," he said, "if that answers your charming little historical question. Once we were married, she burned everything she could find. Pictures, furniture, books. Even some money. Anything she had that belonged to them. She burned it all in the backyard."

"She got rid of her family's stuff," I said. "I always thought you did it."

My father stared. "Why the hell would I have done it?"

"I don't know. Sorry."

A boy—the Benedettis' grandson—threw bread crusts to the gulls until someone shouted out the door and called him in. "So you eloped, right, Dad?"

He shrugged. "I thought I'd have to talk her into it. That still surprises me. She was willing."

"I guess she loved you," I said.

"I guess so." Lights were ticking on in the next block. I felt we were getting somewhere, getting close.

"Proposing marriage is very awkward if you've never done it," my father said.

"I never have." I looked down at the rug, at the spot that Spunk had always favored, by my father's chair. "But Bill has. He's offered to marry me."

My father looked up, clearly shocked. "Offered. What do you mean, he *offered*?"

"He proposed. What else could I mean?"

"He got down on his knees and asked a woman, nine months pregnant with a stranger's child, to be his wife?"

"You could phrase it that way," I said.

"He must be more of an idiot than he looks."

"Thanks," I said. "I haven't said yes or no. He probably thought I'd jump at the chance. I think he's angry, in a quiet way."

My father looked at the clouds, stretching and pulling apart like taffy, miles away. "I assume you're playing hard-to-get?"

"No. Bill Denzer has been nice to me. More than nice. He's been a real comfort. I sound ridiculous saying this because I don't think that I'm in love with him, but he's proposing a certain future, giving me choices. It's good to feel like you can pick this life or that.''

"Your world's a hell of an oyster." My father rocked. His face seemed to sag; his eyebrows looked like they needed to be propped up. "The man rents a floor of my house for years. He writes me checks. Now he wants to marry my daughter. Bill Denzer must be fifty if he's a day."

"He's forty."

"He was your teacher. Wasn't there some kind of hanky-panky way back when?"

"Dad, no!"

My father planted his slippered feet on the wooden floor. Had he hidden a pair of slippers in a closet or driven over without his shoes? "What about the poor bastard who made you pregnant? Why don't you marry him?"

He knew I wasn't going to answer. I remembered when my father's hair began to turn gray, the silver strands coming in straight and thick as wire. Bee and I used to pull them out. "Did Mom's parents dislike you? Or were they just ashamed that she was pregnant? She never talked about them to me. I never knew them."

He wiped his face with the cuff of his shirt. "They disliked me for lots of reasons, most of them stupid. They were Catholic, they had money. Your mother wasn't supposed to go out with me at all."

"And she never went back to her parents after you married her?"

"Once," he said. "One time; that was it."

The refrigerator revved its tired engine behind us

and began to hum. "You shouldn't have sold the house, Dad," I said. "You were born in one of these rooms."

"That's gone," he said, waving. "Under the bridge."

"It's the worst error in judgment you ever made. And it's irreversible, too."

My father smiled. "Irreversible. Now that reminds me of something else. Could we use that word to describe your condition?"

"It's not the same," I said. "I haven't made mistakes that hurt other people."

He sat forward in his chair. "When's the last time you talked to your sister? What's she doing in that crappy two-bedroom place by herself?"

"I didn't put her there—"

"And bringing a fatherless child into the world? That doesn't injure anyone?"

"It doesn't injure you."

He slowly inhaled, as if someone were listening to his chest with a stethoscope. "I helped raise two children. I buried my wife. I wiped the slobber off your chin. And for what it's worth, your sister helped raise you, too. You were a pain—all children are; they run you ragged in a couple years. And I screwed up now and then. What if I did? You can't tell me one solitary thing about my only grandchild's father?"

"You're changing the subject," I said.

"No, this has always been the subject. Every day. You can answer or not answer: Who was this guy?"

"That doesn't matter."

"Humor me. Pretend it matters. Pretend that, right

here, shoulder high, is a ten-year-old kid who wants to know where his father is.''

"He won't be *here. Here* will be gone—''

"Pretend I'm still around when he asks you. What do you say?''

It was getting dark. A fishing boat bobbed like an early star five miles from shore.

"I knew him only for a night,'' I said. "Actually, two. After that I didn't see him.''

"Two nights.'' My father exhaled. "You bring someone into this world for two nights?''

"It's been done for less.''

He nodded. "That's a start. Tell me something more. Tell me his name.''

"That doesn't matter.''

"Was he tall?''

"No. Dad, I don't think it's good to talk like this,'' I said.

"I don't give a good goddamn what you happen to think.''

We rocked. The sun set. "He didn't force you,'' my father said, as if restating a fact to better comprehend it.

"No.''

"If it was only the two occasions, are you certain it was him?''

I nodded. Most of my life I'd been sensible; I kept track of the lapses fairly well.

"Adam,'' he said. "Brian. Carl. Dan. Will you tell me if I guess it?''

"No,'' I said.

"I'll be able to tell from your face. Where did you meet him?"

"In a bar."

"That wasn't smart," my father said.

I agreed it wasn't. It had happened in March. March was the month my mother died; I was always stupid in March.

"Edward. Frank. You were lonely," my father said.

I agreed again, nodding, my voice getting lost in the back of my throat. I tried to recall the exact moment when I let myself go, when I knew I was doing something reckless and didn't care. I knew that I'd sensed the moment and walked toward it, that I'd wanted to submerge myself and enter something new.

"I imagine he was married," my father said. "That's why you didn't tell him. You were unhappy."

I saw myself walking out of the bar, Chinatown, 11 P.M. in Philadelphia, trying to recognize the streets. No matter where I lived, I never knew my way around; there was no ocean, no rushing noise of a heartbeat from the east. I remembered getting into his car for a lift home, I remembered the brown mismatched gloves on the dashboard, the single piece of chewing gum by the stick shift on the floor. I remembered that his hair was black and that I had told myself when he left that second time, Don't forget his face. I struggled with its image for a while, then let it go. He wouldn't matter anymore. He would have a daughter or a son.

"What was his name?" my father asked.

Suddenly I understood what he was asking for: not the facts—that his daughter had slept around, that she was careless and unfaithful even in bed—but a kind of truth that would make sense of what I'd done. I reimagined the moment when I lay down with my child's father; I took away the mediocrity and offered my father a story, like the stories long ago he'd offered me.

"His name," I said, "is Zebulon. He was seven feet tall and a millionaire."

I watched my father smile. We were sitting in the dark on the old wood porch of a house that soon would not exist, but we might as well have been floating out to sea in a canoe. Other than the broken line of white from the rising tide, we were alone. We might have been sitting in my old bedroom, with my mother beginning her slow, uneven voyage toward death in the next room. Bee was right; my father may have done the best he could. He had loved me with the tools he had at hand.

"Maybe one day when we least expect it," I said, "Zebulon will drive down here in a limousine and treat us all to dinner at the Captain's Wharf." My father's eyes were shut. He didn't see the sky change from navy to black; he didn't see the place on the horizon where the stars seemed to be tasting the deep water. By selling the piece of ground beneath our feet, he'd closed his eyes to Sea Haven. Without him it would be a tenuous and unremarkable place: a hill of sand as yet not ruined by water, affixed with fragile wood structures and inhabited mainly by birds, which could relocate, and by a handful of people too short-sighted to do the same.

My father yawned and stretched. He rubbed his eyes and propped his feet on the windowsill. "You'll get one hundred thousand dollars when I die," he said. "Try to spend it well."

"Dad, you look cold," I said.

"Of course I'm cold. I'm sixty-nine years old. It's near December."

I got a blanket from the couch, and he let me spread it over him. "It's a lot of money," I said. "I just wish you still had the house."

My father pulled the blanket up to his chin. "That's how it goes. This world is imperfect; it's a mess. You'd better find yourself a new one."

"I'll look around." I tucked my feet up on the rungs of the rocking chair. "Mom's parents must have been stubborn. I bet they died regretting it," I said.

"Who says they died?" my father said.

I called Murphy to tell him to lock up my father's trailer; he would be spending the night at home.

10

〜

Etymology

From the window of the bus he looks like someone else's father, square and courteous and eccentric, a man with a sense of fun. He stands swaying side to side, hands on his hips, wearing a mismatched shirt and tie probably found in the attic. The skin of his neck is creased and loose; his collar, of course, is folded wrong. He grows inexorably older, aging even as I make my way to the front of the bus. Just before I reach the doorway, it occurs to me that I could sit down again, turn away from the window, and ride back to New York for another plane to Mexico, making him a man who hunts forever for his daughter. Then he sees me stepping down; though my mother dropped me off, he'll take me home. He has come to claim me, as he has in bus stations and schoolrooms, camps and playgrounds, all my life.

"Long trip," he says, looking tired.

We collect my luggage—two large suitcases full of summer clothes, unused film, and unread books.

"I parked on Daniel." My father looks down at the luggage. Daniel Street is a quarter of a mile away. "We'll have to come back and get these with the car."

I can see that, out on the street, most of the metered spots are empty; my father refuses to use them because the meters are new and cost twenty-five cents for half an hour. He thinks that year-round residents of Sea Haven should be able to park downtown for free.

We check the luggage and walk. Oddly, my father heads for the boardwalk, which is several blocks out of the way. He usually avoids it, especially in summer because of the crowds: he hates the whizz and clang of the games, the sunburned, overweight bathers, the crazy bicyclists and musicians, and the collection of end-of-the-worlders holding apocalyptic placards above their heads. "Back again," my father says, whenever he sees them. "I notice this time you've got a tan."

Even at this time of year—February—the board-walk smells of spilled candy, dead crustaceans, spin-paint fumes. A few of the larger stores are open; up ahead a man dressed as a peanut lounges against a wall holding a tray of chocolate fudge. A group of work-men are dismantling the cave of horrors, dumping a nameless rubber creature into a bin. A clutch of girls in baseball jackets, wearing makeup that looks as if they applied it from a distance with wooden spoons, smoke cigarettes and examine the fraying ends of each other's hair.

"I could go for a corn dog," my father says. "How about you?"

I look at him. His eyes are red from the cold; his

jaw tilts at an angle from when it was broken and
misset forty years ago. "Dad," I say, "I think someone should have called me sooner."

He veers off to the right, to a hot dog stand. I study
him: bald spot, bowed legs, accessories from the
1930s. He has been waiting for her to die ever since I
was small, and this is what he'll look like when she's
dead: perplexed and hostile and unready, ludicrous
even in his grief. We will not discuss her death or his
condition. We will communicate, for the rest of our
lives, by innuendo instead of speech.

I follow him to the counter, order a corn dog and a
Coke.

"How was Mexico?" he asks, staring ahead. The
ocean at our backs is cold and gray, the beach a litter
of seaweed and broken shells.

"Warm," I say. "Sunny."

The corn dogs arrive in their paper boats. "I
wouldn't have gone, though," I tell him. "I would
have stayed home. You should have telegraphed right
away. That was stupid. You didn't think of me at all."

My father takes a bite of his corn dog. "When I
was growing up," he says, chewing, "this boardwalk
was a place to take your family on a Sunday afternoon.
People dressed up just to come here, to promenade.
My mother wore gloves."

A pigeon looking for crumbs ruffles its feathers at
my feet. "Let's go. I want to see Mom. I'll get my
suitcases later."

He ignores me and calls to the boy behind the
counter, whom I recognize as the younger brother of
a former classmate of mine.

"Sir?" The boy ducks his head under the menu, which dangles above him on a chain like the blade of a guillotine.

"This corn dog," my father says. "It tastes like horse manure."

"Oh?" The boy glances from my father to me.

"Dad, come on, Bee's waiting."

My father brushes my hand from his jacket; I was trying to coax him toward the car. He looks at me and the boy as if we are plotting together against him. "Don't think you'll ever teach me anything. You're not up to it," he says, and walks away.

I close my eyes and think of Mexico, the bleached white courtyards and endless sun. I try to conjure it up in front of me, to turn it on in my imagination like a bulb. I haven't slept. Instead of the sun I remember the airport, the bus; I smell the hair oil of the man who leaned his head on my shoulder, pretending he had fallen asleep. The light—the sun and shadow—all has gone out.

These are the things that happened in my absence and will continue happening every day of my life, repeating themselves endlessly and without cure. Still nursing her cold, my mother wakes up at night with a low-grade fever; then it goes away. A few days later, she wakes up in a sweat, the sheets drenched, and feels short of breath. Both she and my father have had the flu, so they don't worry about her symptoms. She begins to feel tired during the day. She has aches in her bones. The third week I'm in Mexico she gets a higher fever and checks in with the doctor just to be safe.

Chemotherapy begins the next day. No one calls me because things look good for a week or two, then the white blood count plummets. She begins to shake. She tells my father, with her teeth clacking together and her hands performing a dance across the sheet, that she is doing the tarantella. Bee flies in from Chicago. At this point I am probably tutoring the father of my Mexican family in English: "Do you throw and catch? Do you enjoy playing *fútbol*?" My mother's blood pressure gradually drops. "Why is there so much sand in here?" she asks. I am still not there. Bee tries to phone me at the Riveras' house but can't get through. Briefly my mother dips into unconsciousness, then revives. Bee sends a telegram to the director of the school. She isn't sure whether she should use the word DYING, and she wants to compose an economical message, so she pauses at the telegram window for a while, pen lightly rapping against her teeth. Then she takes the plunge. LYMPHOMA REOCCURRENCE. MOM PROBABLY DYING. COME IMMEDIATELY. She wires me five hundred dollars and returns to the hospital to find my mother in intensive care.

In quantum mechanics, the uncertainty principle suggests that *watching* an experiment affects its outcome. The monitoring presence of the scientist is itself a factor: he is unable to subtract himself and cannot accurately measure what he sees. At the end of a day the scientist feels this nervous lack of knowledge pulling on his strings. This is perhaps why Bee abandoned philosophy and then physics for the surer proofs of mathematics—certainties, no matter how depressing, are more helpful and reassuring in the end. To console herself, Bee works out brand-new theorems on legal pads, striving to come to a single conclusion, one without ambiguities or hope. My father suspects that she's floundering and is disappointed that she hasn't finished a Ph.D. One of her legs is wrapped tightly around the other; to read her handwriting would require a microscope.

Our mother is no longer conscious. Suspended on tubes and wires like a reclining marionette, she seems light enough to float. Urine courses through a byway strapped to the inside of her leg. Fluids enter through her nose. Her wrists, Bee says, were once tied to the metal bars at the sides of the bed, to keep her from pulling out the liquids entering and leaving on their own. Now her hands are face up, perhaps from the habit of being tied, and the pale insides of her arms are inscribed with bruises. What disturbs me most are the dried-out corners of her mouth—even in sleep her tongue creeps up to touch the sore, cracked places. I would like to ask whether we could get a tube of ChapStick, but it seems inappropriate not to think about larger things.

According to Bee, my mother spoke the morning before I arrived. Bee was alone with her and doesn't remember exactly what she said. "I think it had something to do with grapes. She said something like 'Ask him about the grapes' or 'Tell him there are grapes.' It didn't make sense to me, anyway." Now that I sit here waiting, my mother doesn't mention grapes or anything else, even though several times a day I put my ear beside her lips in case there are any messages for me. My mother is a sacred vault, and I am waiting for the password that will allow me to know the secret and let me in. The cracks at the corners of her mouth look like paper cuts: I'm afraid the shell-pink skin inside her mouth is spreading out and will somehow creep, before she dies, across her face.

"Dad wants to take her home." Bee and I are sitting by my mother's bed; I've been here at the hospital for eleven days. "He hasn't been able to get permission."

"She wouldn't see anything," I whisper, because whispering is what we do. "She wouldn't notice."

Bee looks down at her lap. Her cuticles are torn. She chews on them when she's anxious, reviving a childhood habit. "It would make Dad feel better, though. Even if it's just for a couple of days."

It's important, Bee and I know, to discuss these things. We pretend that we are keeping the channels of communication open. I don't tell her, though, that I'm relieved we can't take my mother home. I don't want her struggling for breath while I eat my cereal; I don't want to pretend that there's anything normal or everyday about the underwater pallor of her skin. Bee goes on about the benefits of home care. My mother's upturned hand is inches away from me on the bed. I nod at Bee to show I'm listening, but this is difficult because I see each word emerging from her mouth as an independent creature: they present themselves at the entrance of her mouth as if marching through a door. "You haven't slept enough," Bee says.

"Neither have you."

She touches the veins in my mother's wrist, probably taking her pulse. "I think when I remember this," she says, "I'll remember how much time we spent together. You and Dad and I."

Bee comforts herself by thinking noble thoughts. Her proprietary grasp of my mother's arm makes me insane.

"There are still four of us," I say. "It's a little early for nostalgia."

Bee actually blushes, a splotchy rash quickly spreading across her cheeks. Deliberate cruelty still takes her by surprise: the accidental kind she understands.

"Mom knew you were coming," she says. "We told her you were."

My sister's hair, unwashed, resembles hay, and her clear green eyes are cloudy. She's been awake for several days, reading by flashlight in the lounge when the lights are dim. I feel I can see her more clearly than I ever have: the veneer of self-assuredness, the brusqueness, the deliberate brilliance like a wall between herself and me.

"That idea must provide you with a warm feeling," I say.

Bee lets go of my mother's wrist. "They didn't call me, either, Jane. I called them and found out she was sick. Otherwise I wouldn't have gotten here when I did. So you can take the chip off your shoulder."

My mother's breath makes a clicking sound. All those extra years, all those years we had no right to, and we made so little use of them. I tell Bee softly that it's nice to know that even after our mother is dead I will have two parents to guide me. She picks up her things and leaves the room.

Leaning over the bed I brush my mother's hair from her face; her skin looks like rice paper, impossibly fragile and thin. She has spent her lifetime bluffing, threatening to die. For a fragment of a second I have an overwhelming urge to put the pillow over her face and hold it tightly; then the urge is gone. I would like to remember nothing. I'd like to willfully erase these nights and days as they occur, banish them, hour by hour, from my memory. But as I look at my mother's dormant face, I know its image will refuse to fade; it will bloom in me like a bruise I'm compelled to touch.

The word *lymph*—"a yellowish, coagulable fluid, containing white blood cells in a plasmalike liquid"— used to refer, also, to the sap of plants. Perhaps even earlier, it denoted a stream or spring of pure water. Think of *limpid*. Think of *nymph*. The word has gotten cloudier, thicker, more opaque. As knowledge increased, physicians and pathologists may have harkened back to pastoral, romantic words in order to instill loveliness in what made the average layman squeamish. Nymphs, now, are horny girls. See *dryad, hamadryad, sylph*.

The oncologist, Dr. Strike, is sympathetic. He arranges for an extra bed in my mother's room and allows us to spend the night whenever we like. He's available for questions, though we seldom have them anymore. We introduce him to a few of my mother's friends. At the end of the fourth week we sign, under his gaze, a DNR order—"do not resuscitate." Then we see him less often, presumably because his job is done.

Probably before the last time she lost consciousness, my mother thought about me. Even though I wasn't present, she might have reviewed my birth, my baby-hood, the annoying things I've said and done. If she had compared my sister and me—she wouldn't, of course, but if she had—I doubt she would find Bee better. She would think we were different, each unique. And even if she might have wondered where I was those last few days when she was lucid, I had wondered where she was for most of my life.

She doesn't look so bad for a dying person. I imagined worse. The sore on her mouth is getting better; I touch it with my finger when no one is there.

Words are tricky. In the yellow and white waiting room where Bee and I spend a great deal of our time, I look things up in a dictionary someone left at the nurses' station. Although it is probably considered hospital property by now, I carry it around wherever I go. In its pages I run across things I don't expect. For example, look at *poltroon*. The word might seem to have something to do with poultry, that is, "being chicken." Instead it derives from French and Italian, the verb *poltrire* meaning "to lie lazily in bed," thus not confronting the things you fear.

Recreant, on the other hand, would seem to refer to recreation, but does not. It comes from the old French, *recreire*, "to yield in a contest," and therefore contains an element of treason. *Pusillanimity* is the only one that refers to the spirit. The Latin suffix, *animus*, means soul. *Small-souled*.

Mexicans, though they use the word *cobardía* for cowardice, also use the verb *rajar*, which literally means to split or cleave. But it also means to back down, to show fear, reveal vulnerability, acknowledge a lack of strength. To open yourself up, to spill or confide, is a kind of treason: the ultimate cowardice. That much I learned on my short semester in Mexico.

My father is bearing up, Bee and I agree. He seems to want to set an example, going home to shower every day, to feed the dog, and coming back dressed in a fresh shirt, sometimes a tie. Each day he brings my mother something from the house, perhaps to remind her of who she is. He brings her purse. He brings her silver mirror. He runs these objects through her hands, wrapping her limp and nearly translucent fingers around them: Hold onto this. I can see the faith he has in himself when he takes the objects from their plastic shopping bags.

Sometimes in the face of rituals like these, I think of my family not as humans, but as insects, usually ants in a tiny colony. The insect queen is dying, and the others scurry along the corridors, moving grains of dust here or there, in a senseless attempt to stave off what must come. Seen from above, their efforts are curious and sweet. The ants have elaborate plans for their bodies when they die. The father ant will donate his body to science. Student ants in a separate colony will cut it apart, in a funny attempt to learn how the organs work. "The pickle jar," he calls it. He wants his skeleton to shine. The sister ant wants to be buried at sea because it's less damaging to the environment. Fish will suckle at her toes. The mother ant, the queen, wants to be consumed by fire; the other ants will scatter her ashes in a breeze, probably at sunset from a bridge—the ants love beauty and, surprisingly, are capable of graceful things. The final ant wants to be buried in the ground in a special box. Oddly enough, in death, none of the four ants will meet again.

"They're calling for thunderstorms," my father says. This is the third or fourth time he's said so; he forgets. The sky is perfectly clear and the ocean—at least the piece of it we can see from the hospital window—is calm and gray. All three of us furtively watch my mother, who lies unmoving beneath the sheet, the timid intake of her breath less frequent now.

"I wonder whether she's dreaming," Bee says. This, too, has been said before. We repeat ourselves, using the same words over and over without getting anywhere. The meanings of words seem to disappear. Sitting here talking and waiting gives us the feeling that we're gathering things together or that things are gathering in us. Something is building, coming to a head. We feel it growing and think: Yes, here it is, now I'll understand it, I'll get it right. But when we open our mouths to reveal these sudden truths, we have nothing to say.

Bee eventually goes back to her problems, and my father wanders out into the hall. I pick up the dictionary again. It's a heavy volume, not a paperback, and even so I'm amazed at the poor selection; the words lack variety and seem suited only for expressing the mundane. If I could label what I see, I would feel better. I flip the pages back and forth, scanning the words, but they're inadequate: what I look for doesn't exist or isn't here.

At dinner, as the fluids move through one of my mother's many tubes, the three of us sit in a circle on uncomfortable chairs, eating pizza. We chew the crusts, grinding them. The sound of our mastication is obscene. We watch TV with the volume barely on. By eight o'clock it begins to rain. On the news they discuss storm warnings, thunderstorms, and advise that small craft head for shore. By eleven, though, the rain has stopped. My mother's eyes are closed. I rub my face against her upturned fingertips before Bee and I go to sleep in the waiting room.

I watch the hands on the clock go around. When my father's alone with my mother, he is always talking, talking, talking. He summarizes the news, including house fires, muggings, train derailments in foreign lands. Slow and quiet, uncharacteristically sincere, he sits beside her gazing steadily at her face, trying to keep her, one way or another, in this world.

Without realizing that I've slept, I wake up to the sound of thunder; the storm has come.

Bee's already up. It's five-fifteen. "Listen," she says. Even through the windows, which are closed, the thunder is loud, enormous; it fills the room.

My father is sitting at my mother's side. He lifts her eyelid with his thumb. "Look at the lightning, Caroline," he says.

At home, when we were small, my mother loved storms. She would stand on the outdoor deck until the rain came down, then climb the attic stairs to watch from beneath the overhang on the porch. It was one of the few times she seemed to love living by the ocean: she'd stand with her dress clinging to her legs, her face closed to us, turned away. Only by tugging at her hands could Bee and I make her notice us. She would gradually lose her rapt expression and return, making us wonder who she was when we weren't there. I used to be nervous about thunder, and she would take me in her arms. "Look how beautiful," she'd say, watching the ocean roar up across the sand.

"She can't see anything from here," my father says. For the first time since I arrived he seems confused by his helplessness. He lifts her eyelid once more, and it very slowly shuts on its own.

I say, "Let's turn her around."

My father unlocks the wheels on the bed, Bee moves the tangle of IVs, and I hold my mother's head against my shoulder, propping her up. Her hair is uncombed and smells of seaweed or of sweat.

"Ah," she moans. Or else that's Bee.

"She's saying 'ocean,' " my father says.

Bee walks to the window and forces it up. It should be sunrise but the sky is dark. You can see a vertical slice of the ocean by looking between two concrete buildings. The surf is rough. At home, the water has probably reached the bulkhead. This isn't the same as watching from the deck—we can't hear the wave but all of us want my mother to see. I make in the back of my throat so that she'll th the ocean. A little rain from the window finds its way in.

"Can she see?" my father asks.

I move her head a little to the left. She is so thin and light, I think of her as distilled. "Are you watching, Mom?" I could prop her up with pillows, but I won't.

Bee pulls up the sheet, which lifts and billows like a sail.

More rain comes in. The storm is just beginning—dark clouds come down and cover us like a lid; the smell of salt and brine pervades the room. The thunder resonates like a heart, a ragged drum. "Are you watching?" I ask again. I make the sound of the waves by my mother's ear. We rock a little, like a boat. It is just the two of us at last, the salt air a sweet comfort all around.

The thunder drones. "Oh, God," Bee says. "Lay her down." I refuse. Bee drops to the bed like a sack and puts her head on my mother's shoulder. It's hard work holding both of them, but I do.

"Dad." Bee is sobbing now, holding my mother's hand, stroking her neck.

My father appears beside me and calls my name. But I pretend that I can't hear him for the ocean's roar.

11

⌒⌒

December

I lay on Dr. Subramanian's table, looking at a poster on the ceiling about birth control. A young couple—she, of course, a blond with gently waved hair, he a brunette—looked quizzically at each other as if wondering who would be called on to reproduce. I had studied the poster many times.

"Two centimeters," Dr. Subramanian said. "That accounts for your backache. You are not in labor now, but it will probably begin soon. Is someone here to drive you home?"

"I came by myself."

Dr. Subramanian shook his head. "You are hiding in the sand again. How is your sister?"

"I haven't seen her for a while." In fact I hadn't seen much of anyone. Bill was busy arranging his new condo next to the Christian Brothers rest home, and my father was helping Murphy spruce up his trailer.

Dr. Subramanian started writing things down in my folder. I tried to sit up but couldn't, and he extended a delicate hand. "Beatrice. That was her name, wasn't it? She seemed very eager to help."

I grabbed his wrist with both hands. "Your table got narrower," I said.

He persisted. "You could have the baby quite soon, in a day or two. Or it might be weeks. We can't predict. You might inform your family. Ask them to treat you well, to keep you sitting down with your feet up."

"There isn't much left at home to sit down on," I said. "My father sold the house."

"He probably chose a good time to do so. How is your leg?"

I had begun to like Dr. Subramanian very much. Soon I wouldn't see him anymore. I wasn't sure I was ready to go. "My leg's okay. But I seem to have this large growth in my abdomen . . ."

He sighed and lay his hand on my calf. The veins there now formed a violet knot, and my leg was always hot to the touch. "Support hose," he said. "Not the knee-length; they constrict. No crossing your legs. Do you have arrangements for someone to drive you to the hospital?"

"Of course I do," I said. But I didn't name names.

Everyone said that my mother's parents were probably dead. My Uncle Harold, their only other child, was alive four years earlier but now was gone. "Faulty genes," Bee said. "People on her side don't last long."

"That's not encouraging. We're on her side, too, you know." I had called Bee on the phone to let her know what our father had said about our grandparents.

"We could hire a private detective to try to find them," I suggested.

The answer was typical Bee. "They didn't come to their own daughter's funeral. What would we want to find them for?"

I spent the end of the month getting ready for Christmas, shopping mainly at Stedman's, where I recognized some of the salespeople and shoppers but no one recognized me. Against the cold I wore an oversized sweatshirt and my father's blue windbreaker, unzipped; I was lumpy and wide, ungainly: nothing like the vibrant pregnant women I sometimes saw in magazines or on TV. Except for their stomachs, they were still relatively trim. I was doughy, my bones seeming to have retreated far beneath the surface of my skin.

I bought a scarf and a footstool for my father, a sweater for Bill, a giant beer stein for Murphy, and for Bee a pair of earrings and a calendar. These weren't the most sensible gifts: Bee didn't wear jewelry of any kind—she fastened her watch through the belt loop of her pants—and she never wrote her appointments down, simply remembering instead, where she had to be. The earrings were long, amber tears, like molasses drops; I'd held them up in the store gauging their color in relation to my sister's hair. My father wanted us all to have Christmas dinner in the trailer: I imagined a two-foot vinyl tree with five pieces of tinsel, a toaster-oven turkey, and the sound of eighteen-wheelers on their way to Atlantic City thumping by.

I had gained more than fifty pounds in the last six months. When I walked, cowboy fashion, down the street or along the sand, I felt sudden, sharp pains in my hips and thighs and had to clutch parked cars, railings, and public trash cans so that I wouldn't fall down. Even though my father's new queen-size mattress was free, I still slept in the drafty guest room, the pillows used to prop my arms and legs into reasonable positions tumbling onto the floor, where I would trip on them getting us to use the bathroom. The fetus seemed to have filled its available space; it barely moved except to readjust a cramped leg every now and then.

Sea Haven was cold and very quiet. Sometimes I sat on the back porch and watched snowflakes melting into the ocean like a dream. At night I often woke up and heard the clicking of the clocks in the next room; without my father they seemed louder and more forlorn—he hadn't mentioned taking them to the trailer. Sometimes I opened the door to his study in the dark and stood in the hallway listening to them measure out the minutes we had left: the amount of time until the baby was born, until the house came down, until my father and Bee and I could forget some of the things we'd said and done. Like my mother, I had come back to Sea Haven tentative and dreamy, looking for something elusive: mainly I had succeeded in alienating my sister, causing my father to sell his house, and evicting Bill Denzer from his home.

Bill was polite and sympathetic when we saw each other, which wasn't often: he thought it was better if we spent some time apart while I "considered my decision."

"I don't think I can make any kind of significant

life choice before the baby's born," I said. "It wouldn't be fair. I'm not sure how I'm going to feel."

"You'll feel tired." He sounded sturdy, sure of himself, as if ready to overlook, once we married, the shortsightedness I was currently demonstrating.

"I guess we both know that you wouldn't have wanted to marry me if I weren't pregnant," I said. "For most people that would have been a deterrent, but you've always wanted kids. I came along with a baby nearly made."

Bill exhaled conspicuously through his nose. His condominium was comfortably large enough for three. "I haven't asked any other pregnant women to be my wife," he said.

I tried to imagine having sex with Bill. It would probably be a laborious enterprise, earnest and full of thankfulness and cheer. I knew he would be a good father, though, communicative and understanding. He would forgive all faults, and his children would be suntanned and healthy and satisfied. His wife would sew little outfits for the kids.

"Do you want to have dinner tonight?" I asked.

"No," he said.

"I will make a decision, Bill, really."

Bill had told me that he loved me and asked me only once if I loved him. When I didn't answer fast enough, he'd said, "It's all right, Jane. Ours can be a different sort of arrangement."

"Oh, right," I'd said, before we kissed.

My father had overheard us. " 'Different' sounds like a hell of an understatement to me," he'd said, raising his eyes toward heaven when Bill was gone.

*   *   *

I felt the first pains in the middle of the night. They were mild and in my back, like an intermittent muscle spasm. I turned on the heating pad, and by morning when I got up the pains had gone.

My father called. He warned me that I shouldn't go too far if I intended to walk: storms at this time of year came rolling in much faster than pregnant people traveled, and he didn't want to read about any more rescue missions in the news.

"Dad, it's perfectly clear. I can see to Atlantic City."

"That's a mirage." He sounded cheerful. "It's probably caused by your condition."

I asked him if he wanted to come over for dinner.

"Not tonight," he said. "I'm going bowling, of all things. There's a group of widow spiders here that have their eyes on me. How about tomorrow? You come here and I'll buy a steak—lots of iron for pregnant ladies."

"Okay." I rubbed my back. "Maybe you'll be married again before I am," I said.

He laughed. "Wear your party clothes tomorrow. I'll introduce you to some cronies. I'll put a flag out on the roof so you'll know where I am."

I ate a bowl of rice cereal and threw it up almost immediately in the sink. I brushed my teeth and ate some very small spoonfuls of chocolate walnut ice cream from the container, then felt guilty and fixed some celery and carrot sticks. The backache returned. I wasn't going to let it trick me. I knew the stories about women who went to the hospital too soon and had to be sent home like fools to wait. I wouldn't leave until I was ready.

I remembered a list I had seen somewhere of the items a woman takes to the hospital when giving birth. A rolling pin was supposed to relieve back pain. I was also supposed to have a change of clothes, some underwear, a bathrobe, makeup and a mirror (every list-maker seemed to think that all women needed makeup), a good luck charm, a camera, a couple of favorite snacks, spending money, clothes to dress the baby in, identification (Was this in case you ended up in the morgue?), and the telephone numbers of people to notify.

I had left some of the baby things in the attic. When I climbed up the first wooden step, I felt as if someone had thrust a giant fist and a hairy arm down through my lungs and stomach and kidneys, and the giant knuckles were grinding and pushing against my spine. I caught my breath. When the pain subsided I kept going, holding onto the railing with both hands. I hadn't been up to the attic for several months. It was neat and well arranged. At the foot of the bed Bee had slept in, I found a small canvas suitcase and, taped to its side, my list, like a treasure map of sacred things. In the suitcase already were underwear and pajamas, a book about the Russian steppes, a sweater, a shirt, and a new heating pad, still in its plastic wrapping. Bee. I climbed down the stairs to look for a rolling pin, then climbed back up, barely clearing the landing before the pain returned again, this time scaling my hipbones and twisting around my stomach to the front.

I found the baby clothes folded neatly in a paper bag right next to the suitcase. Bee had bought dozens of things that I hadn't seen: bleached white T-shirts the size of my open hand, miniature socks, a yellow cap with BABY across the front, a suit with a bear stitched flat across the chest, a bag of diapers, pacifiers, and several flannel blankets in neutral tones. It hadn't occurred to me that she would like buying baby things. There was even a silver frame and a blank book with a space for a baby's picture on the front.

According to the list I still needed a good luck charm, a camera, some makeup, and some snacks. I didn't own a camera, but I had to satisfy all the written requirements. If the list had said that I needed a piece of blue chalk, a frog's eye, and a dozen bristles from a broom, I would have packed those, too. In an apple crate I found Bee's old Brownie camera, taken apart and reassembled twenty years ago. I didn't care if it worked. I packed an old lipstick I found dried up on a dressing table, a silver square of airline peanuts, and some gum. To look for the good luck charm I started to ransack Bee's dresser, still full of odds and ends she hadn't yet moved to her new apartment. Under a pile of real estate forms and handkerchiefs (Bee didn't believe in tissues), I discovered three pieces of yellowed construction paper, folded and worn thin.

The pain in my stomach peaked and subsided while I slowly held the letters up to the light. I had given up prying through others' mail, but through the first thin page I could see a child's writing. Maybe it was my own. I paused; then I unfolded the letter.

Dear Mommy,
  Come back. I miss you. We are sad. Come home.

                                   Love, Bee.

The characters were rounded—circles and sticks—and in most places it seemed an adult had guided her hand. My father? Murphy? Bee would have been only four. I opened the second letter.

Dear Mommy,
  Please come home now. I miss you. My birthday is next week. I want a turtle and a pen. I don't like pencils.

                                   Love, Bee.

The letters weren't dated, but Bee's birthday was in July. What year were these written?

Dear Mommy,
  Please come home. We miss you. I don't like the baby crying. Daddy told me I can name her. I call her Jane.

On Bee's birthday in July, I was four weeks old. How long had Bee said that our mother was gone? "Long enough so that she looked different when she came back."

The giant knuckles scraped against my vertebrae again.

I tried to remember what Bee had said about my father feeding me and changing me and singing me nonsense songs. I tried to see his unlined face looking gravely down, his square hands buttoning my clothes. He used to recite nursery rhymes in the car. I remembered that whenever I asked my mother about something that had happened when I was a baby, she'd say, "Ask Beatrice. She has a better memory than I do."

I folded in half next to the dresser, a sword piercing my stomach and a thin stream of clear liquid flowing down my leg into my shoe.

I called Bee. My mother had left me. She hadn't come back to Sea Haven for my birth; she had run away from me after it, leaving Beatrice and my father and me alone.

There was no answer. Bee was gone.

My back contorted again; I called my father—no one home. I dialed Bee's number over and over, thinking, what a legacy, what a mess, what a distance we've built between each other. I called Dr. Subramanian.

"How frequent are the contractions?" He sounded tired.

I didn't call them contractions; most of them were in my back. "I haven't timed them," I said, though I was holding a clock in my hand. I must have found it in my father's study, though I didn't remember opening the door.

Dr. Subramanian coughed. "Twenty minutes? Ten? Or more like five?"

"Sometimes five," I said. "Sometimes they fade." As I spoke, the muscles in my back began to tighten, as if someone had pulled on them all at once, from my thighs up to my shoulders; I arched my back and breathed in.

"You are having one now?" he asked.

I tried to say no.

"I'll wait," he said, and did.

"I'm all right," I reassured him. I thought of my mother, like me, finally drawn back to the ocean, to 5025 Amanda. But when? She had spent her life in a waiting posture, ear cocked to listen, mouth half open as if to speak.

"Of course you're all right," he said. "Now look at your watch." His patience frightened me. His tone said that he was talking to a desperate person, conning a criminal into laying down his arms, releasing hostages, and emerging from the building to be shot, hands up, by the police.

I looked at my father's clock. 11:15 A.M., December twenty-first. When did she come back? How long was she gone? I refused to have this baby until I knew.

Dr. Subramanian was talking, talking, talking. The cold snap was extraordinary, wasn't it? Had I preregistered at the hospital? I could hear a woman and some children in the background. We talked about how close the hospital was. My back started winding up again.

"Now," I said.

"Well, that appears to be under five minutes. But you said that the pains vary and aren't intense?"

I was on my knees.

"Take your time," he said.

I was holding onto the receiver like a lifeline to a world above; I stared at the linoleum, at the tiny cracks and fissures into which I would fall if I let go. "I need to call my sister."

"Certainly. I think you should. In the meantime we can do either of two things. You can go straight to the hospital now and have a nurse examine you, or you can wait a little longer to see if the contractions remain regular."

"I'm not ready yet," I said.

"That's all right. I think many women feel that way. I want you to rest, but don't lie down. Walk, if you like; do whatever is comfortable. Get your bag and ask someone to stay with you. Call again if the contractions remain regular, at four minutes apart or less. Or call at any time if the pain gets significantly worse. Heavens," he said, "call whenever you like. I'll be at home."

I called my father and let the phone ring twenty-five times; then I dialed Bee again. No one was home. I didn't want to call Bill. I brought the phone down next to me on the carpet and dialed Murphy. When he answered I was panting, inhaling dust.

"Hey, how's my favorite pregnant person?" he asked, just as the fist took an unexpected turn and slammed down more forcefully than before. When I breathed out his name, he said, "I'm coming," and hung up the phone.

Murphy found me in the bathroom on my hands and knees, clutching the rim of the toilet, one leg of my navy sweatpants soaked through and another pool of clear liquid on the floor. "Mary and Joseph," he said, throwing towels down around me on the tile, then trying to pick me up by the armpits. When he touched me, I started to scream. "Okay," he said, backing up and disappearing around the corner, dialing the phone.

I heard him swear. "Okay," he said again, wiping his mouth with the back of his hand. "You don't think it's coming now?" He stood in the doorway, looking down; I had crawled out near his feet. "Hospital," I said. Murphy looked green. I was some kind of alien creature at the level of his knees: I might as well have had the body of a spider and the head of a ram. I pushed my hair out of my face and tried to stand up.

"Wait," he said, "I'm going to restart the car." He left with my suitcase, and when he came back I had pulled myself to standing by the door. "Good girl," he said, his big hands patting the empty air. He walked backwards in front of me down the steps, wide-eyed and nodding all the way.

"Murphy," I said, stopping in the cold salt air with my hand on the frozen mailbox at the bottom of the steps. "My mother left right after I was born."

"What?" He continued walking backwards, as if my body was a weapon set to fire.

"Where did she go? Did she go back to see her parents?"

Murphy had opened all four car doors, but I think he sensed that I wouldn't budge unless he started talking. "Here you go," he said. "I don't know a whole lot about it. Right in here." He held my hand. "I've never been this close to a real delivery. Sarah always went to her mother's before ours were born."

"Where did *my* mother go?" I braced myself against the open door and refused to get in.

Murphy sighed. "I don't know. Probably to her folks. Your dad was afraid to go after her."

I folded myself onto the front seat, and Murphy

sprinted around to the other side after slamming the door. He put the car in gear and peeled out. There was almost no one on the road.

"I was a few weeks old," I said. "Who took care of me and Bee?"

He didn't answer.

"Who?" I was doubled over, forehead grinding into the glove compartment latch.

"That was the hardest for your dad," Murphy said. "Two little girls."

"He did it by himself?"

Murphy seemed to be catching every pothole along the way; he was going sixty miles an hour in a thirty-mile zone. "Sarah and I helped. Sometimes we took you in the afternoons. Your dad never wanted you to know."

We turned one corner and another, and I saw the hospital portico, like the drive-up window of a fast-food chain.

"How long was she gone?" I asked.

Murphy blinked. "I think she came back sometime that fall. I know she was here by Christmas."

All my life she had been distant.

"You want me to call Bill Denzer? These days I guess they like to have the fathers there."

"He's not the father," I said. I imagined my own father sterilizing the bottles, washing the diapers, singing me to sleep in the rocking chair. He had sold his own house to give me money.

"No, not technically, I guess. He sure is excited, though."

I knew Bill would be a good father; he would be

generous and loving and very fair. I grabbed Murphy's shoulder. "Listen," I said. "Bill saved my life. But he's not the father in any way. Will you remember that I said that? I'm not going to marry anyone right now."

"Sure." Murphy parked and threw open the door and whistled to a male attendant with a wheelchair.

I pulled myself up, holding onto Murphy's arm. "My father lied to me a lot," I said. "He lied about a lot of things."

"That wasn't all he did," Murphy said. "He did much more."

I had a little nut tree; nothing would it bear
But a silver nutmeg and a golden pear;
The king of Spain's daughter came to visit me,
And all was because of my little nut tree.
I skipped over water, I danced over sea,
And all the birds in the air couldn't catch me.

I was reciting nursery rhymes in my head to dilute the pain. They were coming back to me like charms, like missing gifts.

"Dr. Subramanian's on his way," the nurse said. "We phoned him half an hour ago."

Half an hour ago this nurse—M. HANRICKSON said the tag across her breast—snapped on a rubber glove and inflicted on me the most excruciating experience I ever hoped to know. "Easy," she said, as if steadying a mare. "It's supposed to hurt. Eight centimeters. This baby should be here soon."

If I had lived in the Middle Ages, I would have believed I was being punished. In fact I believed this anyway. "How soon is soon?" I asked, when Hanrickson reappeared wheeling some menacing apparatus. "Babies are born on their own schedules," she said, fitting a belt around my stomach, pinching the skin. She was young, younger than I was, probably childless, with a cloud of blond hair that floated around her face. I imagined she hated me for some obscure psychopathic reason; smiling, she punched a series of buttons on a little ticker-tape machine.

She began to hum under her breath, puttering around the room as if I weren't there. I told her that I was waiting for a shot of morphine; Dr. Subramanian had described a two-minute interval between injection and relief; it would be like hearing my own screams from underwater. "This hurts like hell," my mother had said once after surgery. But she was on painkillers at the time, drowsy and drugged.

With effort I got out of bed, unbuckling the belt and throwing up on the nightstand along the way.

"Good, walk," said a nurse's aide, pushing a call button on the wall. She imagined that I was up and about in an effort to speed the process: a move right out of the manuals, cooperative and up-to-date. In fact I was escaping, dragging my sweatpants along the floor with my big toe. I was past the sink, near the tray of metal instruments covered with cloth, when it hit me again, the pain completely out of proportion with joy, hard work, discomfort, expectation, and all the other euphemisms I had heard.

Hanrickson opened the door and gripped my arm—I was looking my torturer in the eye.

I remembered my mother saying that, when Bee was

born, she had been "knocked out." Was she awake for me, though, spending the hours calling for ether and chloroform?

I threw up again: to vomit felt pleasant—it provided a brief distraction from the pain.

Dr. Subramanian came in smiling, fresh from a haircut, it appeared, and reassured me that things were fine. He will save me, I thought, and I made a polite request for medication as he led me back to the metal side-railed bed.

"At eight to nine centimeters, that is unnecessary." He put on a green hospital gown not unlike the one I was wearing. "At this point, we would mainly be drugging the baby."

"What baby?" I wanted to shout. "Who cares about a baby?" But I felt the pain like the side of a mountain coming again, moving through the narrowest passages, tearing parts of me away, and I was screaming before the worst of it began.

The monitor at my side showed the fetal heartbeat leaping and falling and indicated with green fluorescent peaks and valleys the "productivity" (Hanrickson's word) of my contractions. Watching the screen was like being strapped to the torture rack and observing the tightening of the wooden screws. I wasn't able to look away.

I told Dr. Subramanian that I thought it best at this time to order a cesarean.

He smiled absently, glancing at the small electronic screen.

"Fuck you," I said, so that he would look at me. He did.

"Everything is going nicely. There is no need for a cesarean." He brought a cold washcloth for my forehead, stroked my leg. "Try to relax. That makes it easier and quicker."

"An epidural," I said.

The spindly green line began to climb; I was sobbing in disbelief that anyone could allow me to suffer in this way. I could hear a woman in the next room moaning in subdued and modest tones. Dr. Subramanian was talking to the nurse, but I'd ceased to hear. I knew only the green electronic peaks, predictor and mirror of my suffering. Some looked like the pointed, misshapen roof of my father's house.

Hanrickson fitted an oxygen mask across my mouth and nose. I pictured my father at my funeral, holding a child I would never see.

"I want the painkillers," I said, my voice a tinny echo behind the mask. I was making an effort to sound lucid and not to whimper, but when I looked around the room, I was alone.

The mountain approached with a roar again. Before I could take a breath, it had already reached me, and I pulled down the hanging curtain around my bed in a single effort to get away. The nurse's aide peered in and soon returned with Dr. Subramanian, looking stern. I held the hem of the ruined curtain in my fists. "You're killing me," I said.

"Don't be ridiculous." He snapped on a rubber glove.

"Don't touch me," I warned. I tried to kick him away and he tried to look patient. A few minutes later, after pressing an icy stethoscope to my stomach, he was gone. An hour or two passed in this way, and I began to understand that pain is not related to time and is not an experience. It's a place that one travels to, like a tiny, hideous country of one's own.

Sometime later, during what I once would have recognized as late afternoon, Dr. Subramanian brought out a syringe, a knife, and a scissors, sliced through the skin of my crotch, and told me to push.

I refused.

He looked up, two dark eyes above a mask. "All your might," he said, "now."

My mouth was full of ice chips brought by the nurse. I held them cupped on my tongue and looked away.

"You can't prevent it," he said. "This baby needs to be born. Push hard."

I remembered my mother dying, somewhere upstairs and down the hall from this very room. I hadn't heard her last words: Bee had heard them and forgotten, or wouldn't tell. I pictured my mother sitting beside my bed, worn out and rumpled, her bony hands folded in her lap. "What are you waiting for?" she asks. She wears the light green dress we brought to the funeral home for her cremation.

"I was waiting for you."

"What on earth is the matter?" Dr. Subramanian's face, lightly sweaty, loomed into view.

I couldn't answer because I was sucking the oxygen down. I closed my eyes and willed him away. When the mountain of green lines approached, I would knock

it down; I'd send a wrecking ball through the roof of
my father's house.

My mother fades, returns again. "I came back soon
enough," she says. "I wouldn't have been able to help
you anyway."

"You could have," I tell her. "You never tried."

"You'll need to try harder." Dr. Subramanian
pulled the oxygen mask away, and I got ready to hit
him with my fist.

"You weighed almost nothing," my mother says.
"So small. When I left, I knew your father would love
you best."

"Don't go," I say, and Dr. Subramanian looks surprised. I reach for the oxygen again. We are too far
from water; I could drown in this arid room.

"Jane?" My mother's voice has changed: it's
lower, softer, more sympathetic. I can feel her ap-
proaching like a flood, a wave of rescue. When I open
my eyes to forgive her, I find Bee. I wait the three
long seconds it takes my sister to reach my bed; then
I arch up and let out a noise as horror-filled as any I
have ever heard.

"Push," Hanrickson says.

Bee looks at my face and seems to take me in.
Blood has soaked the backs of my legs and the
bleached white sheets. "Don't look," I whisper,
hoarse, afraid Bee will faint and have to be carried
from the room. She's pale enough already. She spies
the oxygen mask, puts it over her own nose and mouth
and takes a breath. Then she turns the monitor away
and puts a bulging paper bag on the metal table by
the bed. She takes out a red alarm clock. She takes out

a night-light and plugs it in. I feel the roof coming, the edge of the mountain bearing down. She pulls out a rubber alligator, a rabbit's foot, a wooden plaque with our baby teeth glued to the surface—I grab her wrists when the peak tears through me and pull her close, close—then she sets up a ballerina, a bag of marbles, an Erector set, and tapes behind my head a chart of the constellations. She has recreated our room, the one we shared before our mother got sick and went away. Bee tried to protect me as well as she knew how.

Everything's crumbling around me, the mountain coming down in sheets of rock, the roof shearing off and plunging to the ground.

"Push," says Hanrickson again.

Bee holds my hand and looks out the window. "It's dark. The stars are out."

"Bee, I know Mom didn't leave you."

"Shh," she says. "I can see Cassiopeia. I can see Polaris."

"I was wrong. She left me." I want to tell Bee everything, as once I wanted to tell my mother.

But she doesn't let me talk. "That doesn't matter now," she says, touching my hair.

This is all that's left of us, I think.

"Good," Dr. Subramanian says.

I start to cry, remembering the days before my mother died, before Bee slept in another room. That was when we loved each other best and didn't know it. Whatever lay in store, we headed for the worst of it together.

"Ready," Bee says. I feel my skin begin to tear. "Get set."

"Beatrice!" I scream.

She lays her face against my own. "Now you can go."